STICK BREAK

BOSTON BUCKS

CATHRYN FOX

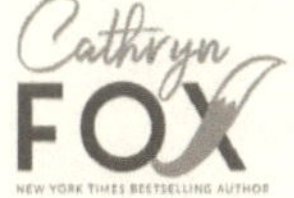

COPYRIGHT

Stick Break
Copyright 2025 by Cathryn Fox
Published by Cathryn Fox

ISBN Ebook: 978-1-998943-96-8

ISBN Print:978-1-998943-95-1

1

RIP

Either that one beer was stronger than advertised, or Goldilocks has broken into the wrong damn fairy tale—and decided my bed was just right.

The wood floor creaks, as I take a measured step closer, and peer at the petite blonde hugging my pillow like it just whispered sweet nothings and promised her coffee in the morning. I lean forward, but with her back to me, I still can't get a good view of her face.

Heck, maybe it's not a real woman between my sheets. Maybe my buddy Gunter, or one of my teammates thought it'd be hilarious to stash a blow-up doll in my bed while I sucked back some suds after a walk on the beach. But no, that theory doesn't add up. Gunter is away on his honeymoon, and only he and his wife Paisley know I'm here at their cottage. Which means, there really is a woman in my bed...and Jesus is that my sweatshirt she's wearing?

I clear my throat. "Um, hello."

"Fftlelle..."

I scratch my head as she mumbles something in her sleep and flops like a fish having an existential crisis, until she's turned my way. That's when I get a good look at her features—very familiar features. Sure, her hair is shorter, and a different color, but it hardly makes her less recognizable. That pretty face of hers has been splashed all over the media for months now. First for winning The Spotlight and second...well, because of a leaked sex tape.

I inch closer, and shake my head. What the ever-loving fuck is reality TV singing star Indie Rhodes doing in Connecticut, in my buddy's beachside cottage? Maybe the better question is, how the hell did she get in? I double checked the door before I went out to stretch my legs.

As I work to puzzle it out, I come to the realization that she's not waking up anytime soon, so I back out of the room and pull my phone from my pocket. Should I call Gunter? Shit, I don't want to bother them on their honeymoon. Besides, Paisley plays four instruments and writes symphonies, which means it's possible that she knows Goldilocks, and she had given her a key. But why would they offer the cottage to Indie, when they know I need to lay low, and keep out of the spotlight while I try to heal?

In the kitchen, a warm breeze rushes in, and that's when my gaze goes to the slightly opened window above the sink—a window that I'd also double checked and made sure was locked. Ah, okay... So, my friends didn't offer up the place to her at all, or give her a key. It's obvious that Goldilocks shimmied the window open and let herself in. I walk over to the counter, and it takes extra effort to tug the window shut. The damn thing must have been painted closed years ago. Little blondie might be half my size, but she clearly has grit and determination, if she got this open.

I turn back around, and that's when I take stock of the empty bowl, dirty spoon and the ripped open, single serving packet on the kitchen table. You have got to be fucking kidding me?

Okay, so not only did this woman break in, tug on one of my sweatshirts before falling asleep in my bed, she made herself a damn bowl of oatmeal—and left the dishes.

Fuck my life.

A tortured laugh crawls out of my throat as I pinch my eyes shut and will myself awake. I mean, I have to be sleeping, right? Not only is this too crazy to be true, Goldilocks is a fairy tale and I don't believe in fairy tales, or happily ever after. Although that fable didn't really have a happy ending, and if I remember correctly, Little Bear was pretty pissed off.

I might not be little bear, and yeah, my nickname on the team is Big Bear, partly because of my size and partly because of the scraggly beard I grow during the playoffs, but I'm pissed too. I came here to heal in quiet. I can't let anyone know that I tore my groin in our playoff game, and that if it doesn't heal properly, it could be a career-ending injury.

The last thing I need is a cute blonde—who's been drawing a ton of media attention—bringing unwanted cameras my way. I stalk back to the bedroom, ready to wake her and send her packing, but the second I do, and see the dark circles under her eyes as she sleeps, clutching the blankets like they're her lifeline, my insides soften. That whole scandal has to be hard on her.

What if she too is here hiding from reality?

Shit, I can't send her out into the dark. There might not be any vacant rentals and the hotel sign down the road has been flashing No Vacancy all week. She stirs again and I go still.

Honestly, if she wakes up now and sees a guy my size hovering over her, it'd scare her half to death, and I don't want that.

I quietly leave the room again, and eye the sofa. It doesn't pull out, but it looks comfortable enough for one night. Mostly. In the closet I find a pillow and blanket and toss them onto the sofa. Should I do the dishes first? While I'd really like to, that could wake her, and I think our first meeting and our first conversation is best left for morning.

I tug off my shirt and debate my pants. I'm not a fan of clothes at the best of times, hence the Ripley Stripley nickname the bunnies gave me. In this situation, however, I think it's best to leave my pants on.

I fling myself onto the couch, where I'm forced to drape my legs over the armrest like I'm posing for a Renaissance painting. Nevertheless the position is perfect...for completely destroying what's left of my groin. Eventually I contort into something that could pass as comfortable, and close my eyes. Sleep, however, is not a team player.

After a very restless night, the first rays of sunlight stab through the window and pull me awake. Groaning, I toss my cramped legs to the floor. Big mistake. Huge.

Not only is one of them dead, the other lights up with pins and needles. Jesus, did I step on a porcupine? To top it off, I've planted myself directly in the sun's death beam.

"Jesus," I mutter, shielding my poor, innocent eyeballs as the sun blinds me. I swear I can hear them sizzling. Bones cracking, I stumble to the kitchen like a man three times my age.

Coffee.

Sweet, caffeinated salvation.

I smash buttons on the machine and when it begins to gurgle, I tiptoe toward the bedroom, praying Goldilocks decided to vanish in the night the same way she appeared—magically and without explanation.

Nope.

Of course not.

With her short blonde hair falling across her face, her arms and legs spread wide like she'd been making snow, or rather sand, angels—we are after all, at the beach—she's still snuggled between the sheets. The covers are down, exposing her legs, and I force my gaze away.

Now is not the time to be admiring the criminal in your bed, dude.

Right. Because later will be a much more appropriate time to ogle Little Miss Fugitive.

No, I mentally slap myself. There will be no later. I'm kicking her out. Nicely. Politely. But firmly. There's no way I can allow her to stay here in this one-bedroom cottage. Not only am I trying to heal in private, I have a damn girlfriend. Well, not really a girlfriend. I have a friend, a girl, who used to be my girlfriend. Lyra and I were a thing during our college years in upstate New York, but now, we're sort of on again, off-again.

Yeah, on again when she needs something, dude.

I push that thought from my mind, and make my way back to the beloved coffee maker. I grab a mug and fill it. As I sip, I lean against the counter. Then I hear movement. The soft rustle of sheets. A thump. Shuffling. And finally...none other than Indie Rhodes appears in the doorway, head ducked, hair a mess, not at all looking like someone who broke into my buddy's cottage.

"Sleep well, Goldilocks?"

Her head snaps up, eyes wide. One hand shoots out and grips the doorframe, like the sight of me shocked her legs right out from beneath her. "I uh...who..." Her eyes bounce around the room, as her other hand grabs a fistful of the oversized sweatshirt. My sweatshirt. Which may or may not look better on her than me, and I'm leaning toward may. "What...what are you doing here?"

I blink. "What am I doing here? I'm pretty sure I'm the one who should be asking you that question."

Her gaze slices to the door, and I swear I can hear the mental math she's doing—distance, speed, angle of escape, odds of success. She looks like she's two seconds from trying a full Olympic sprint when I push off the counter and grab another mug.

"Relax. I'm not going to hurt you." I pour coffee into a big mug with the Connecticut skyline on it, and pretend this is just another Tuesday. I set the mug on the table and take a step back, like I'm trying not to startle a skittish kitten. Nibbling her lip, she stares at it. "It's not poisoned." Her eyes dart to mine, and that's when I see just how blue they are.

"I didn't think it was...until now."

That gets a laugh out of me. I grab the carafe and pour more into my mug and take a big, dramatic sip just to prove I'm not the villain here. I raise it in salute as she tiptoes to the table and scurries right back to the safety of the bedroom doorway.

"Thank you." She takes a sip and a visible chunk of tension melts from her shoulders.

"So, are you going to tell me what you're doing here...in my sweatshirt?"

I arch a brow, watching her tug at the hem like it might suddenly stretch into pants. It rides higher on her thighs instead. Distracting.

She blinks rapidly. "I didn't realize it was yours." She points a thumb over her shoulder. "I found it in the dresser."

"Yeah, because *I* put it there."

Is she wearing anything under that sweatshirt?

She leans against the doorframe, chin tipped up now. She's presenting calm, maybe even cocky, like she's decided bluffing is better than bolting. "I'm renting this place. From friends. Maybe *you're* the one who's lost. All the cottages look the same, right? Maybe you're supposed to be in the one next door."

Nice pivot. "Mrs. Callahan's?"

"I don't know her name."

I sip my coffee, now amused with her antics. "These friends of yours...they forget to give you a key?"

"What?"

I nod toward the window. "Assuming that's why you had to climb in like a cat burglar."

She groans, eyes fluttering shut. "Damn."

"I liked the effort though, and you should be glad you didn't crawl into Mrs. Callahan's place." I mock shiver. "She kind of scares me."

When her lashes flutter open, the bluff's gone. Just like that, her shoulders drop. The whole show collapses. "I'll go. Thanks for the coffee."

She starts to leave, but something in me won't let her. "Wait."

Jesus, what am I doing? I should let her go. I *need* to let her go.

But I ask anyway. "Do you actually have a rental here? Are you really in the wrong place?" She stares into her coffee cup like it might offer an excuse she hasn't thought of yet. "Just tell me the truth."

She finally lifts her eyes to mine. They're raw now—sad and tired and real. It hits like a puck straight to the ribs.

"No," she explains. "I broke in. I needed somewhere to go. Somewhere to…disappear."

She drops her gaze again, distant now, like whatever she's remembering is darker than she wants to say.

I watch her in silence for a moment, then, "How long do you need a place?"

What the hell, man. Show her the door. This is a terrible idea.

And yet…I don't move.

Her eyes flick to mine, wide and uncertain, but there's hope there too, and it's that glimmer that dissolves what little resolve I have left.

"A week, maybe."

I exhale. "There's only one bedroom."

"I'll take the sofa," she blurts, like she's been rehearsing that exact concession. "I'm sorry you had to sleep on it last night." She walks over, bends to pick the blanket up off the floor.

And my sweatshirt rides up.

Way up.

White panties.

Bare legs.

Jesus.

I clamp my jaw tight, fight a groan as my body reacts like I have got zero self-control. Which, apparently, I do. She straightens and turns, totally unaware she just turned my brain to static.

"I really didn't know anyone was staying here," she says.

I roll one shoulder, a stiff ache radiating down my arm. "Yeah, well..." I groan softly as the knot protests.

"You're stiff."

Jesus.

She flinches. "I mean...your shoulder."

"I know what you mean."

"That sofa couldn't have been comfortable. And it was really sweet of you to let me crash in your bed." A smile ghosts across her lips. Soft. Real. The first I've seen. "It was just right."

I bark a laugh. "Sure. And I'm guessing the oatmeal was *just right* too." I grab the bowl and spoon and carry them to the sink.

"At least I didn't break a chair," she offers, playing along.

"Or the window. I think it was painted shut." I glance at her.

She frowns. "I don't recall Goldilocks breaking a window, but I'm not up to date on my childhood fairy tales."

"Right, same. Do you know the owners?"

She nods. "Yeah. Paisley and I have crossed paths a few times. I knew she was out of town, so I—"

"Broke in. Yes, we've established that. Gunther and I—" I catch myself before saying we play together. The last thing I need is for her to connect the dots. "We've crossed paths, too."

"Gunther's a hockey player."

I nod and try to play it cool. "You a fan?"

"I don't love hockey. Do you?"

"Yeah, I do. Play occasionally." Okay, not a lie. But not enough for her to put two and two together right? "So, what do I call you?" I only know her stage name, and I'm not sure if she wants that to ring a bell with me either. I'm guessing not.

"I'm ah..." She hesitates, her teeth tugging on her bottom lip.

"Goldilocks is good," I offer, turning my neck and wincing as pain shoots down my shoulder. Great. Not only is my groin fucked but my neck is too.

"Right. Um... You can call me Charly."

Charly. Not her stage name. Yeah, she really doesn't want me to know who she is either.

"And you are?" she asks.

"Bear. Big Bear, actually." Not a lie. Just not the full truth. She grins, amused.

"Not Papa Bear?"

"I'm no one's papa, and you can call me Rip."

"Rip. As in, Rip who allows women to break into his sanctuary, and doesn't ask too many questions. That about right, Big Bear Rip?"

"Right."

We lock eyes. The moment hums between us like a live wire. The less we know about each other, the safer we both are.

She steps closer, sets her coffee on the table. Her eyes flick to mine. "So... we need to do something about your stiffness."

2

___

CHARLY

___

"Um, what?" he asks, turning his back to me as he refills his already full mug.

"Sleeping on the sofa." I nod toward it, even though he's not looking. "You're all twisted up."

"I'm okay," he practically growls without turning around.

I study him—posture tight, shoulders stiff—and my stomach twists. I stand frozen for a moment, weighing this whole ridiculous, complicated situation. I glance at the door, sensing I've crossed some invisible line. Breaking in, taking his bed, wearing his clothes, eating his oatmeal—maybe forgivable. But mentioning his stiffness? That feels different. Like a sore spot. No pun intended.

Wait. Unless... he thought I meant something else. Some other kind of stiffness.

Oh God.

But there's no way he could've thought I was implying he was attracted to me. And that I wanted to do something about it.

That's wishful thinking, right? Wait no. That's not what I mean at all. I'm wishing my life wasn't a total mess. That I didn't have to break into a friend's cottage and hide out like a fugitive. I swallow hard, fighting back a nearly painful sob.

How the hell did I even get here?

Oh, you know girl, you know.

Right, my ex put me here out of spite and his own desperate need to climb the fame and fortune ladder.

I catch the way Rip's eyes flick to me—curious, maybe a little guarded—and I suck in a quick breath. Does he know who I am? I instinctively lean forward to hide behind my hair. Shoot. Now that it's cut short, there's nowhere to hide. I steal a fast glance his way. But no, he can't possibly know who I am.

With no makeup, my long dark hair chopped short and dyed blonde, and this oversized sweatshirt, I barely even recognize myself. I'm far from the glamorous woman who's been singing her heart out onstage these last months.

I gulp. "Sorry. Your business is your business."

Best to leave it there. He might not know who I am, but I definitely know who *he* is. I'm not exactly a hockey fan—too much violence, too many grown men slamming into things on purpose—but that doesn't mean I haven't caught a game or two. Maybe I fibbed earlier. Call it intuition, but I get the feeling he doesn't want me recognizing him any more than I want him figuring out my identity.

"Yeah," he says, leaning against the counter in that effortless way that reminds me I'm still a red-blooded woman with functioning eyes. "If we're going to cohabitate for a week, maybe we need some rules."

"Rules, right." I try to sound casual, but my heart skips. He seems decent. I mean, he didn't poison me. Are those my standards now? Honestly... after what my ex put me through, they might be. But still, what kind of rules are we talking here?

"Dishes. We do them after we eat. And we clean up after ourselves."

"Done."

He pauses, his brow pinching slightly. "Um... there's only one bed with thin walls, so... no sleepovers?"

A surprised laugh bursts from my throat before I can stop it. He cocks his head, assessing me with a look that's way too observant for my comfort. Yeah, okay, weird reaction to that rule. But sleepovers? With a stranger? Not in this lifetime. I clear my throat. "No sleepovers," I agree. "The bed's yours. I don't mind the couch."

He makes a low, grumbly sound and rubs a hand over his scruffy jaw. No wonder they call him Bear. He's big, broad, and just the right amount of adorably grouchy. Not that I'm going to say that out loud. As the Bucks' infamously hard-hitting defenseman, I'm guessing "cute" isn't his preferred descriptor.

"What?" I ask, when another grumble escapes like he's wrestling with himself.

He shakes his head. "What kind of guy makes a girl sleep on the sofa? My mother would kill me."

Something in me melts a little at the mention of his mom. They say you can tell a lot about a man by how he treats his mother. If only I'd paid attention to that the first time around.

I don't know much about hockey legend Rip Hart—aka Ripley Stripley to the puck bunnies—but hearing him talk about his mom softens some of that tough-guy armor. For a second, I get a glimpse of the man underneath the pads and the scowl.

And I like what I see.

I lift my mug and, hoping to ease his worries, offer a smile. "A guy who makes coffee for Goldilocks, even after she crashes his place and breaks all the rules? That's a true gentleman move." I tug at the hem of the oversized sweatshirt I borrowed. "I'll change and do the dishes. It's the least I can do."

"Don't worry about it," he says, eyes flicking away, but not before he adds, a little too casually, "Maybe just, uh... put on some pants."

Pants.

Oh. My. God.

In all the chaos, I somehow forgot that my legs are completely bare. When I bent over earlier... did I...?

I die a little inside.

Maybe that "stiff" comment really did hit the wrong way.

Nope. That's crazy talk. Totally unrelated. Entirely coincidental.

"Pants. Yes. Of course." I scramble to cover up, my dignity flailing somewhere in the distance.

"Um, maybe you should put on a shirt," I say, equally as casual.

He grins, and I can feel my face flush.

Really, Charly, you had to bring up the fact that he was half naked too?

Trying to spin a joke out of it, before he thinks I like what I see, which of course I do, I pluck at the sweatshirt. "Or am I wearing your only one?"

"No, I've got a shirt." He heads to the fridge, not at all in a hurry to go find it. But then I catch it. His gait. It's not just casual morning stiffness. There's something off. A protective tightness in the way he moves, favoring one leg. Suddenly, it clicks. Jason is a physiotherapist, and I teach yoga at his clinic. I've seen injuries like that a hundred times, an injury he's hiding.

Not *your business, Charly*.

Do not get involved.

I'm halfway through convincing myself to shut up when my mouth betrays me. "Rip."

He pauses, glancing over. "Yeah?"

"I'm doing some yoga on the beach later. Thought it might help with, you know... the tightness." I casually rub my shoulder, trying not to make it obvious that I'm totally calling him out.

He looks down, brow furrowing like he's debating whether to take the offer or pretend he's fine. After a beat, he gives a small nod. "That might be a good idea."

Progress.

He gestures toward the bedroom. "Go get dressed. I'll make us something that isn't oatmeal. Or porridge. Any allergies?"

I shake my head, and he holds up the oatmeal wrapper, crinkling it in mock horror. "Obviously carbs aren't a problem. And hey, I'm not mad about that."

He tosses me a grin, casual and cocky, and it does strange, fluttery things to my insides.

"I was stress eating," I say defensively, even though we both know I would dive headfirst into another bowl if given half the chance.

He goes quiet, his expression softening, something tender flickering in his eyes. "I'm sorry you're stressed, Charly."

I offer a smile, but it's the kind that never quite reaches your eyes. It sits on my face like a mask, brittle and tired. "I'm sorry for dumping that on you." I try to shake it off with a wink. "But hey, a week at the beach...that'll be just right."

He huffs a soft laugh. "Okay, go. I'll get cooking."

I make a quick stop in the bathroom, where I wash my face, brush my teeth, and temporarily pack my emotional baggage. On my way to the bedroom, I sneak a glance at him, fully dressed now. He reaches into a cabinet, pulls out a box of pancake mix, or something equally simple. My eyes betray me, lingering just a second too long on the way his broad shoulders flex and shift.

Nope. Not doing that. I speed into the bedroom, unzip my duffel and sigh at the sad excuse for a wardrobe inside. I'd packed in a panic, bolting from the tiny California apartment I shared with my ex after the story broke. Paparazzi on the sidewalk, neighbors whispering, phones buzzing with fake concern. I barely had time to call a rideshare, let alone think about clean underwear.

At first, I didn't even know where I was going.

Most of my friends—what few I had left—had faded into the background over the years. Turns out singing in bars every night doesn't leave a lot of time for socializing. My ex and I met during a last-minute booking screw-up at a bar. We hit it off, played a few duets, dated for a year... then came The Spotlight auditions. After I won...then came the scandal. A "leak," they called it. I called it betrayal.

I'd made what I thought were friends on the show, but after my name made the headlines again, for all the wrong reasons, people either vanished or turned against me.

I didn't even consider going home to my parents. Not after they acted like I'd *personally* posted the video for clout, and to embarrass them. Because clearly, that's what every daughter dreams of. My brother was the only real safe space left. But he's newly engaged, running his own physiotherapy clinic, and too good to be dragged down by the dumpster fire I've become.

So here I am. Hiding out at Paisley's cottage.

She's one of the few people who's always been in my corner. We met years ago at some recital. She went off to university and classical training, while I headed to smoky barrooms and open mics. Different paths, same dream. We stayed in touch, and I knew about this place. When I saw she was off on her honeymoon, I figured fate had finally thrown me a bone.

I pull out a pair of yoga pants and a snug spandex top from the bag, changing quickly as music starts to drift through the cottage. Not just playing—thumping. Bassline heavy, upbeat, with a little groove.

I crack the bedroom door open quietly... and bite down on my lip to keep from laughing out loud when I spot Rip at the stove, spatula in hand, hips swaying slightly to the beat. He's not full-out dancing, not with his kind of injury, but there's movement. A shoulder roll here, a head nod there. For a big guy, he's surprisingly... rhythmic. The man's got secrets, but he's also got some well-hidden kitchen swagger. And God help me, I'm sort of looking forward to a week here.

"Rip's got moves," I tease.

Okay, so maybe they're a little stiff, but they're moves nonetheless. Like a grumpy bear trying to groove.

He shoots a look over his shoulder, deadpan. "Be nice or no carbs for you."

"I'm always nice."

"I'm not," he mutters, slipping back into his signature grump-mode, but something tells me he's bluffing. "I'm only moving because someone found my bed just right and now my shoulders are kinked."

Kinked.

Well, great. Why did *that* word light up every inappropriate corner of my brain?

"Won't happen again. And hey, look at that, we now know something about each other," I say, trying to steer us away from dangerous territory. There's an unspoken agreement between us. Boundaries. Breathing room. No peeking past the surface.

I step closer, trying to sneak a look at whatever he's cooking. Since I can't quite see over his hulking shoulders, I lean around him, one hand brushing his back, the other resting lightly on his arm.

His whole body goes rigid, like I've triggered some kind of fight-or-flight response, and I instantly retreat a step. "Sorry,"

I blurt. "Didn't mean to, uh, touch you like that. Just wondering what smells so good."

"Pancakes," he says, voice a little lower than before. "Whipped cream and fruit are in the fridge. Can you grab those?"

"On it." I spin around, grateful for the mission. I pull out blueberries, strawberries, and a can of whipped cream, placing them on the table with a little more enthusiasm than necessary.

I already know where the dishes are, so I grab two plates and two glasses, and start setting the table. Music still hums through the cottage, and it helps settle the flutter in my chest. Somehow, we're finding a rhythm, not just in the space, but with each other.

"Do you do yoga every day?" he asks suddenly, breaking the comfortable silence.

As he flips a pancake, one slides off the spatula like it's trying to escape. I grin. "Yeah, I do. I used to teach classes, too."

He nods, thoughtful, and hands me a fluffy, golden pancake. Then he pours more batter into the pan, quiet again, like he's mulling something over.

I pile my plate with fruit and whipped cream, fill our glasses with juice, and slide into one of the chairs. Rip stays at the stove, and I let him be, devouring carbs like it's my full-time job.

God, I've missed carbs. When I was on the show, I had a strict diet—protein shakes, steamed vegetables, no sugar. No soul.

The cameras add ten pounds, Charly.

Yes, Mom. I know.

She didn't want me in the music world, but if I was going to be in it, I guess I had to at least look good in her eyes. I mean, I am a reflection of my family, after all.

But this week? This strange, unexpected week by the beach? I'm doing whatever I want. Eating pancakes. Breathing. Healing.

Well, within reason, of course.

No sleepovers.

He finishes cooking his huge pancake, piles it with fruit and cream, then drops down across from me with a sigh. He takes a slow sip of juice, a deep crease cutting across his forehead like he's trying to solve world hunger—or maybe just how we both ended up here.

"Gentle stretching's good for strains, right?" he asks.

I nod. "Should help your shoulders." But there's more in that question, something about the stiff way he's moving that he doesn't want me to know. "We can do some gentle stretching today."

He gives me a soft smile. "Thank you."

"Hey, I owe you."

"That's true."

I laugh, feeling the tension slip from my shoulders. "There's nothing like the beach to cure what ails you, huh?" He takes a big bite, cream smudging his nose and scruff. "Maybe they should call you Santa." I bet this man can deliver all kinds of goodness.

"Santa?"

I tap my chin and hand him a paper towel.

"Ha. Ha." He snatches it from me, and wipes his face as I bite back a grin. God, could he be any more adorable.

I stab a chunk of pancake, and hold it up. "For the record, this is just right."

He grumbles, chewing, then drops a curveball: "We should probably talk rules."

I arch an eyebrow. "Rules? There's more?"

"There's always more," he grouches.

"I never pegged you as a rule follower."

His fork freezes mid-air, eyes narrowing with a flicker of caution. "That's because you don't know me."

I catch that like a test. He's nervous I might see through him. "That's true," I say, biting into my pancake. "Okay, hit me with the rules. Wait, I don't have to be in bed by eight or anything, right? I only crashed early last night because of the long travel. I'm a night owl."

He looks down. "I'm not."

I glance at the counter. Even after cooking everything is in order. I'd have batter on the ceiling if I were in charge, and probably more whipped cream on his face than he'd like. What am I even saying?

"I'm not a neat freak either," I clarify.

"I am."

Never would have guessed.

"I like late-night TV. Especially B-rated scary movies."

His lips twist. "I read."

Okay, that response was unexpected and that's on me. Just because he's a jock doesn't mean he's not well read or educated. If I remember correctly, he went to college in upstate New York.

"I like to sunbathe," I add, riding the momentum.

"I don't."

Ripley Stripley—clothes-hater extraordinaire—doesn't like to sunbathe.

But that thought brings on another. "In the nude," I blurt before thinking better of it.

Jesus. Why did I say that?

Oh, maybe because I want more than a grunt and two words out of him.

If he really did know me... well, just saying he recognized me from The Spotlight and was on the fence about whether the tabloid sex scandal was true it would no doubt have him leaning toward the 'yes.'

His head lifts, and his eyes lock on mine. Being his entire focus steals the air right out of my lungs. He stares, long and steady, and I can almost hear his mind racing.

"This isn't Vegas," he finally says, "But what happens at the beach stays at the beach."

Okay... what exactly does he mean by that?

3

RIP

Do not think about Charly sunbathing in the nude.

Too late.

Thinking about it.

Which is crazy, and going to make this week long and painful in so many ways.

"Ready?" she asks as I pluck the key from the starfish bowl on the counter.

"Yup."

She struggles with the big blanket in her arms and I take it from her. She frowns. "I didn't pack my yoga mat."

"Do I need a blanket too?" Jesus, I can't believe I'm about to do yoga. But the doctor did say I needed to follow the 'rice' method. Rest, ice compression and elevation, which I've been doing. Yoga with gentle stretching by a certified instructor would definitely help. I just didn't want to seek out a yoga studio. Didn't want to draw any attention to myself. But now that Charly and her skills fell into my lap, so to speak, I should take advantage of her...it...I mean it. The yoga. I'm not, and never have, taken advantage of anyone.

"You don't really, uh, sunbathe in the nude do you?" I ask.

She cocks her head in challenge. "Is it on the list of 'can't do' rules?"

"No. Actually, I just don't want you drawing any attention to yourself."

Or me.

"Mrs. Callahan would likely call in the police." I nod toward the back of the cottage. "There's a quiet spot on the back deck. It's fenced back there. Private. Probably a good spot."

"Sounds perfect."

We step outside and a warm breeze washes over us as I lock up, making a mental note to get her a key so she can come and go as she pleases. I'm not about to keep her captive inside. We walk down the small walkway, cross the street, and step onto the beach. Warm sand squishes between my toes and I pull my hat down low as we walk toward the water. The beach is pretty quiet this time of morning, and usually later in the evening, when I do my nightly walking.

"Have you even been to Haven beach before?" I ask.

"No." she looks around. "it's beautiful here, though. You live in Boston, right?"

I stiffen and she holds her hands up. "Just making conversation, and for some reason I assumed you lived there because that's where Paisley and Gunter live and you know them."

"Right. I do live in Boston. I'm from California, though."

She smiles, some warm memory drifting across her face. "Do you miss it?" she asks.

"My family is still there, so yeah, I miss it. I was actually living in Chicago before moving to Boston last year." Shit, why am I telling her so much?

"Do you like Boston?"

"I do. I have friends there. You ever been?"

"No."

"I think you'd like it. Maybe not the cold winters, though."

She chuckles. "Probably not."

We make our way toward the water and a soft strumming sound reaches our ears. She instantly turns, like she's seen a ghost but then her body relaxes when her gaze lands on a man sitting alone, strumming on his guitar. She watches for a moment, and my throat tightens at the longing, and then hurt that moves across her pretty face.

"You play?"

She snorts out a laugh. "Feels like a lifetime ago."

"Do you want to move further down the beach so we don't hear it while we stretch?"

"Actually, it is kind of soothing. I'm okay with it if you are."

"I am." I glance around. "This looks like as good a spot as any." She nods and I spread out the blanket. "How did you get into yoga?"

"I used to take dance lessons as a kid, and stretching was a big part." She grins. "That's how I knew you had good moves."

"Well then, if you've seen me dance, then it's only fair that I see you dance."

She huffs out a laugh, as she widens her feet and lifts her hands above her head. "I'm not sure that's the rule at all."

"My cottage, my rules, Goldie."

Rolling her eyes, she puts her hands on my arms and then instantly pulls them back. "Sorry, I didn't mean to touch. I was just trying to position you."

"You can touch me, Charly." She hesitates for a second like she's not too sure about that so I add, "You just caught me off guard. I was here for a week by myself."

"And in one week, I will be out of your hair."

I resist the urge to ask her where she'll go. If she broke into a place she thought was abandoned, it means she has no one, and that breaks my fucking heart. Everyone needs someone.

And who do you need, Rip?

Lyra.

But like Mick Jagger once said, you can't always get what you want. She knows I'm here at the beach. We text. Especially when it's late at night and she's feeling lonely. I've always been there for her, but I don't really want her visiting, not that she said she wanted to. But I need to heal in private.

While I've been holding a torch for her since college, it's unrequited most times. Maybe not wanting her here is a sign I'm getting over her. Or maybe it's a sign that I'm worried she'll figure out I'm hurt and use it to further her career.

Which begs the question, why the hell am I still pining for a girl who burned me once, and I believe would do it again? I need my head checked. Of that I have no doubt. Maybe I'll make an appointment with Melanie when I get home. But the truth is, hurting me is one thing, but now, it's not just my secret I have to protect, and I feel weirdly protective of my new roommate.

She puts her hands on me again. They're soft and warm on my arms as she shimmies me on the blanket. She finally gets me where she wants me and stands back. My gaze rakes over tight clothes that showcase her soft curves. I tear my gaze away.

"Why do you need me standing right here?" I laugh, hard and deep and she grins at me. "Is it some sort of sun salute ritual thing?"

"Oh, it's a sun thing." I eye her and she continues to explain. "I need your big body to block it from my eyes."

I laugh, deep and hard. "Oh, so I'm helping you out yet again." I shake my head at her antics.

"Come on, it's a win/win. No sun in your eyes, and no sun in mine. Now stop talking and do what I do."

"Bossy," I grumble, even though I like our easy banter.

She takes a big breath in and I do the same and lift my arms to the sky. I stretch and when she leans to the left, I lean to the left. We continue this for a few more minutes, and then we drop to the blanket, the sand cushioning us.

She stretches out her legs and puts her hands between them. Her eyes catch mine, and there's a deep seriousness there. "Stretch forward gently. If you feel any pain in your legs, even the slightest twinge, back off, okay? I don't need you trying to impress me."

I glance at her and give her my signature bad boy smile. "If I were trying to impress you, you'd know."

She rolls her eyes, unaffected by my charm and that's probably a good thing. Wait, why am I even trying to be charming? I think the lack of sleep and early morning heat is messing with my brain.

"Press your feet to mine."

I do as she says and honestly, it feels pretty damn good to stretch out like this.

"Close your eyes," she says quietly. "Feel the sun on your back. Listen to the water. Smell the ocean air, and let the tension drain from your body as you become one with nature."

I take a deep breath and concentrate on her voice as I engage my senses. I let air out slowly, and it loosens something in my chest, a knot that has been tightening, thickening since our last playoff game.

In the distance, the call of the seagulls mingles with the strumming guitar, and I lean forward a little more. A small twinge has me pulling back and I open one eye to take in the petite blonde facing me, our bare feet touching.

"What are you smiling at?" she asks, and that's when I realize her eyes are open too and she's watching me.

"Nothing," I say quickly. "I guess, this is nice. It feels good."

"Goldilocks got skills." She takes a deep breath. "By the end of the week, Big Bear will be purring like a kitten."

Purring like a kitten.

The sudden image of little Goldie under Big Bear—purring like a kitten—pulls a growl from the depths of my throat.

She arches a brow. "You growling at me, Big Bear?"

"No. Just…maybe let's not talk about purring."

Her smile falters, just a flicker. "Why?"

I glance her way, one corner of my mouth lifting, dry. "It's problematic for me."

She blinks, and for a beat we just sit there, the air stretching between us, charged.

"Right," she says, finally, her voice light but her gaze not quite meeting mine, because yeah, she gets it. "No more kitten talk."

"Appreciate it," I murmur. But I'm already too late. The image is burned in.

She shifts into another pose, seated twist, her spine long, chest open, and I follow, though my joints protest. Not from the stretch. From the proximity. From her.

Goldie, with her tousled hair, her sand-dusted skin, and those eyes that see too much. She exhales slowly, grounding herself. I try to do the same. It doesn't work.

"So, Big Bear," she teases lightly, not looking at me, "Do you growl often, or just when provoked by woodland creatures or when you stretch?"

"I growl when someone pokes the bear."

She snorts at that. "You're not as grumpy as you pretend to be, you know."

"Don't let the pancake-making fool you. I'm a menace before breakfast, after dinner, and always when doing yoga."

"That so?" She lifts a brow and moves into a forward fold. "Guess I'll make a note not to poke the bear during those times."

I'm trying hard not to look, but then she glances at me, upside down, hair spilling toward the sand, a teasing smile on her lips.

"What?" she asks.

I clear my throat and turn my gaze out to the ocean. "Just... wondering if we need more rules."

She straightens slowly, studying me. "So many rules for one week."

Before I can answer, she stands, brushes the sand from her leggings, and offers me a hand. "Come on, Big Bear. Let's go back. You've got rules to write, and I've got sunbathing to do. In something appropriate."

Great, now I'm picturing her in something...not appropriate.

I take her hand, but don't let go right away. Her skin is warm. Her grip steady. There's something really different about this woman.

"We're done, already?" I ask. "Are we going to do it doggy style?" Her eyes go wide and she bites her lip, working hard not to laugh. I shake my head, confused. "What?"

"We are going to take it slow, and it's called downward dog, and we're going to get to that, eventually. Doggy style is something else entirely and no we will not be doing that."

I nearly choke on my tongue. I don't know much about yoga, but I know a Freudian slip when I hear it. "That's not—I didn't mean—obviously we won't be doing that." Fuck my life. "I mean, I don't even want to."

Liar.

CHARLY

I check in with my brother to let him know I found a place to stay. I don't tell him where. Call me paranoid, but I have no idea who is listening or watching. That almost makes me laugh. It's not like I'm a big star. Heck, just a few months ago I was a nobody. Sure, my name, Indie Rhodes, became popular when I won The Spotlight, but it was the supposed sex tape I was in that really skyrocketed me.

Who knew all you had to do was flash the world to become popular?

They say any publicity is good publicity, but I disagree. I really don't want to be known for my sex-capades, even if they weren't mine. But honestly, I have no idea if this will blow over...ugh, bad choice of words...or I'll have to find another career, out of the spotlight.

I read my brother's response. He, of course, wanted me to stay with him, but again, I don't want to bring him unwanted attention. What would he think if he knew I'd crashed in Rip

Hart's bed. He'd probably lose his mind. Everyone knows Rip's reputation. But I'm not about to crawl into bed with him.

No sleepovers.

No doggy style.

A chuckle rumbles in my throat just as a noise at the door gains my attention. I set my phone down, shade the late day sun from my eyes and spot Big Bear stepping into the back yard.

"Something funny?"

"Just texting my brother." Shoot, I shouldn't have said that. We're not sharing details of our lives, and the less we know the better. Although, something does tell me this man can keep a secret. Heck he's keeping one of his own. But I plan to help him with that. He just doesn't have to know it.

"Crispy yet?"

I poke my leg. "Medium well," I say, and sit up. I might have sunbathed nude, considering I don't have a bathing suit with me, but no way would I do it with Rip in the house. I am not leaning into the things the media is saying about me.

He jerks his hand out. "Thought I'd go catch us some dinner."

I angle my head. "You're going to catch dinner? Should I be worried?"

He laughs. "Nah, did you see those rocks today when we were doing yoga?"

He waves his hand, pointing to somewhere far in the distance, but all I see is the fence hugging the backyard. "Vaguely."

"Good fishing spot. I can hook us some summer flounder."

I sit up a little straighter. Honestly, I'm not built for lounging. Sure the backyard is peaceful and quiet, which is exactly what I thought I needed, but I'm already starting to feel like a decoration. A slightly sweaty, restless gnome.

Rip, meanwhile, looks like he was born to recline in silence and look handsome doing it. I don't want to ruin his Zen more than I already have.

"Sounds fun," I respond, like someone pretending to know the difference between a flounder and a door stop.

He turns, about to walk off, then hesitates. "I have an extra rod, if you want to tag along."

"I've actually never fished before," I blurt out, already scrambling to my feet like this is a limited-time offer and I have to react. My body is halfway to the house when my mouth tries to play it cool. "But I don't want to get in your way."

Jeez, way to act casual, Charly. Maybe throw in a cartwheel next time.

"Kind of seems like you do," he teases as I brush past him.

"It's just that I don't like to half-ass anything," I shoot back as I flash him a grin over my shoulder. "Mother always told me if you're going to do something, do it right."

"So she means, if you're going to be a nuisance, you're going to be an award-winning nuisance?

"I don't do amateur hour, Rip." His laughter curls around me as I shut the bathroom door. I wash up quickly, buzzing with way too much excitement for what is technically a yucky fish-based activity. Heck, I thought I wanted quiet and calm.

Turns out calm is kind of boring without my guitar, and nothing is boring around Big Bear.

After washing up, I step into the living room and find it empty. "Rip?" Did he leave without me? The place isn't big and there are no spots a man his size can hide. Rustling sounds from outside reach my ears, and I slip on my flip flops and step out front to find him pulling rods and a toolbox from the small shed. I stand back for a moment and take pleasure in the strength of his big body.

While I'd like to suggest he ice his groin, I'm not supposed to know about his injury. There are ways I can probably get around that, though.

I walk up to him. "Need help?" I ask and he jumps. "Sorry."

"I'm going to have to put a bell on you," he grumps.

"Or you can just remember that you're sharing this place with me now. Have you forgotten already?"

He hands me a rod. "No, of course not."

Okay, why is he saying it like that?

Maybe because you really are an annoyance, girlfriend.

A wave of guilt seeps through my blood. If I had anywhere to go, I would. I guess all I can do is try to make this week easy on him. Help him out with cooking and cleaning, and healing and whatever other things he might need help with, like yoga, stretching...doggy style.

Nope not going there.

He sets the toolbox on the ground, and I'm about to flick my hair over my shoulder before I bend to pick it up. That's when I remember it's cut short. My stomach tightens. I probably shouldn't be out on the rocks, parading around the beach where someone might recognize me.

Rip's phone pings, and he tugs it from the side pocket of his shorts. His entire body goes stiff as he reads the message, then he stands there like he's debating his next move.

"Everything okay?"

"Yeah, it's…ah…she's uh…"

"You don't know who she is?"

"She's my girlfriend," he blurts out, and that takes me by surprise.

"Oh, yes, of course. I'll just be over there, to give you privacy?" He rubs his eyebrow as I step away, which appears to be some kind of nervous tick. Are they having a fight? Is that why he looked unsure, maybe even a bit nervous when the message came in? Does she know about his injury? Is he hiding it from her, too?

Wow, for a girl who doesn't want to get to know her roommate, I sure have a lot of questions.

Not your business, Charly.

Unless of course it is my business and he's worried his girlfriend would be upset to find out he was cohabitating with a strange woman.

I walk away, and stand in the small driveway. I'm guessing Rip must have taken an Uber here too, since there's no car in the driveway. If there had been, I probably wouldn't have shimmied the window open and snuck inside.

I examine the fishing pole and tug on the line, pretending to know something about the contraption as his fingers fly over his phone. A moment later, toolbox in hand and fishing rod in the other, he steps up to me.

"All set?"

From the frown on his face, to the deep line in his forehead, it's easy to tell he's not okay. I'm not about to ask. Asking questions leads to more questions and I don't want any of those directed at me.

"Those rocks over there?" I say, pointing off toward the coastline, hoping to steer the conversation toward something he obviously enjoys. My finger arcs through the salty air, and Rip follows the line of my hand. "That's where we're going?" He nods, and I ask, "Have you been fishing this week?"

"Nearly every day."

We fall into step, our feet crunching over a mix of crushed shells as we cross the road and reach the beach. We head toward the waterline.

"Catch anything?" I ask, brushing a wind-whipped strand of hair from my cheek.

A grin tugs at his mouth, and his shoulders lift in a dramatic shrug. "Yesterday I caught an old pair of gym shorts, followed by a wave of disappointment."

I snort, nearly tripping over a driftwood log. "Tragic."

"Don't laugh," he says, bumping my shoulder with his. I stumble sideways with a mock gasp, nearly losing a flip-flop. "I worked hard. I thought I had something big on the line."

"I'm sorry," I say, still giggling as I regain my balance. "Really, I am."

Rip shoots me a sideways look. "Don't be. There's a fish market down the street. This is about relaxing."

We reach a flat stretch of wet sand and slow our pace. I glance over at him. "So... did you keep them? The shorts, I mean."

"No."

I tap my chin. "Hmmm."

"What?"

I stop short, plant my feet like I mean business, and toss a hand on my hip. "Let's have a contest."

"A contest?" Rip turns, raising an eyebrow like I just challenged him to a duel instead of beachcombing. He adjusts the fishing rod on his shoulder with a practiced ease that really shouldn't be so attractive.

"Yeah. Let's see who can reel in the most useful item today. Winner keeps the loot."

He gives me a crooked smirk—equal parts charm and trouble. "Define useful."

"If it's clothing," I say sweetly. "We have to wear it. No exceptions."

Rip narrows his eyes, full of suspicion. "I'm not putting on a dress. Or anything with sequins. Or feathers."

I grin, already imagining him in something tragic and glittery that smells faintly of seaweed and regret. "Then maybe you don't want to play?"

He steps closer, and his eyes flicker with a cocky gleam. Why did I know this man would never back down from a challenge? "Oh, I'm playing. Just want it on record that if I end up in someone's discarded wedding gown, I'm blaming you."

"Why do I feel like this isn't hypothetical?" I squint at him.

A grin tugs at his mouth as he steps up on a rock and extends a hand to help me over. "Let's just say I've seen some things in Vegas that no man should ever see. Including a groomsman in a tiara."

This isn't the first time he's mentioned Vegas. "You spend a lot of time there, or do you just live in a Hangover movie?"

"My grandfather owns a resort out there," he says with a shrug, then winces, like he accidentally dropped a secret.

Truthfully, his secrets are safe with me, as long as mine are safe with him. I pinch my eyes shut playfully. "Now I'm never getting the vision of you in a wedding dress out of my brain."

"It wasn't me." He laughs. "But my buddy nearly ended up in one. Fortunately, he found himself in a Mrs. Roper dress."

"From that old seventies show?"

"Yup.'

"That is fortunate," I say with a laugh, not exactly sure how that is better.

"He was helping a girl out, one who needed to get away from her fiancé."

"Okay, clearly I broke into the wrong cottage. Does your cross-dressing hero friend have a place nearby? He'd obviously be up for my game." I glance around casually.

For the briefest second, something flickers across his face. Jealousy? No. Couldn't be. Could it?

"Nope," he says smoothly. "And he's married to that runaway bride now."

I stick out my hand. "So, we got a deal? No backing out if you catch a wetsuit and a tutu?"

He shakes my hand, his grip firm, warm, and just a little too smug. "You're on," he says.

"Prepare to be dazzled by my sea trash couture," I tell him, eyes twinkling.

He sets the toolbox down, and takes my rod from me. I watch as he gives a detailed explanation on how to cast my line, and I like that he's not watering it down for fishing dummies 101. "First we need something shiny to attract the fish." He gestures with a nod toward the box.

"Open the tackle box and grab me a lure."

"Is that what this is called?" I ask, as I pop it open. "I thought it was a toolbox. I just wasn't sure what tools we used to fish. I thought maybe you kept a hammer in here and bopped them on the head."

He chuckles. "That's okay. You didn't know. Now see that shiny lure there. Grab me that, and grab that bobber."

"Bobber?"

"The red and white thing."

I laugh. "I thought this was a grenade." I pick it up and examine it. "Kind of looks like one. You don't use this to blow the fish out of the water?"

"No, we're not blowing anything."

Blow.

God.

We both go deathly silent for a second and when he clears his throat and holds out his hand, I place the bobber in his palm. He goes about doing something fancy as he ties it to my line.

"Come here." He places his hands gently on my arms and draws me in, chest to back, no space. No air. Just heat. "This is how you hold it."

He positions my fingers with careful precision, and I swear my brain short circuits. His thighs brush mine, his chest is solid and warm against my back and I can feel his heartbeat thudding against my body in a steady rhythm that seems to be hypnotizing me.

Focus. Focus...

His callused fingertips skim the line, and all I can think about is how those same fingers would feel tracing down my bare skin.

Get it together, girl.

I move against him and a sound catches in his throat as my ass brushes against his... Wait, what was that I just brushed against? He shifts to the side and I clear my throat and struggling for something other than what that might have been pressing against me, I blurt out, "This doesn't seem too hard."

Hard...

Ugh.

I instantly regret every life choice that brought me to that cursed sentence.

"Okay," he murmurs, his voice deeper now. "You hold your finger on the line here, pull it back like this, and as you cast, let go." The line releases. I watch as the lure plunks into the water and the little bobber bounces like it's doing the macarena.

"If that bobber dips, it means you have something nibbling."

Nibbling...

Why is everything about fishing starting to sound suggestive?

"And if I get a nibble, what do I do?"

"You tug. Like this."

Tug...

He gives my line a firm pull, just enough to jolt the breath right out of me.

"That will hook the fish and you can reel it in." He steps away from me, finally giving me room to breathe, or possibly combust. I wet my dry lips. "Why don't you reel it in, and give it a try yourself, while I get my rod ready."

Rod...

Fantastic. I am officially thirteen years old.

I steal a quick glance at him as he fiddles with said *rod*, and take a cautious step closer to the edge of the rocks, trying to shake off the weird things I'm feeling, but...bad idea.

A rogue wave surges up out of nowhere and suddenly...

Whoosh.

I'm on my ass, slipping into the water, which I hit with zero dignity. I gasp, cold, wet. Mortified.

Before I can even curse, he's there, arms around me, hauling me up like some damn romance hero who just happened to be waiting for the perfect moment to rescue a flailing disaster of a woman in distress. Which I'm not. I'm capable of rescuing myself, but maybe I'll just let this play out for a second.

"Are you okay?"

I nod, but the words don't come. Not because I've swallowed half the Atlantic, but because I'm in his arms.

And I *really* like it.

He must see something on my face—something worrisome—because his expression shifts.

"Shit," he mutters.

Then, before I even realize what's going on, I'm flat on my back in the wet sand, and this man, this gorgeous Big Bear, a guy with as many secrets as I have is leaning over me.

And giving me mouth-to-mouth.

Oh. God.

Do I stop him?

Do I tell him I'm fine?

Or do I let him keep going...because well it's so good.

Seriously though, I really need to put a stop to this.

Yet, here I am, a moan threatening as I enjoy his mouth on mine, even if it's for unnecessary, medically questionable reasons.

His lips are so warm. Firm. He smells like saltwater and sun and every mistake I want to make twice. Then...that sound escapes. It's just a tiny one. Barely a sigh. But he hears it.

Believe me, I *know* he hears it, because he freezes, just a breath away, eyes locked on mine.

"You're not drowning," he says.

I blink up at him. "Technically, no."

He stays close, the warmth of his breath on my face when he says, "You let me do mouth-to-mouth."

I offer a shrug, which is hard to pull off when you're flat on your back in wet sand. "I panicked."

His gaze flicks down to my lips again. "That noise you just made. What was that?"

"Accident," I offer.

"Accident?" he echoes, but it's a question.

"I think it was just a bit of air escaping." Also known as a sigh...one full of pleasure, if we're being honest, but we're definitely not being honest.

What even is my life right now?

Rip leans back just enough to give me space, except now he's straddling my legs, the heat of him pressing through the chill of my soaked clothes. His brow lifts, droplets sliding down the sharp line of his jaw. I have the overwhelming urge to follow one with my fingertip. Or my mouth.

"So just to clarify..." he says slowly, like he's solving a puzzle. "You accidentally fell into the ocean, then accidentally sighed while you accidentally let me kiss you while fully conscious?"

I narrow my eyes at him. "Kiss me," I shoot back with a snort, trying to play this cool. "Dude, that was mouth-to-mouth." A beat and then, "Wasn't it?"

His eyes glaze over for a second. "It was a lot of mouth." He doesn't sound mad about it.

Yeah, me neither.

I sit up too fast, and we nearly headbutt each other. We moan, then laugh, awkward. Breathless.

"I'm okay and you're okay," I mumble, brushing sand off my chest like that'll somehow erase this moment. "Let's get back to fishing. I'm itching for a new pair of cargo shorts."

But his eyes are still on me, trailing down my face, low and slow. But then his search stops, right where my soaked shirt clings tightest. Right where my cold, very awake nipples are making an undeniable appearance.

"But..." he pauses and scrubs his face like he's in total agony.

Join the club, buddy.

"But what?" I ask, when he can't seem to finish the sentence.

He swallows. "You're all wet."

Wet.

Yes, yes I am and God help me...

5

RIP

I try to keep my focus on the fishing line. Really, I do. But the woman next to me is soaked, her T-shirt clinging in ways that should probably be illegal, and her hard nipples are doing absolutely nothing to help my concentration.

A warm breeze drifts over us as she shifts her stance, brushing damp strands of hair from her face.

"If you want to run back and change," I offer, keeping my tone casual, "I wouldn't blame you."

She waves me off. "Nah, I'll dry soon enough." Then she wipes her brow and shoots me a smile. Open, grateful, genuine. It knocks me off-kilter more than her wet T-shirt ever could. That's probably not a good thing. She lowers herself onto the rocks beside me, shoulders sinking like the last of the tension is finally melting out of her. "Actually, Rip... this is the most relaxed I've felt in a long time." She lifts her face to the sun. My God, she's pretty. Like really pretty.

I drop down next to her with a quiet grunt, stretching out my legs. My groin is already protesting. The stretching this morning was helpful, but apparently, standing on rocks for an hour isn't part of my healing regimen.

"I'm glad," I say, because it's true. She's been through a lot lately, and if I can help out a bit, help her forget real life, even for a week, then I'm happy to do it.

The Atlantic stretches out in front of us, sunlight bouncing off the waves in sharp glints. She watches the ocean like she's memorizing it. What is going through her mind?

"I had no idea fishing could be like this," she murmurs, enlightening me to her thoughts. She gives me a grin. "Maybe I'll take it up when I leave."

A knot tightens in my chest at the word *leave*, but I shove it down.

"There's lots of good fishing in California," I say, trying for casual. "You can charter a boat, do some deep-sea stuff." She grunts at my suggestion. "You don't like the idea of that?"

Her nose crinkles as she puckers. "I kind of like being on the rocks." She pats the smooth surface beneath us.

"You don't like boats?"

"I actually fell off one once. When I was young. It was an accident, but..." Her voice trails off.

When she doesn't continue, I lean forward. "Jesus, I'm sorry, Charly. That must've been terrifying."

"It was." She pauses, then adds, "My parents were super mad."

That makes me blink. "Wait... You had an accident and your parents were mad?"

She gives a hollow chuckle. "But that's me. Troublesome Charly. Too much. Disobedient. Out of control."

"I'm sorry." The words are automatic, but a wave of anger rises in me like a tide. How could her parents be mad at her for nearly drowning?

"Not your fault," she says. Another humorless laugh. "Wasn't mine either, but that didn't seem to matter. My brother and I were playing. He accidentally knocked me in. But he's the golden child. He can't do anything wrong."

I go quiet. We have this unspoken rule — no sharing, no digging — but she's clearly handing me a piece of herself. And it feels fragile in my hands.

"You get along with your brother?" I ask gently.

"I do. And don't get me wrong. I love him to pieces. He's a physiotherapist, and is my parents' pride and joy." A warm smile touches her mouth. "I'm so proud of him too." Her voice softens.

"I'm sure your parents are proud of you too."

She swallows. "I never followed the path they wanted for me." She rolls one shoulder. "See, rebel."

"Nah, we have to follow our own hearts, Charly."

"Maybe. But look where that got me." She stares out over the ocean, but it's easy to tell her thoughts are miles away. "My brother was the only one who believed me when—" She cuts herself off, the words dying suddenly.

"What is it your parents wanted you to do?" I ask.

"They thought I'd be a good teacher, or even lawyer, since I was so good at arguing."

I cringe. "That sounds more like a dig than a compliment. I take it your teenage years were hard."

"On all of us. I thought I could show them with…" She shifts, sits a little straighter, like she's pulling armor back into place. "Wow," she says with forced brightness. "What is it about fishing that has me dragging up past hurts and bringing the mood down?"

"It's all good, Charly. Fishing can be a quiet time, a time to reflect, too. And you only brought up the past because I asked about boats."

She nods, her gaze drifting out across the water. Silence settles for a moment, comfortable now.

Then I ask, "Do you think you'd ever get on one again? You know what they say about falling off a horse."

She grins, just a little. "I don't know. Maybe. For the record I've never been on a horse, so I don't know what I'd do if I fell off."

I do an air checkmark. "Adding horseback riding to our list of things to do," I say playfully. "But seriously, I could rent a boat. We wouldn't have to go far. And I can put you in a life jacket and water wings."

"Water wings?" Her eyebrows lift.

I grin. "Lots of my friends have pools and their kids wear them. You know—" I raise my arms and wrap a hand around one bicep, miming the inflated floaties. "They blow up and keep you afloat. Pretty stylish, honestly."

"Well, I mean, if there are water wings involved…" Her eyes light up with amusement. "Will you be wearing them too? Because if so, then yes, I *have* to see that."

"I'm not sure they make them in men's sizes," I say, chuckling. "But if they do, yeah, I'll wear them." She leans a little closer, and I catch another whiff of her sweet scent. Sunshine and warmth.

"Really?" she murmurs. "That wouldn't embarrass you?"

I meet her gaze, and something warm blooms in my chest. "Nope. Not if it gets you back on a boat. I'd wear a whole inflatable suit if I had to."

That earns me a laugh, an unguarded, genuine sound that wraps around me and squeezes tight. God, I love that laugh and it's crazy how much I enjoy her company. How easy it is to sit here with her, just talking. I don't usually do this, talk with women. Not like this. The women I've been with before, they wanted something else from me. Attention, maybe. The image. The body. But never this. Never the part where we trade memories and dare to be honest. That's not to say I'm not attracted to her. Hell, I am. But this is just really...nice.

"You don't have to answer," I say, nudging her gently. "I'll leave that with you. I mean, we've got to do something to pass the time this week."

Pass the time.

There are about ten things I could think of to make the week go faster... or slower. Or just plain more interesting. All of them start with her and end somewhere I probably shouldn't be thinking about right now.

"Okay," she says, her voice quieter. "I'll think about it."

I glance at her again, then shift a little on the rock. "What do you usually do to relax?" I ask, even though we promised to keep things surface-level. I can't help it. I want to know more. I want to know *her*.

She doesn't answer right away, and for a second I wonder if I pushed too far. But then she tucks her hair behind her ear and says, "I write and play music."

I blink, like I'm surprised by that. Actually, maybe I am. I knew she sang, but I didn't know she wrote music too. "That's awesome. I have, like, negative music skills. I can't play anything. My singing is strictly shower only, and you're welcome," I tease.

She laughs, her eyes sparkling. "What's your go-to shower song?"

I smirk. "That's classified."

"Oh, so it's embarrassing," she says, clearly delighted. "Let me guess... something dramatic. Whitney Houston? Celine Dion?"

I gasp. "I'll have you know I nail, 'My Heart Will Go On.' The acoustics in the bathroom are phenomenal."

She grins and bumps her shoulder against mine. "Now I have to hear it."

I raise an eyebrow. "You volunteering to sit outside the door while I shower? That's bold, and a little creepy, Charly." Jesus, I can't think about her climbing into the shower with me. I do not need to be sporting a boner while fishing.

Her cheeks flush, but she doesn't look away. "Maybe I just want to know what kind of guy I'm stuck with for the week."

"I'm full of surprises," I say, a little softer this time.

She holds my gaze, and for a second, the teasing fades into something quieter. Warmer. The air between us shifts.

Then she looks away, lips curving. "I think you're full of something."

"Hey," I burst out.

She laughs. "Tell me, do you incorporate your 'moves' when you're belting out Celine?"

I grin. "Be nice. You weren't supposed to see that. My disco skills are also highly classified."

She laughs, really laughs, and it's the kind that makes your chest feel lighter just hearing it. I'd do a hundred more ridiculous dance moves if it meant I could hear that sound again.

"I guess I'll have to get a bell after all," she teases with a gleam in her eye. "A woman can only take so much of those moves."

"Does that mean you like them, or hate them?"

"They're not bad, Rip. I mean, I've seen worse."

"That's the nicest thing anyone has said to me today," I joke.

She grins, eyes on the water. "I can teach you to play. Least I can do after you introduced me to the relaxing world of fishing."

I narrow my eyes, scanning through a mental inventory of the beach house. "Did you bring a guitar? Must've been a tight squeeze getting it through the window."

She laughs, but there's no real joy behind it. More of a hollow echo than a belly laugh. "Right. No. Didn't bring it."

Her smile fades, her rod twitching as she watches her bobber like it might reveal the secrets of the universe.

"What's Rip short for?" she asks, casual but curious.

"Ripley."

She turns slightly. "I like it. It suits you."

"Charly suits you," I say. So does Indie Rhodes, but that part stays behind my teeth.

"I'm named after my dad," she says softly.

"I'm named after a fictional alien-slaying badass." Her brows shoot up. "Yeah. My mom was a superfan of the Alien franchise. My older brother's name is Easton. I guess they saved the weird name for the second kid."

"Weird?" she teases.

"It came with nicknames," I sigh dramatically. "You know what kids called me growing up?"

She perks up, lips twitching. "Do tell."

"Some went with *Believe It or Not.*" I pause, giving her a second to connect the dots.

She frowns, then her eyes pop. "Oh, *Ripley's Believe It or Not.*"

"Yup." I snort. "Yeah, those kids weren't exactly comedic geniuses." She's already giggling, so I pile on. "I also got *Rip Cord. Rippy Longstocking.*"

"Oh, that one's solid," she laughs, clearly delighted.

"Wait, there's more. Teenage years? I had a breakout moment and became *Zitley.*"

"Oof. Harsh."

"Yeah. And then there was the time I got caught in a rainstorm and some genius coined *Dripley.*"

That gets a real laugh out of her, loud and free. "Dripley. That's gold."

"Oh, you like that one, huh?"

She nudges me with her elbow. "You know, Rip... I find it very hard to believe you were ever the guy getting picked on at recess."

"Oh yeah? What gives you that idea?"

She waves a hand slowly, up and down. "Just a hunch. Something about the whole... six-foot-something, FAFO energy you give off."

"FAFO?" I ask and then laugh. "Oh, fuck around and find out."

"Yeah."

I chuckle. "I wasn't always big. And honestly, the names never really bothered me."

"Well, that's good," she says. "Because I might start calling you Dripley from now on."

"Great. Can't wait to hear that in public again."

"Now you're Big Bear," she says, grinning.

"And Ripley Stripley to some," I reply before I can stop myself.

Her head tilts. "Ripley... *Stripley*," she says quietly like she's heard it before.

Wow, way to draw attention to who you really are, dude.

"Uh, Rip?" she asks.

"Yeah?"

"Do you think your girlfriend's going to be upset that I crashed your place? I mean, I don't want to come between the two of you."

"She's not really my girlfriend," I blurt.

She blinks. Her face shifts just enough for me to catch the flicker of surprise, and maybe confusion, before she looks away. I open my mouth, then shut it again like a malfunctioning fish.

"It's just that...uh."

"You don't have to explain anything to me," she says softly.

"I know. I just..." I scrub a hand over my face. "She used to be. We're on again, off again. Mostly off these days."

Charly goes quiet, and a shadow moves across her expression. She must be thinking about...him. The guy who leaked that tape. My hands tighten on my fishing line, the tension running up my arms. What kind of asshole does that? I don't care how mad you are, you don't break someone like that.

"You're currently... off?" she asks.

"Yeah." Just that. Simple. Not simple.

She looks like she wants to say more, but I nod to her bobber. "You've got something."

Her eyes go huge. "No way." She jumps up, nearly dropping her rod, but I help her with it. "Oh my God, is it a fish?"

"Not sure." I drop my line and move behind her. "Easy," I say, close to her ear.

She shivers, and I get the sense that it has nothing to do with the catch on her line.

"Come on, Mama needs a new pair of cargos," she says, grinning as she works the line.

I chuckle just as a summer flounder leaps from the water. Charly squeals like she just won the lottery. "Ohmigod, it's a fish."

"It's a fish," I say, laughing at her pure joy.

"I caught a fish. I can't believe I caught a fish."

I reach down, cover her hands with mine to help her reel it in. "Nice and slow," I murmur, guiding her.

Her scent drifts up—coconut and something sun-warmed—and for a second I forget we're reeling in dinner.

The fish flops onto the rocks and Charly jumps back like it might lunge at her. "Ah, nope. No thank you."

I take the rod and crouch beside the flopping flounder. "Now we take it off the hook. Then I slice down the belly and clean it."

I glance back, and she looks...horrified.

"Are you... going to kill it?"

"That's kind of how this works."

She shakes her head. "I... I don't want to do that."

"I can do it."

"Maybe we could just... have peanut butter sandwiches for dinner?"

I pause, then nod. "Okay."

Walking to the water's edge, I release the fish gently. It floats for a second, stunned, then flicks away into the surf.

When I turn back, she's hugging herself.

"Hey." I step close and wrap my arms around her, pulling her in. "You okay?"

She nods against my chest. "I guess I never thought about what happens after you catch one."

"It's okay." I smooth a hand over her back. "We can do catch and release. There's a market down the road if we want fish."

She lets out a breath, shoulders still tight. "Sorry. I know you wanted to catch dinner."

"I wanted to relax," I say, simple and true. "Fishing helps me with that."

She looks up at me, cheeks pink, lashes fluttering. And I don't know if it's the sunrise, the salt air, or the fact that she just squealed over a flounder, but I might be in trouble here.

CHARLY

"You sure you don't mind?" I ask, as I hold one of Rip's big T-shirts against my chest.

"Nah, I have lots. We can run to town later, though, if you like, and get you some new clothes. I usually like to go for a walk after the sun goes down."

The thoughts of going into town makes my stomach knot. Recognition, whispers, phone cameras. It's the kind of attention I'm trying to avoid. Still…I didn't exactly pack for an extended hideaway. No big comfy clothes to lounge in. No chill out vibes. "I supposed we could go later, after dinner," I say casually. Breezy. Not at all panicked.

Is that why he waits until after dark, so no one will notice him?

"There's also a pub that does karaoke." He wags his brow playfully. "You could show me your singing skills."

"Only if you show me yours."

He puts his hands on his hips and shakes his head at me, looking utterly adorable. "Haven't we been over this?"

I snort and duck into the bathroom before his ridiculous cuteness can fry the last of my brain cells. I get out of my sun-dried clothes and into his roomy T-shirt with my only other pair of yoga pants. I check myself in the mirror. Flushed cheeks. Beach hair. An oversized shirt that smells like him. Honestly, not the worst look. Not that I'm trying to impress anyone here.

When I come out, Rip has changed too. He's in a clean T-shirt, new shorts, beachy and delicious like an ad for rugged seaside living. He jerks his thumb toward the door. "I'm going to the market. Join me?"

I hesitate. I want to. But Rip likely draws attention like a lighthouse in the dark. Even if no one here knows he's an NHL star, that face and body would break necks anywhere.

"I think I'll stay here."

"Okay." He doesn't press and I'm grateful. "So...dinner. No fish?"

"I'm not opposed to fish that I didn't have to catch, or..." I gulp. "Well, you get it."

"Did you see the fire pit outside? I thought fish over the grill for dinner would be nice. Then maybe later, after the sun sets, we can have a bonfire."

"I love that." A weird little bubble of excitement wells up inside of me. The last time I grilled fish over a fire was...never.

He grabs his wallet off the table and shoves it into the side pocket of his shorts. "Be back in a minute. Anything you need?"

"I'd like to make something to go with the fish?"

"Salad?" He blinks, looking hopeful and something tells me the only vegetable he's eaten lately has come on his fast-food burger.

"Sure and maybe potatoes?" I grin. "I'm getting my carbs when I can."

"Right, carbs. Fish with only salad is stupid."

"For a minute there I thought you were a monster."

He lets out a deep belly laugh, one that makes his whole-body shake. It does something funny to my insides.

"What do you need?" he asks when the laughter dies down. I reach for my purse and he waves a hand to stop me. "I got it, Charly."

I arch a brow. "I crash a peaceful cottage getaway and now you're grocery shopping to feed me. I must have won the jackpot."

"Seems like you did."

"Healthy ego." I give him a slow nod. "I like it. But seriously, I'm all about paying my own way, Rip."

"You will." He flashes a grin, one hand on the doorknob. "I'm not letting you off that easy."

My stomach flips. What exactly does he mean by that?

He pauses, his smile softening. "The truth is, I'm benefitting too," he continues. "A man can't live on fish alone and I wouldn't know how to put a salad together without a step-by-step YouTube tutorial."

I laugh. "A fish you have to buy because I made you throw that one back."

"It's possible I'm still bitter about that," he teases, even though it's clear he's not.

"I'll make up for it by making salads all week."

"Then you're forgiven."

"But hey, you know what they say, buy a man a fish and you feed a man for a day, teach a man to fish and you feed him for a lifetime."

He lets out a loud snort and I have to say, I love our easy banter. "I did teach you to fish and look how that turned out for my dinner." He laughs. "Honestly, you're saving me from living off takeout and junk," he says, patting his admittedly rock-solid stomach. "I've missed my morning runs lately. When this vacation is over, I can't roll back into real life looking like a couch potato. I don't want..." he catches himself, hesitates a beat. "I mean...yoga is a good replacement for running."

I don't ask him why he can't run. I already know. "Well," I say gently, "That makes me feel a little less guilty for crashing your solitude."

"Guilt is overrated." He pulls out his phone. "Give me a list." Just as he taps the screen, it buzzes. He goes still.

A flicker of something—tightness in his jaw, the subtle flattening of his mouth. He reads the message, doesn't respond, just swipes it away and opens a notes app instead.

Maybe it's his ex. Maybe she's ready to be "on again."

"Everything okay?" I ask, heading for the fridge.

"Yeah." The answer comes a beat too quick. He taps again, posture casual but eyes just a little distant. "Tell me what you need."

Wow. Loaded question.

But no, girlfriend. You do not need to see this man naked. You do not need his hands on your body, his mouth on yours.

That's a want, not a need, and I don't give in to wants anymore.

I open the fridge. It's practically empty, just energy drinks, milk, and bottled water.

"How long have you been here?" I ask.

"A couple of weeks."

I glance over my shoulder. "We seriously need to get something green into you."

"You're not wrong."

I rattle off a list of vegetables, and when I'm done, he tucks his phone away.

"Back soon," he promises.

The door closes with a soft click, and silence folds in around me. I cross my arms over my chest and stand still, just for a second, letting the quiet settle. I thought I wanted quiet. After months of grinding it out in noisy bars, after weeks on that chaotic reality TV show, I was craving peace. Stillness. Anonymity.

But now...I don't know. Maybe it would have been different if I hadn't woken up to find Big Bear in the kitchen. He's easy to be around. Too easy. I'm adjusting to his company faster than I should be. Craving it even.

I move through the small cottage, checking the cupboards and drawers. It's a single guy's setup—oatmeal, protein powder, cereal, Pop-Tarts. Of course Rip Hart eats Pop-Tarts. Somehow that tracks. I shake my head, smirking, and head for the door.

Outside, a warm ocean breeze kisses my skin. I sink into one of the folding chairs and let the sun work its magic. Some-where down the beach, kids are playing, their laughter drifting on the wind. Seagulls circle overhead, scavenging like feathery pirates.

God, I'd forgotten how much I love the beach.

I close my eyes and, for the first time in ages, my thoughts aren't consumed by my ex. Or the tabloid disaster that has flattened me. Instead, I think about the man I'm sharing a roof with.

Kind. Thoughtful. Funny as hell. And now I'm grinning like an idiot, picturing him in a pair of cartoonish water wings. Honestly? I might need to find a boat, just to make that dream come true. Inside, my phone pings, and my eyes snap open. Rip?

Nope. We didn't exchange numbers. And it's not like I have friends regularly checking in on me. I push to my feet and step inside, spotting a message from my brother. Just a check-in. I text him back, and soon we're chatting about his wedding in the fall. I try to match his excitement, but the knot in my stomach tightens. The thought of facing our parents again, the hovering cloud of media attention—it's all going to be the icing on a very bitter cake.

Needing air, I wander around the cottage, ending up in the lounge chair tucked into the fenced backyard. I close my eyes and let my mind drift—to music, lyrics, melodies. This whole hideaway could become a song one day. A whole album, even.

Eventually, I open my phone and dive into a book. The words pull me in, and for a while, I forget where I am. Until I hear the door. I'm up in an instant, practically skipping toward the sound like a kid on Christmas morning.

"Hey," I say, trying to rein in my enthusiasm. *Cool, Charly. Be cool.* "Did you get everything? I'm starving."

"Got everything," Rip says, holding up a bag. Then, grinning, he pulls out a box. "And this."

"S'mores?" I gasp. "What was that you just said about being a couch potato?"

"I won't tell if you won't."

"Deal."

"At least I'm not sneaking cinnamon rolls every night like my buddy Roman."

"Roman?" I tilt my head. Is he referring to Roman Marinelli?

"My best friend growing up," he supplies. "Still is."

"Nice," I say, trying not to sound envious. "I lost touch with most of my high school friends." Something in me clenches tight, and I quickly turn to the bag to hide the sudden pang of loneliness. I start unloading fresh produce. "This looks amazing. Wait, did you remember—"

"Potatoes?" he says with mock seriousness. "Of course. I value my life."

"Smart man." I laugh, washing a cucumber and placing it on the cutting board. Rip sets the potatoes beside me, and the sound of my stomach growling fills the space between us.

God, I've been depriving myself for so long, maybe trying to earn my mother's approval, maybe punishing myself for being so difficult, disobedient. But not this week. This week, things are being done differently.

Rip must catch something in my expression. "I still don't get why your parents think you were disobedient," he says gently. "Teenage years are brutal for everyone. I was no saint."

"I never actually thought you were," I tease, slicing the cucumber.

I hold a piece out for him to take. Instead of grabbing it, he leans in and eats it—straight from my fingers.

All righty then.

He bumps his shoulder into mine, playful but firm enough to make me sway. "Don't act like you know me," he warns playfully.

If only he knew...

"Careful," I reply, grinning. "I'm the one with the knife."

I toss the cucumber into the bowl, pretending not to feel the sizzle in the air between us.

"Yeah, well..." he mutters, clearly improvising as he pulls a butcher-paper-wrapped package from the bag. He unfolds it proudly. "I'm the one with the fish."

I raise a brow. "And that's supposed to mean...?"

He shrugs, already chuckling as he folds foil around the fish. "Absolutely no idea."

We're both laughing now, shoulder to shoulder in the tiny kitchen, and suddenly the world feels a little lighter, the future a little less terrifying.

"Thanks, Rip," I say quietly.

He looks over at me, his smile softening into something that hits low in my chest. "You're welcome, Charly," he says, like he knows that thank you goes deeper than giving me a place to stay, and food to eat. Then he adds, "Thank you too."

It's simple, but there's weight behind it. Like he knows more than he's letting on.

Maybe he does.

Maybe he knows I do too.

It's interesting, because we're both in hiding, but I have the feeling the universe brought us together for a reason, and that we're both exactly where we need to be.

Then again, I've been wrong before.

7

RIP

Crouched over the fire, I peel back the foil and catch a rush of steam that smells like lemon, herbs, and deliciousness. My stomach growls. I test the baked potatoes with a knife. Smooth glide. Perfect.

"That smells amazing."

I glance up to see Charly heading over from the house, barefoot and radiant in the golden hour glow, balancing a bowl of salad on her arm, and plates and utensils in her hands. She sets everything down on the rickety table I rescued from the shed, then pops open two lawn chairs like this is exactly where she belongs.

"Drink?" I ask, flipping open the cooler.

She brushes a leaf off her seat and drops into it with a sigh. "Yes, please."

"I've got soda, beer, and sparkling water. I didn't know what you liked. Goldilocks didn't raid my beverage stash."

She sticks her tongue out at me, and I grin. "I'll have whatever you're having."

I crack open a beer and hand it to her, then crack one for myself. We clink cans before I sink into the chair across from her.

"Thanks," she says, taking a sip. Her shoulders relax, her eyes scan the ocean. "This is... really nice."

"Yeah." I nod, staring at the glittering water as the sun dips low. "I might never want to go back to reality."

"When is that?" she asks softly.

I glance down, play with my can. "Couple more weeks."

She doesn't ask what comes after. She doesn't need to. Just like I don't ask what she's running from. It's an unspoken deal—we're not here to dissect the damage. We're just... here.

I stand, check the fish and potatoes again. "Dinner is served."

She passes me a plate. I grab the foil with my bare hands like a genius, trying to do it fast and smooth.

"Ow. Ow. Ow." I hiss, juggling the hot foil while attempting not to look like a complete idiot.

"We have these things called tongs, or a spatula," she says, biting back a smile.

"Okay, *Mom*," I shoot back, then grin as she shakes her head. "But hey, admit it, that was extremely manly."

She lifts a brow. "Oh yes. My ovaries are in full revolt."

That gets a real laugh out of me, deep and uncontrollable. "Was it the 'ow, ow, ow' part that did it for you?" I tease.

She leans forward just a little, her eyes sparkling. "That and the interpretive fire dance. Truly primal."

I laugh again, and damn if it doesn't feel like something's shifting between us. Not a big moment. Just a little spark. A warm, flirty, dangerously tempting one.

I set the plate in the center of the table, steam curling upward as I peel open the foil. "Glad I could deliver, Charly."

She leans in, eyes lighting up. "That looks so good."

"Let's hope it tastes as good as it smells." I spear a generous piece of fish and slide it onto her plate, followed by a potato. She bends low and inhales, closing her eyes like she's at a five-star restaurant instead of sitting barefoot in a folding chair.

"Speaking of Mom," she says as I slice into my own potato, "Does your family still live in California? Are you guys close?"

"Yes and yes." I scoop a solid dollop of butter. "As close as we can be, considering I'm in Boston."

She grabs the salad tongs and helps herself before passing them my way. "Do they visit much?"

"Just once so far. I've only been there about a year. When I get a bigger place, I think they'll come more often."

A look flickers across her face, something wistful. Soft. It guts me a little. She's not close with her family. Doesn't have a real crew of friends, either. Damn. If she lived in Boston, the WAGs would adopt her on sight. But she doesn't. And she's not dating or engaged to any of the guys who would bring her into the circle. Weird how the thought of her with any of them makes me want to snap a hockey stick in half.

"You said Easton was older?"

"Yeah, I'm the baby."

She smirks. "Biggest baby I've ever seen."

"Damn, girl. All these compliments," I say. "My ego just can't handle it."

She laughs, and the sound ripples right through me. "I mean that in the nicest possible way, of course."

She takes a bite of the fish and moans—actually moans—and I forget how to breathe.

Fuck.

"Rip, this is so good."

Fuck me again.

I clear my throat, trying to will away every X-rated image that just ambushed my brain.

"Glad you approve." My voice is a little rough. "Want seconds or a cigarette?" I tease.

She chokes on a laugh, cheeks turning pink. "Wow. Look at you. One perfectly grilled fish and you think you're Gordon Ramsay in a romance novel."

I grin. "Hey, I didn't hear a no."

"You're right." She licks her shiny lips. "I'll probably have seconds. I haven't tasted anything this good in ages."

I focus on the tomato in my salad, needing something —*anything*—to distract me from the way she just licked her lips. I stab the cherry tomato a little too hard. It explodes. Juice hits me right on the cheek.

Perfect.

A groan escapes me before I can stop it. Thankfully, I can blame it on the damn produce instead of the image currently playing on loop in my head—Charly, licking her lips while I have my mouth on her body.

"You've got tomato juice on your face," she says, laughing as she grabs a napkin and leans in. Her hand reaches for me. I catch it. Her skin is soft. Too soft. And the contact short-circuits every reasonable thought in my brain. Especially the one trying to keep blood flow *above* my belt.

"Thanks," I say, my voice rougher than I intend as I take the napkin. She sinks back into her chair, and I quickly wipe my face, then toss the napkin into the fire like it's evidence of a crime.

When I glance back at her, she's smiling.

"Let's try this again." I pop a tomato into my mouth, this time gently. It bursts with flavor. "Salad's great, Char."

She blinks. "Char?"

"You don't like that?"

"No, it's fine. No one really calls me that." Her lips twitch. "It's nice, *Dripley*."

I groan. "Can we not?"

She grins. "Does Easton enjoy hockey too?" she asks.

"Nope. He's a lawyer. Like our dad. Academic type."

"And you didn't want to follow in their footsteps?"

I shake my head as she scoops a scandalous amount of butter onto her plate. Now that's my kind of girl.

"Maybe that's why we get along so well," she says. "You're a rebel like me."

I chuckle. "Graduated with a poli-sci degree, but my heart was never in it." It was just a backup in case...in case I needed it. She grows quiet for a beat. "Do you regret not going to college?" I ask.

"I was a daydreamer, not a desk kind of girl."

Her gaze softens. "The world needs daydreamers too."

She swallows, like my words hit her right in the chest. "Thanks for saying that, Rip. I think I needed to hear it. But if you really want to know the truth, there are times I do regret it. College isn't for everyone, I know that. My parents pushed it so hard, I think that's why I chose not to." Under her breath she adds, "Probably not my smartest move."

"It's never too late. If that's what you want."

She nods, and we eat in a comfortable rhythm, birds chattering above us. A breeze ruffles her hair. I swear she glows in this light.

After a few quiet minutes, she speaks again. "You never did tell me what you do for fun. Besides fishing and open-fire barbecues." She slides her fork into another piece of fish, eyes locked on mine as she brings it to her lips. She doesn't know what she's doing.

Or maybe she does.

I take a long swig of beer before I say something stupid. When I set it down, I deadpan, "I marry people."

Her brows lift. "You what?"

"Yep. Reverend Rip at your service."

Her laugh bursts out so fast she nearly chokes.

I lean back in my chair, grinning. "Certified. Online. Comes with a PDF and everything."

"Wait... you've actually officiated weddings?"

"Surprised?"

"Very." She cocks her head. "Wait, are you being serious? You actually...marry people."

"Yup, in Vegas, in backyards, even on beaches."

Her head tilts. Suspicion is thick in her eyes. "You really have a license?"

"I know, it's kind of hard to believe. But when my brother got married, I got certified so I could officiate. Figured it was a one-time thing, but turns out I enjoyed it. So now I've done a few more."

She blinks, processing. Then blurts, "That's what you do for fun?"

I laugh. "That's what I do for fun."

"You're really not messing with me."

"I'm really not." I give her a playful wink. "If I was messing with you, you'd know it." Her cheeks turn pink and I clear my throat. "I have the license on my phone." I pat my pocket. "Actually, my phone's inside. Want me to grab it?"

She waves me off, eyes still narrowed. "No. I believe you. I mean, who lies about something like that?" She shakes her head, clearly baffled. "It's just... I think that might be the last thing I ever expected you to say."

"Why?" I ask, even though I already know.

"Because," she says, motioning toward me. "You're... you. You fish and light fires, like a feral man."

I grin. "Uh...thank you?"

"Does this mean you're, like, a closet romantic? That you believe in true love?" She says it like the words taste bad. Can't blame her, not after her ex dragged her through hell.

I jab my fork into a cucumber slice harder than necessary, imagining her ex's smug face on the other end. Then memories of my own messed up relationship claws its way into my brain.

"I don't know," I say after a moment. "I guess... yeah. For other people, sure. Just not for me."

She lets out a short laugh. "We really do have a lot in common."

"Yup." I glance at her. "Sucks to be us."

She smirks. "I actually think that's a pretty cool hobby, Rip."

"Speaking of hobbies..." I wipe my mouth and stand, tucking the napkin under my plate as the breeze kicks up. "I have a surprise for you."

Her eyes narrow. "Oh God. I hate surprises."

I pause, caught off guard by how much those words sting. "Yeah," I say softly. "Me too."

She doesn't ask why, but I see the question in her eyes, the same way I see the echo of betrayal in hers. I clear my throat and gesture toward the side of the cottage. "I found something while I was out earlier. Thought you might like it."

"You found something?" she echoes warily.

"It's a good surprise. I swear. I also swear it will be the last one. No surprises for either of us."

"Fine and I guess you owe me a surprise after I surprised you by breaking in."

"That wasn't a bad surprise, Char," I say quietly as I disappear around the corner and return with her surprise cradled in my arms. Her jaw drops.

"Rip...no."

"You don't like it?"

She shakes her head, blinking like she's not quite sure she's seeing this right. "I don't understand. You found a guitar? Like... it was just lying on the beach or something?" Her eyes widen. "Rip. It must belong to someone. Maybe that guy playing while we did yoga forgot it. We have to return it."

I laugh, holding up a hand to stop her before she goes full rescue mission. "Relax. It doesn't belong to anyone. I found it in a resale store."

Her jaw drops again. "Rip, no. I can't. That's too much."

I shift the guitar in my hands. "Okay, here's the truth, Char. This gift? It's not really for you." I let out a long-suffering sigh. Her brow arches like she's about to call me on my bullshit. "It's for me," I say solemnly before she gets the chance. "I've been doing some thinking. It's incredibly selfish of me to keep this voice..." I pause and with both hands gesture to myself. "...confined to the shower. It's time the world experienced the magic." I nod toward the firepit. "Bonfire. S'mores. Guitar. This voice."

She snorts. "Wow. That's awfully generous of you, Rip."

"I know. It's a burden being this talented, but I persevere. So if you play... I'll sing."

Her grin hits me square in the chest and does dangerous things to my insides.

"Will there be moves?" she teases.

I gasp. "Charly, there will always be moves. So what do you say?"

She laughs, but her gaze softens as her fingers brush the guitar's neck. "You kind of had me at magic," she says. "But moves? That was like an overtime goal. I didn't stand a chance."

"Hockey metaphor." I cock my head and take in the warmth on her cheeks. "Thought you weren't into hockey."

"I'm not..." Her words fall off as she blinks at me, like she could actually be into me.

Dammit.

I might actually be into her, too.

But I'm off bunnies and bridesmaids as I try to work through whatever it is I have with Lyra.

Ah, but Charly is neither of those things dude.

CHARLY

I finish up the last of the dishes while Rip fusses with something outside. Since he handled dinner, I volunteered for cleanup duty. Normally, I'd let the mess sit until morning—my usual rebel move—but Rip's clearly a clean-freak and, well, I'm technically squatting in his beachside hideaway. Not exactly the time to be a slob.

I tuck the final plate into the cupboard and freeze mid-step. Wait. Was I just... humming? I blink at the sink. Yep. Okay. That was definitely humming. A sound I haven't made in—wow—a long time. Not since life got a little too real. But somehow, here, in Rip's borrowed kitchen with the scent of garlic still hanging in the air, I feel... lighter.

I glance out the open window I *may* have crawled through once upon a time, and there he is. Rip. Watching me.

I lift my hand in a wave, a little sheepish, and he lifts his in return—stiff, awkward, like waving might physically pain him. Then, like I caught him doing something scandalous, he snaps his gaze away and pretends to be very, *very* interested in the grill tongs.

Okay... weird.

I let myself watch him a little longer. There's a tightness to his movements, a guarded stiffness in his stride that makes my chest pinch. He's hurting. Not just physically—though the limp's still there—but in that big, silent way men like Rip try to hide their worry. His career's dangling on a string, and I'm guessing he's not thrilled about his fallback plan involving dusty textbooks and political debates. He's not built for boardrooms. He's built for ice and speed and cheering crowds.

But if he won't let anyone help him, I'll help without making it a thing. No pressure, no pity party. Just sneaky, subtle care. Ninja nurturing, if you will.

I check the freezer. Full ice tray. Perfect.

Then my phone starts jittering across the counter like it's possessed. I glance at the screen and my stomach drops. Of course. *Her.* My fingers twitch, but I don't move. I just let it ring. And ring. And—

It stops.

Then immediately starts again.

And I still just... stare.

"Are you going to get that?"

I whip around so fast I nearly dislocate something. "Holy crap, Rip. Ever think of knocking?"

Hand to my chest, I try to slow my racing heart. A different kind of racing heart this time. Because he's close. Like, closer than should be legal close. His eyes search mine, his voice soft.

"Didn't mean to scare you."

"Maybe we really do need to think about getting bells," I mutter, trying to play it cool even as my pulse still tap dances in my throat.

He doesn't laugh. Just drags his finger slowly over the scruff on his jaw, eyes flicking to the still-ringing phone. "You don't want to answer."

"It's my mom." I sigh.

"Are you okay?"

"I'm fine," I say quickly, my usual response, but when he cocks his head, I continue, "Today's been... good. Really good. And she has a way of, you know, pouring rain on good."

"Then don't answer," he says simply, picking up the phone like it's radioactive. He holds it out. "Let's ditch these things for the rest of the day."

I grin, surprised. "Really?"

"Really," he says. "It's our vacation from reality, remember?"

"Okay," I say, and I mean it.

I watch Rip's back muscles flex as he hauls the phones into the bedroom. A drawer slides open, and then slams shut. He reappears, somehow looking even sexier than he was seconds ago.

"Going for a walk?" I ask.

"Yeah, I like to stretch out after dinner."

I grin, drying my hands. "Mind if I join you? I could use some stretching myself."

He nods and I'm sure he knows what I'm up to, even if neither of us are saying it out loud. He grabs a ballcap, pulls it low over his brow, and we head out. Once outside, he locks the door, and suddenly, our bodies are close as we cross the narrow road, our feet instantly sinking into the cool sand.

The beach after dark is a whole different world. Quiet, calm. Families have retreated to their cottages, kids tucked in or roasting marshmallows by their own fires.

A dull ache presses in the center of my chest.

"You okay?" Rip's voice breaks the silence.

I laugh, trying to shake it off. "Yeah. Just thinking about how quiet it is now. So different from this afternoon. All those kids building sandcastles, believing in fairy tales."

Rip smirks. "I gave up believing ages ago... Until I found Goldilocks in my bed."

I nudge him playfully. He pulls away just a bit, but the warmth doesn't leave his eyes.

"Come on, Rip, we both know you're a hopeless romantic."

He steps back in close again, fingers brushing mine like it's the most natural thing in the world. "You want a family someday?"

After dating Colby for the last year, and winning the contest, I thought my life would be somewhere else by now. But here I am—kind of a hot mess, drifting nowhere.

I shrug. "I have to figure out what *I* want first. Can't bring kids into this chaos just yet. How about you?"

Rip exhales slowly. "I need to get my shit together too."

There's a long pause, the kind that hums with unsaid things. Knowing he's talking about his ex, I ask gently, "She's hard on your head, huh?"

He rubs the back of his neck. "Yeah. How do I still want her, Char? One minute, she's all love and promises. The next, she's gone—bed cold, off doing God knows what with God knows who. What's wrong with me? I thought other women would fix this. They didn't."

His honesty catches me off guard. It's like all the love and pain he's been bottling up is finally spilling out. He trusts me. And honestly, I'm not sure why because I barely know him. Maybe we're trauma bonding, maybe not. But in a week, I'll walk away with his secrets locked tight in my heart, and maybe that's why it's easier for him to talk to me now.

I'm definitely not the person who should be doling out advice, but here I am, trying anyway. "Rip, you're a good guy. There's nothing broken about you." My voice feels small, almost fragile in the quiet night. "Sometimes the heart wants what it wants—no logic, no rules. But you have to protect yourself. You can't let anyone string you along like a puppet. She's dangling you, and that's not fair. Not to you."

We fall silent, words slipping away like sand between our fingers. Our knuckles brush, just a whisper of contact as we keep walking, lost in our own thoughts. The second my feet hit the harder sand, I stop.

"This would be a good place to stretch."

His voice barely carries, soft and hollow. "Okay."

I lift my arms above my head, and he mirrors me. We move slowly, the world narrowing to the rhythm of our breathing and the quiet stretch of muscles. I ease into some gentle groin stretches, watching his jaw tighten, then relax, then tense again. When I think he's done, I shift back to the dry sand and flop down.

Rip slides down beside me, his body warm against the cooling night air. He points upward. "There's the Big Dipper."

I smile, teasing. "I thought I was laying beside the Big Dipper."

He rolls onto his side, facing me, and my breath catches. The moonlight softens his sharp features, makes everything about him glow. "I'm the Big Dripley. There's a difference."

I roll toward him until our bodies align, our mouths just inches apart.

God, what am I doing?

The beach, the day, the food, Rip—they're all conspiring to mess with my head. His fingers reach out, rough pads brushing back the stray hair that falls across my face.

Before I do something reckless—like kiss him—I flinch and flop back onto my back.

"I see the Little Dipper."

He follows, landing with a soft groan. When he stretches his arms out, our fingers brush and finally clasp.

"How was the stretching?" I ask.

"Really good."

"Maybe we should get in the cold water." I try to sound casual, but my heart's racing. "I like to use ice or cold water after yoga. Helps with inflammation."

"Something's inflamed, alright," he mutters, a grumble beneath his breath. And I can't help but love the way he reacts—gruff, but honest. That little moment reminds me how much of a mess I am. How much I shouldn't want this guy. How much I shouldn't be thrilled he might want me.

But here we are.

He stands, walking to the water's edge, bathed in silver moonlight, looking like a god or a gentle giant straight out of a fairy tale. I laugh softly.

He throws a glance over his shoulder. "What's so funny?"

"Nothing." I push myself up and step closer. "Going in?"

He shrugs off his T-shirt and starts unbuttoning his shorts.

I blink at him. "What are you doing?"

"Going in. Didn't you just ask me that?" He's grinning like he knows exactly what he's doing—stripping to throw me off balance.

"You're getting... naked?" *Way to state the obvious, Charly.*

Rip looks around the empty beach like a mischievous child caught sneaking cookies. "I don't see anyone here." Then his gaze snaps back to me, that playful grin spreading wide enough to melt ice. I swallow hard, heat creeping up my neck. "You don't think I got the nickname Ripley Stripley for nothing, do you?"

He tugs his shorts down, and his boxers follow like it's the easiest thing in the world.

I whip my head away. Either look like a total gawker, or pretend I'm not staring at his... well, everything.

I shake my head but I shouldn't be surprised. Everyone knows his rep.

Once he's stripped down, he steps into the water, and my eyes sneak to his back—to the way every steely muscle ripples. No wonder he's a force on the ice. He glances over his shoulder, catching me mid-stare, and his grin just dares me to look again. How can I resist? The man *is* a walking sculpture.

Heart pounding, I reach for my top. Am I really doing this? Looks like it.

I peel it off as he wades deeper, water almost up to his chest. "It's warm," he calls out, voice teasing.

"Is that why your teeth are chattering?" I shoot back, wrapping my hands around my bra strap, debating if I want to lose it too. Skinny dipping isn't usually my thing, but it's dark, it's just us, and I'm not about to ruin my bra with salt water.

Before reason can take over, I unhook it and toss it on the sand. Then I grab the waistband of my yoga pants, sliding them down, panties and all, with a little rush of adrenaline.

With his back turned, I slip into the water, and holy hell, it's like cool silk against my warm skin. I swim out, shadows hiding me as the moonlight sketches Rip's silhouette. Inches from him, I stand up, careful to keep just enough water to cover me.

He wipes water from his face, smiling like he owns this moment. "Nice, huh?"

"So nice," I whisper, feeling the chill and the thrill all at once.

I dunk under and swim away, feeling the cool ocean close around me. When I surface, Rip's already some distance off, and I float on my back, eyes tracing the stars scattered across the sky. I close my eyes for a moment, ears submerged in silence—blocking out every word, every feeling.

Then, catching me by surprise, big hands suddenly scoop beneath me, lifting me up like I'm weightless.

"Whoa," I yelp, twisting, but his grip shifts and suddenly my chest is pressed against his, my legs curling around his back like they were made to fit there all along. It's strange. This man, with all his scars and secrets, somehow feels like the safest place I could be.

"Sorry, didn't mean to scare you," he breathes, voice deep and rough.

I'm painfully aware of how my nipples press hard against his chest, the electric pull between us thick enough to cut with a knife. Trying to play it cool as I hold tight to keep afloat, I tease, "You're out of breath. Guess I'm heavier than you thought?"

His hands tighten, and I shift lower, feeling.... Oh, God.

"No, you're a lightweight," he murmurs, voice low and ragged. "I'm breathless because... fuck." He slams his eyes shut, his mouth twisted like he's in total agony. One hand slides up my spine, cups the back of my neck. When his eyes open, they lock on my lips like they're the only thing that matters. "Because I want to kiss you."

My lips part instinctively, and I swipe my tongue over them. But I clamp down on the moment. Someone has to be in control here. "Probably not a good idea."

He exhales hard. "No. I'm pretty sure it's not."

"We just met," I say, voice barely steady, "You have that girlfriend."

"Not girlfriend."

Okay, that's not helping.

I shift a fraction, and swear if I move one more inch lower, we'll be crossing a line that can't be uncrossed.

He groans low, a sound that drifts through the night and curls around me. "Charly."

I gulp and unwrap my legs, planting them on the ocean floor with a shiver—not from cold, but from something electric buzzing under my skin. "We should head back."

"Uh huh."

I turn and swim away.

Why is kissing him such a bad idea, again?

Oh yeah, because we just met, and my life's a chaotic mess. Not only that, kissing a guy like him would be a disaster. But...warm hands. The way he touches me. The comfort, the safety, the reckless spark of wanting...

And maybe an orgasm or two.

So yeah, nothing good....and everything wonderful.

But if he knew who I really was, knew about the sex tape scandal, I'm sure it would change the way he feels about me. Honestly, my ex likely ruined me for any good man out there.

I swim back to shore, scramble into my clothes, dripping wet in all the wrong ways, cheeks flaming. Rip dresses beside me, both of us silent as we walk back to the cottage—yet the air between us is crackling with electricity.

"Maybe we can have s'mores and sing tomorrow night," I suggest, voice croaky like I swallowed a frog.

He grins. "Sounds like a plan."

He slides the key into the lock, opens the door, and moves to the side to wave me in. My gaze falls on the guitar. "That was so nice of you, Rip. I promise some music tomorrow." I stretch my arms over my head. "I think I just need a good night's sleep."

"Yeah, me too."

"Would you mind if I borrowed your sweatshirt again?"

"Not a problem." He walks into the bedroom, and comes back with it. I graciously accept it and resist the urge to bring it to my nose to smell his scent on it. I guess I should have known it had been worn recently when I first pulled it on last night. Call it exhaustion.

He jerks his thumb out. "I'm going to grab a shower. Did you want to go first?"

"No, I'm okay. You go ahead." I walk to the sofa and shake out the blanket. "I'm going to make up the bed."

"Charly," he groans, his voice thick with something like frustration or...desire. "I can't—"

"Yes, you can."

"It's not right."

"How about this. We take turns." I don't mean it. I have no intention of taking the bed and letting him sleep on the sofa.

"I...I don't know."

"Good thing I do. Tonight, I'm on the sofa. No way am I putting you out two nights in a row, Rip."

As soon as the words leave my mouth, they take on a sexual meaning, and we both freeze, that charged silence stretching tight between us.

His gaze drops to my mouth. Lingers.

I swallow hard and the sound must do something to him. He steps back like the air burned him. "Goodnight, Charly."

He shuts the bathroom door behind him with a quiet click. I drop onto the couch and stare at the ceiling, heart pounding. What am I even doing? I came here to hide, not to feel. Definitely not to want.

And yet...

As the water starts running behind that door, all I can think is—

What if I opened it?

9

RIP

My eyes snap open.

A sound. Faint. From the other room. Not that I was sleeping. At least not deeply. Not after what happened. Or almost happened.

Charly.

That almost-kiss. Her legs around my waist, nipples tight against my chest. I can still feel the heat of her breath against my jaw. The cold ocean did nothing to help. The cold shower...even worse. My body's been on high alert since she touched me. Since she looked at me with heat. Jesus. I was one second from sliding inside her. Right there in the goddamn water.

Fuck.

I shift, adjusting the pillow under my knee, trying to elevate the throbbing pain away. Not sure if it's my torn groin or something else... The room is pitch dark, quiet. No honking horns. No shouting neighbors. No footsteps pounding overhead. Out here at the cottage, silence hits differently, every little creak amplified, stretched. Maybe I imagined the sound. Could've been the sofa creaking when Charly rolled over.

Charly. On the sofa.

I groan. Honestly, I still can't believe I let her sleep out there while I'm sprawled across this massive king bed. I was going to fight her on it again, but when I came out of the shower, she was already asleep. Or pretending to be. Probably pretending. That near-kiss spooked her. Hell, it spooked me too.

It's a bad idea. Obviously.

...Right?

I mean, I don't have a girlfriend. She doesn't have a boyfriend. We're two hot messes, alone in paradise. Adults. Consenting. Wanting. Sure, we're both kind of in a bad place. But maybe broken plus broken doesn't equal disaster.

Maybe it equals relief.

Maybe it's what we both need. Someone else's skin to quiet the noise in our heads. Her mouth on me, mine on her, just enough to make us forget for one goddamn night.

There it is again.

A sound. Clicking this time. I sit up, listening hard. Should I check on her? Just to be sure she's okay. Or to see if she sleeps naked?

Jesus.

I push to my feet slowly, stretching the tightness from my groin. Once the ache fades, well, not every ache, I creep to the door and crack it open. Silence. I step into the living room and scan the space. My gaze swings toward the sofa and my heart stutters when I find it empty.

She's gone.

Did I scare her off?

Was one almost-kiss enough to send her running?

Jesus, I hope not.

She doesn't have anywhere to go. I know that much. If she did, she wouldn't have broken into the cottage to begin with. She's stuck, just like me. Drifting. Looking for something to hold on to. My eyes adjust, chasing shadows in the dark. The front door is shut tight, a sliver of moonlight sneaking beneath it. Then, suddenly, that light disappears, as though something just moved past it.

Someone.

I go still.

When the glow returns, I step forward, cautious, easing the door open inch by inch. A whisper of sea air greets me, cool and damp. And then I see her.

Charly.

She's standing just beyond the door, her back to me, arms crossed tightly over her chest like that's all that's holding her together. The sight of her hits me in the gut. She looks so fragile, exposed, alone in the moonlight. My first instinct is to go to her. To hold her. But maybe she wants the quiet. Wants to be alone with whatever's clawing at her chest.

I start to turn away but the damn door creaks. She spins around, startled. Her face is damp. Eyes glossy.

Shit.

She's been crying.

"Charly…" My voice is soft, apologetic. "I heard something. I didn't mean to interrupt."

"Actually, it's okay," she says, voice barely above a whisper. "I could use the company."

I step outside, careful not to disturb her, and she turns again to look out at the waves. The moon lights her hair like silver. My sweatshirt swallows her frame. She looks breakable. Beautiful.

"It's breathtaking here at night," she murmurs.

My gaze drifts down her back, her legs bare beneath the hem of my sweatshirt. "It's not the only thing that is," I say, before I can stop myself.

She doesn't comment. Just breathes.

"Couldn't sleep?" I ask, moving in beside her.

"Not really." She casts me a fast glance. "You?"

"Restless."

I turn toward the ocean. "Lots on your mind?"

"A few things." I catch the way she hugs herself tighter, but it's doing nothing to quell the shiver running through her.

"You're cold."

"No… I don't think I am," she says, voice off. "It's just, my body's reacting weirdly."

"Stress?"

A low sound leaves her throat, part scoff, part sob. "Something like that."

I want to reach for her but hold back. She didn't take her mother's call earlier. Her voice cracked when she said she was fine. She isn't. I know that now.

"What can we do to de-stress you, Char?" I ask, quietly. "Anything you can think of?"

"I usually play guitar. But it's late. I don't want to wake anyone."

She shivers again. It's not the cold. It's whatever she's holding inside.

"Do you want me to grab you a blanket?"

She sniffs, and that one small sound slices me open.

"No," she says, too fast. "I'm okay."

"No," I say gently, honestly. "I don't think you are."

She swallows hard. The sound of it seems to echo in the night.

"Rip…"

"I'm here."

She hugs herself tighter, like she's trying to keep from unraveling.

"Thanks," she whispers. "For letting me stay here…for being here, right now."

I lift my hands slowly, letting her see them first. "Can I… touch you?"

She's silent. The moment stretches. Then she nods. "Yes."

I move to stand behind her, and pull her carefully back against my chest. My arms wrap around her. My hands slide up and down her arms, slow and steady, chasing away her tremble. I feel her body slowly settle, inch by inch.

When she finally stops shaking, I tug her closer and sit on the fold out chair, pulling her into my lap. She melts into me like she's been holding herself upright for far too long. My arms tighten instinctively, pulling her closer. We don't say anything for a long time. I just keep tracing light strokes up and down her arms, slow, soothing, repetitive. It's all I have to offer her right now.

"Rip," she says softly, breaking the quiet.

"Yeah?"

"It's really nice to be... touched."

My throat tightens. I don't answer right away. Not because I don't want to, but because I don't trust what might come out if I do.

When I don't respond, she tries to laugh it off. "God, I don't know what's wrong with me tonight. I had a great day. I forgot everything for a while. But the second I closed my eyes..." She breathes out, shaky. "Real life rushed back in like a flood. Maybe I'm just feeling sorry for myself."

"It's okay to feel that way, Char. I'd be lying if I said I haven't felt the same these past few weeks." I snap my fingers softly. "Your whole future, everything you thought was locked in, can disappear in a second."

She pulls back just enough to look at me, her eyes shadowed but open. "I think I'm just... lost," she admits. "I used to know what I wanted. Life was all about chasing the dream. But now, that dream turned into a nightmare. And suddenly, I don't know what I want anymore. I only know what I *don't* want."

"That's scary," I say quietly.

She nods. "Scary for you, too."

I touch her face, fingers brushing along the soft curve of her cheek. She doesn't flinch. Instead, she leans into the contact like it's the only thing keeping her from breaking. Then when she lets out a little sigh, it tears something open inside me. Maybe what she needs tonight isn't advice, or solutions, or someone telling her it'll all be okay.

Maybe she just needs...

To be touched. To be held. To feel something other than loneliness. Just for a little while.

"For the record," I murmur, voice low, "I like touching you."

I slide my hand around her back, draw her in tighter, let my thumb skim a line up her spine. She moans, soft, breathy, unguarded.

"That is nice," she whispers.

She tucks herself into me again, her hand pressing against my chest, fingers splayed over my heart like she's trying to memorize its rhythm. I groan, quiet but rough, her touch doing things to me I can't hide anymore. My body reacts without permission. My dick stiffens, thick and insistent and pressed between us.

She freezes.

Her hand stills.

I stop breathing.

"Rip..." she says, her voice unsteady.

"Yeah, Char?" I whisper back, afraid to move, afraid to speak too loudly and break the spell.

"Everything about today was perfect," she whispers. "But I'm such a mess, Rip. I want this—God, I do want this. But I also don't want to...use you. You've been so good to me. I don't want to take advantage of you, or the situation."

She's unraveling right in front of me, not in a chaotic way, but in the quiet, brave way people do when they're finally safe enough to speak the truth.

She feels safe with me.

I keep my voice low, steady. "This doesn't have to be anything it's not, Charly. No promises. No pressure. Just two people needing something real right now. A fleeting moment that becomes a memory—a good one. One we can hold onto when everything else feels like it's out of our control." She looks up, eyes glassy. "But," I add gently, tapping my temple, "If this is going to make things harder for you in here... if it's going to tangle things up more..."

"I want this, Rip," she cuts in, sure now. Her voice is soft, but her conviction is steel. "Tonight, I want you. I want to feel something that isn't shame or fear or regret. I want to make a memory that doesn't hurt."

Something tightens in my chest. She chose me. Me. The guy with a torn groin, and an unsure future, and I won't treat that like it's nothing.

"Okay," I say. "But you need to know something before we go inside."

She tilts her head, the flicker of uncertainty back in her eyes. "What?"

I gesture toward the cottage. "If we go in there, if you let me make you feel something else, it might be longer than a fleeting moment."

She laughs, and it's like the sky cracking open. A warm, rich, full-bodied sound that breaks through the tension and wraps around my chest like a balm. I want to bottle it. Memorize it. Hear it every damn day for the next seven days... maybe longer.

"I didn't want to say anything," she teases, wiping an imaginary bead of sweat off her brow. "But I'll admit, I was a little concerned. I mean, a guy with your stamina on the ice..."

She says that like she knows I'm an NHL player, but we're not delving into the specifics. "If we're being totally honest here, I've wanted you since I first laid eyes on you asleep in my bed. Wanted to put my hands and mouth on you. Wanted to taste every inch of your body. So with much shame..." I hang my head in disgrace. "I admit, it's entirely possible that the first time might be a little fast..."

She arches a brow, her grin playful. "You mean there will be more than one time?"

I meet her gaze and let a slow, wicked grin tug at my lips. "I can pretty much guarantee it."

Her laughter bubbles out again, warm and unguarded, and something inside me unclenches. For the first time in weeks, maybe longer, it feels like the world isn't crumbling beneath my feet. I want to sweep her into my arms, carry her to my bed, lay her down and fulfill a promise, but before I can figure out how to navigate that with my injury, she slips off my lap and sways toward the cottage with a flirty little wiggle in her step.

She glances back, over her shoulder. "Guess this solves the bed-sharing dilemma."

I don't even hesitate. "Get your ass inside. On my bed. Now."

She squeals, disappears through the door, and I follow her in, close the door behind me, and lock it. My eyes sweep the room, my buddy's beach cottage, where none of this was supposed to happen... and yet here we are. A rustle of bedsheets pulls my gaze down the small hallway. I walk slowly toward the bedroom, my pulse thudding in my ears, and then I see her.

She's under the covers.

My sweatshirt is on the floor.

"You're..." My voice comes out rougher than I mean. I swallow. "You're naked."

She laughs, eyes sparkling. "Not the first time you've seen me naked tonight, Rip."

I grin. "Yeah, true. But now you're naked for me, which means I get to touch you. Big difference."

Still rocking just my boxers, I feel my cock stir, thickening like it has a mind of its own. I grab the waistband of my boxers and peel them off with a sly smile. Her eyes practically pop out when she sees me fully revealed.

"Don't act like you haven't seen this before," I tease, wrapping a hand around myself. "I caught you peeking earlier."

She lifts her chin, cool as ice, but I know she's a hot mess beneath that façade. I know, because I am too. "You're right. I did peek earlier."

"Unfortunately, I was already in the ocean, with my back to the shore, when you got undressed. So while I didn't really get to see, I did get to feel."

Her eyes widen and she shivers slightly.

I close my eyes for a moment, remembering. "Fuck, you felt amazing wrapped around me."

I step toward the bed, trailing a finger teasingly around the blanket she's clutching under her chin. Slowly, deliberately, I drag it down her body, uncovering every inch of her soft, glowing skin.

My heart thunders. My cock thickens even more.

She lies there, wide-eyed under my gaze, squirming a little under my intense stare.

"Char," I whisper when she shifts, "You are absolutely gorgeous."

Her smile flickers, a shadow of worry crossing her face.

"Char?"

"This..." she starts quietly, biting her lip. "This is about escaping reality, right? It's about who we are right now, in this moment. Not about who we are outside this bubble?"

I tilt my head, reading between the lines. Is she worried about the mess she's running from? About me thinking less of her?

"Like I said," I say softly, "This isn't Vegas, but what happens in this bubble we have here at the cottage stays at the cottage."

She nods, a small smile returning. "Except for the memories. We get to take those with us."

"Yes, beautiful," I murmur, my fingers brushing a stray lock of hair from her face. "We get to take them with us."

She relaxes, sinking deeper into the mattress, looking soft, warm, and absolutely ready. My eyes roam over her again, and when they meet hers, I see the fire burning there — fierce, hot, and explosive.

Goddammit, I'm so ready to make her forget the real world.

"Nice," she whispers.

"Really nice," I say as I lean closer.

She parts her legs like an invitation. "Now, what was that about putting your hands and mouth on me? And I believe I remember something about tasting every inch?"

My brain shorts out, fireworks exploding in my chest as need zings through me.

I growl low and wild—like some feral animal about to claim its prize—and climb onto the bed, sliding between her silky thighs.

Just like that, the world outside ceases to exist.

It's just us.

Want. Need. Heat.

Two broken souls chasing one perfect moment before reality drags us back.

And I swear, I am going to give her a memory worth keeping. I'm not sure why it's important, I only know that it is.

CHARLY

y heart pounds fast as the man between my legs leans over me, his lips seeking mine. My lids flutter and I'm about to close my eyes, to slip into this real-life fantasy, but stop when he whispers, "Keep them open. I want you to see me, and I want to see you."

God, no man has ever said that to me before. Not like that. Not with so much quiet conviction and care.

One big hand touches my hair, and he rubs a lock between his fingers before he gently pushes it from my face. I lay still, and honestly, I'm not sure what I expected from Ripley Stripley, but tenderness…that wasn't anywhere near the top of the list. It actually wrecks me a little.

But until this moment, until his body was on top of mine, I hadn't realized that it was tenderness and safety that I craved all along.

"Rip," I murmur, pouring everything I feel into his name.

And somehow, impossibly he gets it. "I know, babe," he breathes. "I know."

His mouth meets mine, and the sound he makes—a low, hungry moan—shakes me from the inside out. His kiss is slow, sizzling, like he's trying to imprint himself on my soul. Like we've got all the time in the world and he wants to savor every single second.

I curl my hands around his back again. Only this time, I'm not pretending it's to stay afloat. I'm not hiding anything. I want to touch him. I want to feel every inch of this man. My hands roam—exploring, mapping, claiming—and when he groans against my mouth, I feel the tremor of it echo inside me.

"For the record," he mutters, breaking the kiss just long enough to brush his nose against mine, "I like when you touch me too."

So I do.

God, so do I.

I run my hands down his spine, over the ridges of muscle, memorizing the hard curves and lean strength that make up Ripley Hart. He draws back a little, like he's trying to get a better look at me, but I cling to him—desperate to keep him close. It's like this man has somehow become my lifeline.

"Babe," he says, voice rough with need and something deeper. "I want you."

I swallow hard. There's no pretending now. No games.

"I want you too, Rip."

He starts with the softest kiss, barely brushing my mouth, then moves to my nose, my eyelids, the curve of my cheek.

Each one lands like a promise of more to come before he drifts lower.

When his lips reach my neck, he breathes me in, like he needs the scent of me to survive. Then, with slow, open-mouthed kisses, he charts a path along my skin, easing lower, sinking his body against mine until the mattress holds us both. Heat pools deep inside me, anticipation simmering just beneath the surface.

His mouth finds my breast, and I cry out before I can stop it.

"Oh God, Rip, that feels so good."

He groans against me, the sound vibrating through my skin as he pulls my nipple into his mouth. He doesn't rush—he lingers, sucks, flicks with his tongue, like this is a feast and I'm the first course he's ever truly wanted. His hand cups my other breast, kneading and teasing, stroking every nerve ending with unhurried care.

My fingers slip into his hair, holding on—not to guide him, not to rush him—but to anchor myself to the sensation of being completely wanted.

When he moves lower, kissing a trail over my stomach, my thighs tense in anticipation. Then, when his lips hover at the apex of my legs, he parts me gently with his fingers. His gaze flicks up, locking on mine, and I rise onto my elbows, needing to see him see me.

"I like everything I see, babe," he says, voice rough, reverent. "And I bet you taste just as sweet."

"Ohmigod," I whisper. "Rip."

He chuckles softly. "Yeah, babe?"

"You just—I mean, I just—"

His thumb strokes my hip. "How about you stop thinking and let me take care of you?"

There isn't any part of me that can argue with that. I nod, as I tremble under his gaze.

He slides his hands beneath me, lifting my hips like I weigh nothing, and cradles me to his mouth. And then he devours me.

The first stroke of his tongue, hot and slow from bottom to top, pulls a sound from my throat. My spine arches, pleasure slicing through me. He laughs, a low, sinful rumble, and the vibration nearly undoes me.

My fingers clutch at the sheets, at him, at anything, as his mouth moves in dizzying, perfect circles around my clit. He's not guessing. He's not fumbling. He's tasting me like I'm the only thing that's ever mattered, like he has all night and all the skill to bring me apart, piece by glorious piece.

And when my hips twitch, desperate for more, for him, I nearly reach down to grab his head and guide him home.

Nearly.

Because I think—no, I know—he's already on his way, and my only job here is to relax and let him take care of me.

He glances up at me with a knowing grin—the kind that says *yeah, I'm going to take you there...eventually*.

Oh, he wants to play games, does he? Fine. I'm game.

Or at least I was.

Until he slides a finger inside me.

My thoughts scatter. All I know is that his finger feels like it belongs there, like it was made to be inside me. My muscles clench around him, involuntary and intense, and his groan vibrates through my core.

"So fucking sweet," he murmurs, almost to himself, like he's just tasted heaven and can't believe his luck.

I lift my hips, nudging into his face, and when I see the shine of my slick on his mouth—see the way he licks his lips like he's savoring me—I nearly lose it.

My arms give out, and I collapse back on the bed, breathless and boneless, but I don't look away. I won't. He asked me to keep my eyes on him, and I don't want to miss a single second. His mouth finally closes around my clit and then he adds the pressure of his teeth—just the lightest graze—and crooks his finger inside me.

I swear my soul leaves my body.

"Rip..."

He answers with a low, contented *mmm* and keeps going, steady and focused, like he's chasing something—and that something is my orgasm, which seems to be more important to him than his own.

Then he adds another finger, the stretch deep and snug, and the pleasure shoots through me like lightning. My hips twitch, my legs tremble.

"Oh God, Rip."

"You like that, Goldie?" he teases, his voice deliciously thick with arousal.

I huff a laugh, breathless. "Oh yes, Big Bear. I love your moves. I was hoping I'd get to see them one way or another tonight."

He grins like I just made his whole damn year, then goes back to devouring me with maddening precision, tongue swirling and stroking like I'm the sweetest thing he's ever tasted—and he's determined to finish every bite.

"I want you to come in my mouth," he says, eyes hot and hungry. "I want to taste all of you."

My heart gallops at the bluntness, at the need in his voice, and suddenly I need it too. Desperately. I reach for him, threading my fingers through his thick hair and pressing him closer. I grind against his mouth shamelessly, chasing the edge like a woman with nothing left to lose.

Because I don't. In a week, I'll be gone. This is a moment out of time, a memory I'll carry like a secret, and I'm going to take every damn second of it.

"Yeah, babe," he growls against me, voice low and rough. "Do what you need."

And I do.

I move against him, chasing every spark of pleasure as he works his fingers inside me—deeper, slower, faster—shifting pressure and rhythm until the heat boiling in my belly explodes outward.

"Rip," I cry out, and then I break apart.

My body spasms, pleasure ripping through me in wild, uncontrollable waves as my hot release spills over his face. He groans in satisfaction, holding me through it, tongue sweeping to catch every drop like it's the only thing that matters in the world.

When he finally pulls back, he slips his fingers from inside me and slides them into his mouth, eyes locked on mine. He sucks them clean, slow and decadent, and God help me, I feel the aftershocks hit all over again.

Then he leans back on his heels, and my gaze drops—straight to the heavy length of his erection, hard and waiting. Even with my body trembling and my brain still swimming in post-orgasm bliss, I rise up, shifting closer to him. I slide my legs around his, wide and wanting, and his eyes drop between us.

"What are you doing?" he asks, voice ragged.

I wrap my hand around his cock and stroke once, slow and sure. His head falls back.

"Fuck," he groans.

I grin, breathless but teasing. "Aww... you guessed it," I purr.

I wrap my fingers around him, stroking slowly, letting my palm glide from base to tip, savoring the silky heat of his skin. When I give a gentle squeeze, a bead of pre-cum gathers at his slit, and I can't help myself. I lean in, tongue flicking out to catch it, moaning softly at the salty-sweet taste that's so him.

Then I draw my tongue into my mouth, letting the moment linger, and when I peek up at him through my lashes, his eyes are nearly black with lust. His chest heaves. His legs look wobbly, like he's one deep breath away from collapse.

Yeah. Not exactly an ideal position for a guy who's injured.

"How about we get you a little more comfortable?" I murmur.

I gently guide him back, nudging and coaxing until he's stretched out on the bed, flat on his back. That gorgeous body—all lean muscle and heat—invites me in. I crawl over him, letting his cock press into my belly as I slide up his chest. My lips find his mouth, and I lick along the seam before diving into a kiss that's deep and slow and full of everything we've been holding back.

When our tongues tangle, I taste myself on him—intimate, intoxicating—and it only makes me hungrier.

He threads his fingers through my hair, sweeping it away from my face so he can see me. Really see me. And then he whispers, voice hoarse and full of want, "I want to be inside you. I need to fuck you, Char."

A tremor rolls through me. I could give in right now. I *want* to.

But I also want to drive him just a little bit crazy first.

"There are so many things I want to do to your cock," I whisper, tracing his lips with mine. "It's only fair... don't you think?"

He groans, eyes squeezing shut. "Babe, if you put your mouth on me again, this moment is going to be over before it starts, and I *need* to be inside you."

I pretend to ponder that, tapping my chin. "Hmm. Dilemma. We had a bed dilemma earlier and solved it like pros... so now we just do what any reasonable adult would do."

His brow lifts, half-wild with tension. "And what's that?"

"We go for round two later."

His agreeing grin is immediate and devastating. I move my hips, grinding slowly against him, letting the thick ridge of his cock slide against me through my slick heat. His breath stutters, and then—

"Fuck," he grits out, hands flying to his head as he grabs fistfuls of his own hair.

I freeze. "What?" I ask, eyes narrowing as I search his face. "What's wrong?"

"Fuck," he breathes, his chest heaving as he pushes up on his elbows, eyes stormy. "I... I don't have any condoms. I didn't bring any. I wasn't planning on..." He trails off, and then cups my face like I'm something precious, like he can't believe I'm real. "You."

That one word, wrapped in softness and awe, hits me straight in the heart. Untangles something tight in my chest I didn't even realize I'd knotted up.

"I wasn't expecting you either," I whisper back, voice a little shaky with the weight of everything we didn't plan but still somehow landed right in the middle of.

He exhales, resigned. "Which means you didn't bring any either... and it's too late to go out tonight."

"There's always tomorrow."

He kisses me lightly. "Yeah. First thing tomorrow. As soon as the store opens, I'm buying every damn box they have."

I laugh. "Every box? I'm only here for a week, Big Bear."

He levels me with a serious look. "Exactly. And I plan to take advantage of every single day... at least three times each day."

A thrill hums low in my belly at how much he wants me. "Then I guess we don't have a problem after all." I wiggle my brows and start sliding down his body. "Because if you can't be inside me tonight, then there's really no reason to hold anything back, is there?"

His cock pulses against my belly, and I don't wait. I wrap my hand around him, warm and eager. He grabs the back of my head. "There is a reason to hold back... I don't want to come in your mouth."

I flash him a grin. "Oh no, Rip. You are coming in my mouth. And maybe all over my face, too. Fair's fair after what I did to you."

He groans, like I just ruined his life in the best way. "Jesus, Char. You can't just say stuff like that."

I cock my head. "Why? You don't like the visual?"

"Oh, I fucking love the visual," he rasps. "I'm just trying to stay conscious."

I lean in, playful and hungry. "Then I better get to work."

And I do.

I take him into my mouth, savoring every inch, every taste, the way his body trembles, the way he mutters my name. My hand slides lower, cradling his balls, and he jerks beneath me. So close. So fast.

He tries to pull me off. I don't let him.

I want this. All of it.

His thighs shake. His hands tangle in my hair. His control shatters with a raw cry that lights me up inside. He spills into my mouth, and when I can't take all of it, I slide back just enough for the rest to land across my cheek, my lips, my throat. When I finally look up at him, his eyes are wide with awe. I think I just wrecked him in the best way possible and I can't deny that I'm a wreck too.

He reaches for me instantly, pulling me to his chest like he can't stand the distance. I melt into him, face pressed to the wild rhythm of his heart.

"Char," he breathes, voice rough and full of something that feels suspiciously like amazement.

"Rip," I whisper back, because I can't say anything more.

His hand strokes my hair and he exhales like I'm the answer to a question he didn't know he was asking. "You're fucking incredible."

I swallow hard, because this man is incredible too. Too bad his heart belongs to someone else. Not that you'd know it from the way he's looking at me. But it's a path I can't—won't go down. Not again. Hell, if there's one thing I know, it's that fairy tales don't exist and perhaps this Goldilocks crawled through the wrong damn window, after all.

RIP

I peel my eyes open, and for some reason, I feel... lighter. Happier. Like my soul did yoga in its sleep. Then last night rushes in with the force of Ash Wheeler, our team's toughest defenseman—after me, of course—and I smile.

Charly.

I turn, expecting to find her curled beside me, but the bed is empty. Just like last night when I heard a sound, checked the couch, and found that empty too. But this time, I don't panic. Because somehow, I know she's here. My gut says so, and my heart... well, it's pounding a little too hard with that knowledge.

That's concerning as hell.

I barely know the woman. We're both keeping secrets, but still... I like having her here. I like talking to her, cooking with her, sitting by the fire with her, and don't even get me started on how much I liked what we did in bed last night. What we plan to do for the rest of the week.

Which, I wish was longer.

I shift in bed, and that's when I feel something soft under my knee. A pillow. I didn't put it there. At least I don't think I did. I toss off the blankets and stand, stretching out like I normally do, and much to my shock, my groin doesn't throb like a war drum.

Huh.

Maybe the sex cured me.

I snort. *Sure, dude. That's totally how anatomy works.* It's the yoga. The relaxation. The cold dunks in the ocean. I tug on a pair of sweats, and head to the kitchen. That's when I spot it. A bag of ice in the sink. Or what's left of it. A soggy, melted mess. I didn't ice myself last night. Which means this was all on Charly.

She iced me.

Propped up my leg.

Took care of me while I was snoring without a care in the world.

I blink at the sink, suddenly full of feelings I wasn't prepared to have. Gratitude. Wonder. Maybe even the tiniest spark of—

Nope. Not going there.

Honestly, for someone who's pretending not to know about my injury, she's doing a damn good job of knowing exactly how to help. I'm not sure how I feel about that.

It's sweet, Rip.

Sweet.

Right.

I grab a mug, pour some coffee, and open the door to let in the morning. Seagulls cry overhead. Kids laugh in the distance. And then I see her.

Charly.

She's sitting in the pulled-out lawn chair, sunshine in her hair, a pan, two plates, utensils and food on the makeshift table beside her. She's barefoot, humming, completely unaware that she's making my chest feel like it's too small for my damn heart.

"Good morning," I say, voice low and still a little rough from sleep.

She turns, and the smile that blooms across her face nearly knocks me on my ass. My God, she's beautiful. Not in a trying-too-hard kind of way, but in that effortless, just-woke-up, no-makeup, tank-top-hanging-off-one-shoulder kind of way. Her short hair is pinned back, her cheeks are a little flushed, and there's something new about her, something glowing, soft, content.

And I can't help but hope I had something to do with that.

"Good morning," she echoes, taking a sip of coffee and motioning to the chair beside her. "I was waiting for you."

"You could've woken me," I say, moving to sit.

She shakes her head, smiling gently. "No way. You were out cold. You needed the sleep. Especially after a night on the sofa." She tosses me an apologetic look.

"It wasn't so bad," I shoot back, even though we both know it's a lie.

Her eyes skim over my face, slow and searching. When they meet mine again, something tender pulses in my chest. "Did you sleep better last night?" she asks.

I nod. "Can't remember the last time I slept that good."

She chuckles. "Same. I lit a fire." She gestures toward the pit. "I hope that's okay. Found some eggs and bacon, figured I'd make us breakfast."

"That's great, but you didn't have to do all this."

Her eyes meet mine again, a flicker of something deeper behind them. "I wanted to."

She turns back to the pan, putting it on the grate over the fire. The sizzle of bacon fills the air, mingling with the salty breeze and the crackle of wood. I sip my coffee and just... watch her. The way she moves without effort. Like she belongs here. Like we both do.

After a long moment of silence, both of us simply enjoying each other's company as the early morning sun climbs higher in the sky, she cracks a couple of eggs. "Over easy?"

"Perfect," I say, and mean it way more than I should.

That one word—perfect—feels like it belongs to this moment. To her.

"Char... about last night—"

"Incredible," she says before I can finish, using the one word I was able to muster after pulling her into my arms. She grins at me over her shoulder. "We've already established that," she adds. "Oh, and we already established that it's going to happen again, right?"

I laugh, the sound catching on something warm and wild in my throat. "I don't think that was a question, but just to confirm, yes. Absolutely. As soon as I've got food in my stomach..." I point to some spot down the road. "I'm off to the store."

"Yes, to buy up *all* the condoms," she says, a small grin on her face as she flips the bacon and looks out over the ocean like she, too, is thinking about all the ways—positions—we're going to get ourselves into. Positions I wasn't sure I'd ever find myself in again.

She turns to me, sees how I've gone serious, and raises a brow. "What?"

"I just wanted to thank you." I swallow. "For the pillow. And the ice."

She softens. "Right. I... uh... hope I didn't overstep. My brother's a physiotherapist, like I mentioned. I've seen injuries like yours before." She gives me a wink, a little spark of humor lighting her eyes. "And, you know, I did put you through a workout last night." A small shrug and then, "Thought I should make sure you didn't sustain any more injuries. Because I definitely want more like last night. So really, this was all very much about me."

I lean in, inhaling her soft, beachy scent as I take a slow sip of coffee. "I figured as much. You ate my oatmeal. Stole my bed. Honestly, I should've known you're only in this for yourself."

"It's good we're on the same page." She smirks as she grabs a plate. She slides a few pieces of bacon on it, then adds two perfectly cooked eggs.

"This looks amazing."

She hands me a fork, then serves herself. "Not bad for a city girl, huh?"

"Nope. Not bad at all."

She settles into her chair, plate balanced on her lap. I toss a piece of bacon into my mouth and nearly groan—it's crisped to perfection.

She glances at me, sun catching in her lashes. "I have to say... I think I could get used to beach life." She glances out over the ocean again, a wistful look on her face. "Cooking over an open fire. You. Me. This."

My heart trips over that last part—*this*.

It's crazy how much I like this too. But is it because of how much I like her, or because in this bubble, we don't have to think about what our futures might hold?

"This bacon is delicious," she says, pulling me from my thoughts.

"I got it at the market. I'll get more. Do you...want to come to the market with me today?"

She frowns, sets the bacon on her plate, and my stomach tightens. Dammit, I didn't mean to bring the mood down. "I know you need clothes," I say quickly, my mind going back to the time in Vegas when I had to bring clothes to my buddy Roman after he saved a runaway bride. "I could just get them for you. Size six? Eight? I've bought clothes for—"

Her head lifts, a curious look in her eyes. "You buy clothes for women a lot?"

I give her an indignant look. "Who says they're for women?"

That pulls a big belly laugh from her. "Fair enough." She gives me a once over. "I must say, though. I can't imagine any women's clothes flattering Big Bear's physique."

"Go ahead," I tease. "Tell me you like what you see."

She puts a big slice of bacon in her mouth. She points to it, and mumbles something about not being able to talk with her mouth full, but goddammit, it reminds me of last night and the way she used her mouth on me. I shift in my chair, my oversized sweats suddenly a little too small.

I finish the food on my plate. "Since you cooked, I'll do dishes."

"Nope. I have to earn my keep," she responds.

"Babe, you earned all the keep…"

She grins. "Maybe I'm just saying that so it will get you moving." I arch a brow and she continues. "Store. Condoms."

"I do love a woman who knows what she wants." Without thinking, I bend forward and give her a kiss. When I inch back, and note the surprised look on her face, I realize how intimate that seemed. "Just giving you something to think about while I'm gone."

I'm about to walk away, when she stops me. "Don't you think you should put on a shirt, and maybe change out of those sweats."

"Right. Shit. I don't know what I was thinking." Actually, I do and it's damn hard to think when there's not much blood left in the brain. I hurry inside and go straight to my room. I tug on a T-shirt, boxers and a pair of shorts. When I come from the bedroom, she's at the sink, humming softly, and it stops me. I watch, mesmerized by the sway of her hips, and as she moves, oblivious to me watching, my heart pinches tight.

She's been through so much in the last couple of months. The competition, which had to be brutal, and then for her ex to throw her under the bus. It's no wonder she ran away from reality for a while. But what is next for her? Where does she go at the end of the week? I really don't have the answer to those questions, but one thing I do know is that she's been helping me, and I want to help her too. Other than giving her a place to stay, I'm not sure what else I can do.

"Be right back," I say, and she gives me a smile as I head out the door. I walk along the beach path, my hat pulled low as people go by on bicycles and cars. It's a lazy town, a vacation place, and most people keep to themselves, which is nice.

A mile down the road, I reach the shops. It's mostly touristy stuff, souvenirs and restaurants, but there is a grocery store where one can find everything they'd need. I hurry inside and go straight to the pharmacy at the back. I grab two boxes of condoms when I hear someone clear their throat. My own throat tightens, when I turn and see Mrs. Callahan standing there. She owns the cottage beside my buddy's and I met her a week or so ago. A nice, elderly lady, who suddenly, doesn't seem like she's minding her own business.

"Good morning," I say, as her gaze drops to the boxes in my hand. Shit. Why do I feel like I'm doing something wrong here?

"Ripley," she says. "You're out and about early."

"Early bird gets the worm." Now why the fuck would I say that. As I mentally curse myself, she purses her lips and it reminds me of my strict grade school teacher. That woman scared the bejesus out of me.

"I can see that."

"I should get going," I say, and hold the boxes up in salute. What the fuck is wrong with me today? I'm a grown ass man and can buy condoms if I want. It's also the responsible thing to do.

"I noticed you have company?"

"Ah, yeah."

"You know, this is a nice respectable community. My great granddaughter is coming to stay with me for the week. I don't want her to be exposed to…well, let's just say I'd like to keep her morals and values intact. No need to expose her to *things* too early."

I gulp. "Things?" What does she think we're doing over there? Wait, no I don't want to know.

"No loud parties, no loud noises. No outside of marriage…sexcapades."

Sexcapades?

What is happening in my life?

"No one sullying up this reputable seaside town," she adds, with pursed lips.

"Oh, yeah. Of course. My fiancée and I are pretty quiet."

A huge smile lights her face, and the lines around her eyes relax. "Your fiancée, how delightful."

"Yeah, so no worries. The most noise you'll hear is her playing guitar."

"Guitar, you say." She nods, seemingly pleased by that too. "My great granddaughter has been asking for lessons."

"You don't say." I inch back. "I should get going. It's going to be a nice beach day."

She nods, but follows me around as I grab a few more things. I pay for my stuff and hurry outside. As an afterthought I stop into one of the tourist shops and grab a couple of items. Once done I head down the path home, but when I glance back, I find Mrs. Callahan walking behind me. Bags tucked under my arm, I hurry my steps, being careful not to hurt my groin in my great escape from a little old lady. I casually glance over my shoulder again, and Mrs. Callahan is right there.

How is she so damn fast? I can't seem to out walk her. Jesus, we should get her on the team.

When the cottage is in sight, I veer off the path, and cut across the road. When I spot Charly sitting outside, strumming her guitar, and realize Mrs. Callahan is following me home, I hurry to her.

"Hey," I say and when she glances up at me, I press a soft kiss to her cheek. When Mrs. Callahan clears her throat, I put my mouth near Charly's ear and whisper, "Pretend we're engaged, okay."

12

CHARLY

hat the ever loving...

I blink up at Rip, who suddenly looks like he swallowed a bug and isn't sure if he's going to hurl or swallow it. Before I can ask what that was all about, he shifts, trying to block my view, but that's when I see her. A woman in her seventies, standing behind Rip. Her eyes are locking on mine, and I search Rip's face for help.

If a look could say, *please play along*, that's what Rip is giving me.

"You must be the fiancée," the woman says, her eyes narrowing, a deep assessment.

I set my guitar down and stand so fast my chair nearly falls backward. "Ah, yes." I give her a big welcoming smile. "And you must be..." I let my sentence hang like an unfinished song lyric.

"This is Mrs. Callahan," Rip pipes in, his voice about three octaves higher than usual. "She's in the cottage next to us. I told you about her. Remember?"

He told me about her quickly and vaguely, but I nod like we discuss Mrs. Callahan over breakfast every day. He looks almost relieved at my enthusiasm. "She knows Paisley and Gunther well. They told her I'd be staying at the cottage this month. They must have forgotten to tell her you'd be stopping by for the week."

Okay that was a whole lot of information in one breath. I run my fingers through my hair, and work to play it cool. "Oh, I'm sorry they didn't let you know I'd be here. Paisley and I go way back," I explain.

Fine lines around blue eyes crinkle as she steps closer, like she's running facial recognition software on my cheekbones. "You look familiar."

Rip coughs. "Oh, that's probably because she's been here with Paisley before. Nothing scandalous." His laugh is forced, and my gaze flies to his.

What the hell? Wait, does he know who I really am? Is he trying to cover for me? He scrubs a hand down his face. No. He's just babbling. But something is definitely going on with him.

"Yes, that must be it," Mrs. Callahan says. "Rip here says you play guitar."

"I do." When exactly did the two talk about my musical resume?

"My great granddaughter is coming for a visit." Warmth crosses her face as she beams. It's easy to tell she loves her family, which is wonderful, even though it hurts my soul because of my family situation. I love them. I just don't love the way they don't believe me, or believe in me. "She's seven, and has been asking for lessons."

"Oh, that's great. I bet she'll love playing." Wait, is she asking me to give lessons? I'm not sure, but I quickly add, "I'm not certified to teach."

She waves her hand. "Being able to play is all the certification one needs. She's here for the next month."

Jeez, pushy much?

"I'm only here until the end of the week," I say, trying to sound casual and not like I'm already planning a fake relocation to Fiji.

"We're planning to lay low for the week," Rip jumps in with that same too-smooth, too-practiced tone. "We just want quiet time and privacy."

She leans in, as if we're co-conspirators and whispers, "Lots of people who vacation here are trying to lay low. Did you know Mr. Ford once stayed in that cottage?" She points down the beach.

I'm not sure which Ford she's referring to, but I do get the sense that she's telling us our identities and privacy will be protected here, and that gives me a measure of comfort. Although, if she knew I was Indie Rhodes, involved in a sex tape scandal, she'd be shooing me away from the beachside resort, and her great granddaughter, I'm sure.

But seriously, maybe it would be nice to get out and socialize. Not that I'm not enjoying being locked up in the cabin with Rip. That's been an unexpected highlight of this escape.

When she doesn't look like she's about to give up, Rip says, "But we've got a wedding to plan."

I whip my head toward him so fast I nearly sprain something. I'm sorry, what now?

Wedding. He just said *wedding*.

The lie rolls off his tongue like he's been rehearsing in the mirror all morning. Honestly, maybe he has.

"Oh, I can't wait to hear all about it," Mrs. Callahan beams, already ten steps ahead of this whole charade.

"Ah... sure," I manage, which is the universal code for *I have no idea what's happening but I guess I live here now*.

"Community dinner tonight," she declares. Rip and I both open our mouths, probably to scream, but she steamrolls right past it. "It's potluck. Bring a casserole and your guitar. Be there at five." And just like that, she power-walks away like she didn't just hijack our entire evening.

I stare at Rip, who's staring back at me with the same expression I imagine people wear after being abducted by aliens.

"What just happened?" I ask.

He blinks, then shakes his head. "I'm not sure. Did we just get drafted into a community casserole cult?"

"Why exactly are we pretending to be engaged?" I ask, arms crossed.

He groans and sets a couple bags on the table with a loud thud. From the brown paper bag, he pulls out not one, but two boxes of condoms.

His cheeks flame red, and it's so cute I briefly forget how fake-engaged I am. "And...?"

"She caught me buying them," he mutters, like it's a confession to a priest. "I panicked, okay? She made this disapproving face, and started going on about her great granddaughter visiting, and how this is a 'respectable community' and I swear to God, Charly—she said *sexcapades*. A little old lady with blue hair threw the word *sexcapades*. At me. Like a weapon."

"And?"

He shudders dramatically. "I blacked out. Words just started falling out of my mouth." He grips his hair. "It was either that or die in the pharmacy aisle. She even said something about sullying up the place."

"Am I sully?" I bite back a laugh even though Rip looks mortified.

"I...think so."

I laugh hard. Big Bear here has been bluffing his way through the most awkward ambush in romantic comedy history, and now he's all flustered and red-faced and weirdly adorable.

I step up, rub his back in sympathy. "Aww, Rip."

"It's not funny," he grumbles, but the way he's hiding behind his hands suggests he knows it is.

"Oh, it's hilarious," I say, rising up on my toes to kiss him.

He blinks, startled. "What was that for?"

"In case she's watching us from her window," I whisper with a wink. "Just doing my part for the neighborhood surveillance committee."

He groans. "Now she's going to expect wedding updates. Like cake flavors. And venues. And color schemes."

"You seem to know a lot about weddings."

"I officiate them, remember?"

"Right."

"God, what have I done?" He buries his face in his hands, and I swear I see a glimpse of the kind of troublemaker he must've been as a kid—charmingly reckless, always caught, never punished.

I gently tug his hands away. "It's going to be okay," I say, maybe trying to convince myself too. "We'll go to dinner, bring a dish. I'll sing a few songs, we'll clap politely at old people's potato salad, and we'll come home. How bad can it be?"

Rip gives me a look that suggests I might have just escaped an institute.

As long as no one recognizes me, it should be okay. Plus she said that whole thing about Mr. Ford, and basically that privacy is respected. As far as her great granddaughter goes. She's into music, but I can't imagine she'd know who I was either. She's seven. So, unless she's super into scandalous reality TV at bedtime, we're golden.

His shoulders slump and he gives a resigned sigh. "Okay, I guess you're right." I run my hands up his back and his muscles ripple. "Oh, and just so you know," he adds. "I may have also told her we'd be...uh quiet. You know. When we have sex."

I gasp, equal parts amused and horrified. "You did not."

His sheepish little smile screams, I absolutely did. "Not in those words," he admits, "But...yeah, kinda." I shake my head slowly, like he's just doomed both of us.

"Rip. Rip. Rip. That's unfortunate."

He lifts a brow. "Why's that?"

"Because now you're going to miss out on me screaming your name." I give him my most innocent smile. He does not take it well.

He growls, a deep, low, dangerous kind of growl that sends heat skittering through me. "You've got to be kidding me?"

"You did this," I remind him sweetly, turning to sit, but he catches me and pulls me back into his arms. I bump into his body and—oh, hello there. "You've got no one to blame but yourself."

"I want you screaming my name, babe," he says, his voice gone gravelly.

I shift slightly against him and feel the way his body responds. My pulse spikes with excitement.

But then...

I turn. "Did someone just clear their throat?"

Rip freezes as he looks past me. "Mrs. Callahan," he whispers.

We both stare at her cottage, the curtain shifting ever so slightly. He shakes his head. "So much for bending you over that table and taking you right here."

A shiver races through me as my mind conjures up the image of him doing just that. "Rip," I push out, suddenly breathless.

Heat blisters in his eyes. "Oh, you like the idea of that, do you?"

"Yeah. I kind of do." But then suddenly, as if having second thoughts, he straightens, his face somber. "What?"

He gives a hard shake of his head, looking like he'd just been hit with a hockey stick and it sobered him, quickly. "It's not going to work," he grumbles.

My heart studders, confused. "What's not going to work?" Is he done with me? Has this charade gone too far? Yeah, it probably has, now that his neighbor is involved.

"I want you, Char," he begins, then lowers his voice even more, "I want nothing more than to take you inside and put my mouth all over you." My pulse jumps with excitement, but when he grimaces, and gestures with a nod toward the cottage next to us, unease makes its way through my body. "The problem is, she's going to know what we're doing. And if I know she knows...ugh, I'm going to have performance anxiety." His shoulders sag. "Cockblocked by Mrs. Callahan."

I burst out laughing. "Wow, now she's living rent free in your brain." I pick up the plastic bag. "I guess we'll have to find some other way to pass the day then." I open the bag and find a sundress, a two-piece bathing suit, a big touristy yellow hat, and water wings. "These for you?" I tease.

"The dress and bathing suit are for you." He snatches the water wings and tears into the packaging. "These are for me."

My insides soar with laughter. God, this man is so much fun to be around. How could his ex string him along like she's doing? Doesn't she know a good guy when she sees one? "Rip, you're insane."

He blows one up and can only manage to get it to his wrist. He holds it out and examines it like it's a jeweled bracelet. "Perfect fit."

I turn and look out over the water, my happiness waning a little. "Does that mean you want to go boating?"

"Hey," he says quickly, his voice soft, full of understanding. "I don't want to do anything you don't want to do, but it could be fun. You remember what I said about riding a horse."

Teasing, I nod toward the house. "I thought that's what I was going to do."

He growls and pulls me against him. "You were about to ride Big Bear," he says, voice low and rough, "Just so we're clear, that offer's still on the table."

I eye the flimsy patio table between us and give it a little test rock. *Creak.* I pucker my lips thoughtfully. "This one?" I rock it again. "I don't know, Rip. I'm not sure it's built to take that kind of pounding."

He lets out a bark of laughter, clearly delighted. The kind of delight that makes his eyes dance and his mouth curve into a grin I feel everywhere.

Pounding.

Honestly, who even *am* I right now?

Apparently, someone he likes. A lot.

"How did we never meet before?" he asks, still grinning.

"Well," I say, "We live on opposite sides of the country. Also, you were apparently in a committed relationship with a woman who doesn't appreciate your floaty-wearing, casserole-bringing, fake-fiancée-having self."

"Tragic," he deadpans. "So. Boating?"

He's fiddling with his water wings again like they're a vital part of the plan. "I promise to stay close to shore," he says, all serious now. "And if you're uncomfortable at any time, we come right back in. No questions asked."

That melts me a little. I mean, how is this man real?

"That could be fun," I say. "You know, to pass the time."

"Not as fun as some other things I could think of," he says, and gives me a playful swat on the backside that sets me into motion. "We need to get moving. We've got to be back for Mrs. Callahan's five o'clock early bird special. No time to waste."

I scoop up my guitar and rush inside to stash it safely, then head to the bathroom to change. Which feels... silly, considering the man has already seen me naked. But still, I close the door anyway.

I hold up the bikini he bought. Of course he found the tiniest one in existence. I grin and shake my head. The audacity. Still, I put it on, and damn if it doesn't fit perfectly.

I slide on the new sundress and when I step back out, Rip's sitting on the edge of the sofa, staring at his phone like it's giving him bad news. He doesn't say anything, but his face is all tight lines and tension, that faraway look again. I don't need to ask who it is. I know it's...her.

I make a noise and he glances up, and just like that, the weight lifts. His eyes lock on me and boom, we're back.

"That fits you," he says, voice a little husky.

I give a little twirl. "It's cute. You have surprisingly decent taste for a man who voluntarily purchased water wings."

He narrows his eyes playfully. "Am I going to get to see what's under that dress?"

"Seriously, Rip? You couldn't find a smaller bikini?"

He bites his bottom lip like he knows exactly what he did. "Kind of the point."

I shake my head, laughing. "At least you're honest. And no, you are not getting to see me in it."

He pouts dramatically. "Maybe later?"

"Maybe," I say, and glance at his outfit. "You planning to swim in those shorts?"

"Right." He hops up.

"And for the love of God, take off those water wings."

"Hell no. A deal's a deal." He pumps them up and I just roll my eyes. "Also, I'm leaving the door open in case you want to sneak a peek."

"How generous of you."

"I'm obviously the better fake fiancé," he says with a wink.

And then, true to his word, he heads into the bedroom and leaves the door open. He turns his back, kicks off his shorts, and glances at me over his shoulder just to make sure I'm watching.

I am. Oh, I definitely am.

As he pulls on his swim trunks, I find myself staring and smiling, warmth blooming in my chest.

How did we never meet before this?

But that thought dims as quickly as it came. Because while this feels like a bubble—safe and shiny and full of promise—I know what waits outside it. The world still remembers the girl in the sex tape. The scandalous career. The headlines. No man wants to sign up for that.

And Rip... Rip's still tethered to a woman who doesn't know what she's got, but owns a piece of his heart anyway.

So, no. No matter how good it feels here in this cottage, in this moment, there's no future for Rip and Charly. Not in the real world.

13

RIP

After signing the rental papers for the ski boat, we head down the sun-warmed wharf. The scent of salt and gas mingles with sunscreen and grilled hot dogs from the shack nearby. I jump in first and hold out a hand to Charly.

She pauses at the edge, eyeing the boat like it might bite. "If I die doing this, I hope you know I'm haunting you forever."

"You'll have to get in the boat to do that," I say, grinning. "Come on. I got you."

She takes a steadying breath, then grabs my hand, and there's a flash of something in her eyes as I pull her in. Trust. Nerves. A little thrill. Maybe all three.

Once she's on board, I tighten the straps on her life jacket and glance down to double-check the fit. "You good?"

"I think so," she says, but her eyes flick toward the water. "You do know how to drive this thing, right?"

"I have a boating license." I give her a mock-wounded look as I put my hand over my heart. "What kind of man do you take me for?"

"Maybe I should ask what license don't you have," she says. "Honestly, I still can't believe you marry people."

I chuckle, leading her to the big, cushioned seat beside mine. "You might get your chance to sunbathe naked."

Her mouth drops open. "Excuse me?"

I gesture to the bow with my chin. "Just saying, that front deck's practically begging for it. If we get out far enough, no one will be no one around…"

She swats my arm but laughs. "You're clearly determined to see me in my bikini."

"Determined to see you *out* of it," I growl.

She smirks. "You do realize Mrs. Callahan is probably looking out her window at us right now."

"She won't be able to see once we're out there." I point to some distance in the ocean. "Unless she has military-grade binoculars, I think we're safe."

"I'm not putting anything past her."

I start the engine, and the boat vibrates beneath us, purring like it's itching to run. I untie us from the dock and ease away slowly, the water lapping gently against the hull.

"You comfortable?" I ask as she wiggles in her seat, shoving her hair into her hat and lifting her face to the sun.

"Shockingly, yes," she says. "Though I reserve the right to panic if we go too fast."

"This will be fun. I promise." I slowly pick up speed, letting her get used to it.

She squints into the horizon. "Wait, are there sharks in these waters?"

I laugh. "This isn't a movie, Charly. 'Jaws' was filmed in Massachusetts, not Connecticut."

"Close enough."

"Relax. You don't even have to get in the water."

"Right." She breathes out and visibly relaxes. "This is actually really nice, Rip. Like… ridiculously nice."

My body warms as I steer us past a couple on jet skis, wave to a pontoon full of drunk twenty-somethings, and catch her smiling. Then a guy flies by on water skis, cutting across the wake with ease.

Charly's eyes track him. She sits up straighter. "That looks… kind of fun."

I tilt my head. "You look like you want to try it."

She snorts. "Uh, no. My balance is limited to yoga."

"Come on. You'd kill it."

"Do you water ski?"

"Yup."

"Surf?"

"Yes."

She studies me with narrowed eyes, like she's not sure whether to be impressed or annoyed. "Show-off."

"Hey, I'll prove it. You, me, beach, one board—I'll even let you watch me wipe out in glorious slow motion."

She grins. "Now that I'd pay to see."

"We probably can't make that happen. At least not on this trip," I say, and though I keep my voice light, she hears what I don't say—that I'm talking about my injury. About how she's never going to see me water ski or surf. Not this week. Probably not ever.

She nods, a small frown tugging at her mouth, and for a beat we're both quiet. There's this mutual awareness hanging between us—once this trip is over, so are we. Back to real life. Back to her silence and hiding. Back to me pretending I'm not injured, or pining after a woman who keeps me dangling like a shiny lure.

If I do see Charly again, it'll be on a screen. But even that's not a guarantee. Her ex did a number on her—scandal, betrayal, a full-blown smear campaign. She vanished from the spotlight, and now I'm not so sure she wants any part of it, and that sucks for her.

Another boat zips past, kicking up a foamy wake. I wave casually, and Charly cocks her head at me. "You're really not embarrassed wearing those water wings?"

I glance down at the bright orange floaties snug around my forearms. "Nope. Might not ever take them off." I shoot her a wink. "Could be the next evolution of hockey gear. A guy takes a hit, and bounces off the boards like a human ping pong ball."

She snorts. "You're a menace to society, Rip."

"And proud of it."

Her grin lingers, soft and wide, and something about seeing her like this—sun warming her face, hair escaping the hat in wild strands—makes my chest go tight. She's beautiful when she laughs. She's even more beautiful when she forgets to be scared.

The engine hums beneath us as we drift farther from shore, wrapped in the shimmer of sunlight on the water. After a few minutes, she slips off her hat and leans her face to the sun like a sunflower finding its way.

We reach a secluded stretch of coastline, and I cut the motor. The world goes still, save for the gentle lap of water against fiberglass.

"Not too far," I say when she glances back at the shoreline. "You could probably swim it if you had to. But you don't."

"I trust you." She says it simply.

I gesture with a nod. "Want to stretch out? I'll set anchor and help you out of your seat. You won't fall. Promise."

She raises a brow. "Trying to get me horizontal, Rip?"

"Always," I deadpan, and she bites her lip as she offers me her hand.

I drop the anchor with a clunk, then grip her fingers and guide her toward the front of the boat. We both ease down onto the cushioned floor, side by side.

"Not so scary," she says softly.

"Not nearly as scary as Mrs. Callahan with her binoculars and judgmental glare."

"Speaking of..." I take in the way the sun kisses her face as I shift a little closer, until our shoulders brush. Her hand slides across the cushion, grazing mine—just a touch. But then she threads her fingers through mine, and damn I like it, *a lot*.

"We need to come up with a plan," she murmurs.

I turn my head toward her. "Where would you like to get married, Char?"

She gasps dramatically and presses her hand to her chest. "Ripley, I thought you'd never ask."

"Smart ass."

She laughs, but it fades quickly. Her expression shifts, thoughtful now. She turns her head, meets my gaze.

"I really thought I'd be somewhere different in my life by now."

I squeeze her hand gently. "You thought you'd be married?" I ask and when she nods, I continue. "You were engaged?"

"No," she says, and the boat rocks gently as if it knows we're drifting into deep waters. "But I was dating a guy for a long time." I shift slightly, and the motion rolls me into her. Our arms brush. She doesn't move away. "I thought marriage was the next step. You know, natural progression."

"I'm sorry," I say, instinctively.

"It's just the way things went down." She shrugs like it's no big deal, but the tightness in her voice says otherwise.

"You're not sorry?" I press gently.

She exhales. "Let's just say I'm glad I found out who he really was before we ever walked down the aisle. Timing sucked, but truth is better than a lifetime with a conniving, jealous jerk."

I squeeze her hand. "I'm glad you found out too. But that probably doesn't make it hurt any less."

Her gaze slides to mine, and for a heartbeat, we just see each other. There's no act, no banter—just understanding. Shared scars.

"You get it," she says softly, not as a question.

I nod once. "Was there someone else?" I ask, my mind on my relationship with Lyra.

She gives a dry, humorless laugh. "Yeah. His ego." She looks out over the water, jaw set. "Turns out he couldn't handle my success. The more I rose, the more he tried to pull me down. When he realized he couldn't, he set out to destroy me instead. All because he couldn't stand not being the brightest one in the room."

Her voice doesn't crack, but it's close. She's holding it together—barely.

I sit with that for a moment, the weight of it settling between us. "Bastard."

She lets out a huff of breath that might be a laugh. "Yeah, that's one of the nicer things I've called him."

"To his face?"

"No." Her voice softens, laced with disappointment. "Just... quietly. Alone. After. I wanted to scream at him. After everything, especially when my parents basically took his side."

She glances down at our hands like she's ashamed of something. "Instead, I ran away. Hid out. And crashed in your bed."

My chest tightens. I let out a long, low whistle. "That's brutal."

She nods. "Yeah."

We sit in the silence, boat swaying gently, sun casting lazy gold over everything.

"You know," I say, glancing around. "We're out in the middle of the water. Nobody around. You could scream. Say all the things you've been holding back. Scream it to me. The fish. The water." I point. "That one grumpy-looking seagull."

She laughs—a real one this time, soft and surprised. "Tell me something, Rip."

"Anything."

"Were you engaged? You and…"

"Lyra," I supply, watching the way her brow twitches at the name. "Lyra Truman." I laugh at that because it's hysterical, really. Lyra who lies, yet her last name is Truman. "No," I say. "We weren't. But… like you, I thought I'd be somewhere different by now."

"Was there someone else?"

"Yeah," I admit. "There's always someone else with Lyra. Some guy she keeps going back to. But every time it falls apart, she shows up at my door and every time…"

"You love her." It's a quiet statement as her fingers curl more tightly around mine. "It's not returned?"

I nod. No sense in denying it. "The truth is, she loves one thing, and it's her career. It always comes first. She'll do anything to get ahead."

Charly's brows pinch slightly, and there's pain in her eyes, pain for herself, because she knows first-hand what I'm talking about. But there's also pain for me. I expect her to ask what Lyra does for a living.

"I'm just a convenience," I admit.

"People suck," she says finally, voice low and honest.

"I'm not going to argue that," I agree, and this time, I'm the one lacing our fingers together.

"I'll do it if you do it," she says, eyes locked on mine, wind teasing her hair.

"Scream?" I ask, half-laughing, half-curious.

"Yeah. I'll scream at Colby if you scream at Lyra. Might do us some good."

Colby. As in Colby Saunders—a fellow contestant from The Spotlight. Jesus. I never liked that guy, even before I knew what a garbage human he turned out to be. Plastic smile. Zero depth. All ego.

"Okay," I say, shifting upright. "On the count of three."

She sits up with me, knees brushing, determination written across her face. We count together, "One. Two. Three—"

Then we unleash hell on the quiet cove.

"LIAR!"

"CHEATER!"

"MANIPULATIVE ASS!"

"EGOMANIAC!"

"USER!"

"CLOWN!"

"PATHETIC!"

"GASLIGHTING NARCISSIST!"

And a few other... colorful choices.

We keep going until our lungs give out and our voices crack from the effort. Then we collapse back, breathless, gasping for air like we've just sprinted a mile.

Our eyes meet—and then we lose it. Full-on belly laughing, uncontrollable and cleansing. It's not pretty. It's real. When we finally catch our breath, I release a long, contented sigh.

"Holy shit. I had no idea how cathartic that would be."

"Right?" she says, wiping at her eyes. "I feel ten pounds lighter."

I roll my head toward her. "Okay, now that we've shouted our trauma into the void... where are we getting married?"

She hums, thoughtful. "Somewhere far from here."

"Vegas?" I ask with a smirk.

She grins. "You and Vegas. Is that, like, your default suggestion?"

I shrug. "Like I said, my grandfather owns a resort there. My brother got married there, and I guess it's sort of expected that I do too."

"But it not what you want?"

"Not really," I admit. "It's a beautiful place, don't get me wrong. But at the end of the day, I want to get married wherever my fiancée wants to get married."

She tilts her head, a teasing smile curving her lips. "Well, since that's me... I was thinking somewhere outside the U.S. Somewhere private. Somewhere no one knows me."

I nod. "Yeah, I get that. I've got a buddy who got married in Santorini—white buildings, blue sea, wine for days."

"Sounds like a dream."

I pull out my phone and scoot closer, our shoulders touching. I search *Best places in the world to get married* and tilt the screen so we can both see.

"Amalfi Coast is number one," I point out.

She scrolls, her fingers brushing mine, her skin warm and soft. "Oh look, you can get married in a palace in Portugal." She gasps. "They do horseback entrances."

That's when I notice her hand again. Bare. No ring.

"Shit. We don't have a ring."

She holds up her fingers, examining them with mock horror. "We'll just say it's being sized."

"Great idea," I say. "Just make sure you tell Mrs. Callahan it's massive. Like, five karats minimum. Ice rink on your finger."

"Wow," she says dryly. "You're so generous." She wiggles her finger again. "If I were into bling, that would be lovely."

I smile but something tugs in my chest. "My ex loved jewelry," I murmur. "I think I bought out half of Tiffany's during that relationship."

Her posture shifts slightly, like she no longer wants to dredge up the past on this glorious day.

"Come here," I say softly.

I slip an arm around her and guide her closer until she's curled into my side, her cheek resting against my chest. I breathe her in—sun, salt, something sweet and uniquely her—and hold her like we've always fit.

She lets out a sigh that melts into me.

No spotlight. No cameras. Just us, floating in borrowed peace.

She sighs, the kind that melts into bone and breeze, and as the sun warms her skin—and mine—her voice goes all soft and sleepy. "Okay... so five-carat ring, Italian wedding. Next summer?"

"That sounds about right," I murmur, letting my hand drift in slow, lazy strokes along her arm. Her skin is warm from the sun, smooth under my palm, and I want to memorize how she feels right now—safe, close, real.

"I like sage, and other shades of greens," she adds, the words slurring gently with drowsiness.

"That works for me, too."

"You in a tux, and me in a ballgown dress," she whispers. "I love the ballgown cut."

Of course she does. She's the kind of woman who could pull off classic, dramatic, and fairy-tale all at once.

Fairy tale, something you don't believe in, Rip.

"Roman's wife, Gabby, used to design wedding dresses," I say. "She's insanely talented. Doesn't do it full-time anymore, but she made Paisley's dress. She still takes on projects for friends. I bet she'd jump at the chance to design one for you."

"That's sweet," she murmurs, eyes still closed, her cheek resting over my heart like it belongs there. And maybe it does. Maybe it always did.

What the hell am I even saying? None of this is real. Just a game. A fake story to fool our neighbour. Except... if it's fake, why does it feel like this?

Her fingers trail down my chest. "Do you think our friends will come? I mean... Italy's a big ask."

"Oh, they'll come," I say without hesitation. "No way will Roman miss the chance to make an inappropriate toast."

She gives a sleepy little laugh. "So, he's your best man?"

"Of course." I glance down at her, catching the tiny flicker of uncertainty in her features. "What about you? Who's standing beside you?"

There's a pause. It stretches between us like the space between stars.

"I'm not sure yet," she says finally.

"That's okay. You've got time."

And I wish—selfishly, foolishly—that I could see her with the other WAGs. That she could meet them, laugh with them, feel what it's like to be part of something. Because I know, without a doubt, they'd adore her. And she'd have too many options for maid of honor, not too few.

"Char?" I ask, because the thought of her leaving in a few short days claws at something inside me.

"Yeah?" Her voice is barely a breath.

"You don't have to leave at the end of the week."

The silence that follows isn't empty. It's full of all the things we're not saying.

14

——

CHARLY

"**O**w. Ow. Ow!"

"I said I'm sorry!" I wince as Rip does a not-so-graceful hop around the living room like he's avoiding hot coals. "Stop moving. You're being a big baby. I just need one more dab."

He glares at me dramatically over his shoulder, skin pink and angry across his back and arms. "How did you not get burned?"

I dip my fingers into the cooling salve and arch a brow. "Maybe because I didn't dive into the water like a golden retriever after we fell asleep on the boat? SPF and swimming don't mix. You have to reapply, but you didn't." He grumbles something unintelligible, which I take as reluctant agreement. "Come on," I coax, holding up my fingers. "Just let me get right here—"

With featherlight strokes, I smooth the salve across his bicep. His muscles flex under my touch, and even though I'm trying to be clinical about it, my stomach flips like a teenager with a crush.

"Mmm." He lets out a low, appreciative sound. "Okay, that actually feels good."

"Of course it does. I have magic hands."

He arches a brow, clearly biting back a joke. "You're right... you do?"

I shoot him a look. "Keep your pants on. We have a casserole party to get to."

He winces. "Fine, but I don't know if I can keep a shirt on. Everything feels like sandpaper right now."

"Do you have something loose? Linen? Polyester? A toga?"

With a grunt, he disappears into the bedroom and comes back holding a breezy, lightweight shirt. "This one's good. Should've worn it on the boat, I guess."

I take it from him, inspecting it. "This is actually a sun shirt, Ripley. It's literally designed to protect you from the sun. Why didn't you wear this?"

"You were wearing a bikini under your dress. I don't think there was enough blood left in my brain to make critical decisions."

"Just be careful putting it on." As he winces, I turn back to the counter and get to work tossing my salad masterpiece. Rip leans over my shoulder like a nosy roommate.

"That's not a casserole. Mrs. Callahan is going to flip."

I snort. "It's a light refreshing salad, not a nineteen-eighties potluck. Besides, you think she'd notice one missing casserole?"

"I'm the one who doesn't want to go missing." He mock shivers.

"I'll claim responsibility for the salad." I slice a cucumber and hold up a sliver. He doesn't miss a beat, leaning in and biting it right from my fingers. A familiar zing shoots through me. It's the second time he's done that.

"You've got a weird thing of stealing food from my hand."

"You keep feeding me like I'm a stray cat with a cucumber deficiency. What do you expect?"

"I expect manners," I tease, popping a cherry tomato into his mouth before he can make another joke, he bites into it—and immediately juice squirts from the corner of his lips.

He blinks. I blink.

"That was... a juicy one," I tease, trying not to laugh.

"Are you flirting with me through produce?" he asks, mouth still full, eyes dancing.

I shrug, smug. "Depends. Is it working?"

"What are you going to do if she asks you to give her great-granddaughter lessons?" Rip asks, bumping my hip gently with his.

I shrug, but there's this little bubble of excitement rising inside me. "Honestly? I've been thinking about it. I don't see the harm. I could teach her a few chords. Just the basics. You know, future rock star starter pack."

"I'm sure she'll love it."

He leans in and brushes a kiss against my lips. Soft, easy, like it's the most natural thing in the world. Like we've done it a thousand times before. And somehow, with him, it feels like we have. This effortless comfort. This...rightness.

His ex must be out of her damn mind. Really, who walks away from this? And worse, who strings someone like him along, making him question his worth? I hate the damage she's done. How it's still hanging over him. How he still pines for her. I hope he finds someone soon, someone who makes him forget she ever existed, and remind him what love is supposed to feel like.

God, that person can't...can't be me.

Right?

"Okay," I say, snapping myself out of it. "Let me pour the dressing and we're good to go."

I drizzle the citrusy blend over the quinoa and toss everything together with practiced confidence. It smells like summer and fresh herbs and I know Mrs. Callahan will love it. I scoop up the bowl and nod toward the guitar propped by the door. "Can you grab that?"

He slings it over his shoulder and follows me out, locking the door behind us. We make our way down the narrow rock path between the cottages, my bare feet brushing the uneven stones. The air is warm, the kind that clings to your skin and makes you feel alive. I'm about to say something, probably something dorky, but then—

I stop short.

Rip collides into my back with an "oof," and I nearly lose the salad to the sand.

"What's wrong?" he asks, steadying me with a hand on my hip.

I blink at the scene in front of me. "I didn't think the entire community was going to be here."

A sea of unfamiliar faces fills the yard. Laughter, lawn chairs, beer bottles, children darting between legs. It's a full-on block party. My skin suddenly feels too tight.

I scan the crowd, searching for anyone who might recognize me. But I don't see anyone familiar. That doesn't mean they don't know *me*.

"Want to head back?" Rip murmurs, his voice low and protective. "I don't want to be recognized either."

I nod. "Yeah. Me neither." I don't explain why. And he doesn't either. We might be sharing kisses and sunscreen and quinoa, but the deeper stuff, well, that's still locked up.

I take a breath and steady the bowl in my arms. I came here to disappear, to outrun the mess I left behind. The scandal, the betrayal. The video. The fallout. But I can't run forever. People are going to connect the dots eventually.

Then again, I don't even look like her anymore. That girl had dramatic makeup, long dark hair, and a stage persona that sparkled louder than her voice. This version of me is muted. Bare-faced, sun-kissed, and blonde. I barely recognize her myself.

I hover on the edge of retreat, every part of me torn between going back and stepping forward.

Rip leans in, his breath brushing my ear. "I can go grab your hat if you want."

I glance up at him, his brows drawn in a worried line, and something inside me settles. "I think..." I inhale slowly. "I think it'll be okay."

I smile, but I know it doesn't quite reach my eyes.

He must sense it, because he smirks. "Want to pick a safe word?"

My head jerks in his direction. "A safe word?"

"You know," Rip says, his voice low and secretive, "A signal between us. For when we need rescuing or want to make a discreet exit. How about casserole?"

I laugh despite the knot in my stomach. "Why does that sound oddly appropriate?"

"Because casseroles are comforting," he says with faux sincerity, "And no one in this crowd will question a casserole emergency."

I chuckle. "It has to be subtle." I grin and give him a playful poke in the chest. "Just so we're clear. A safe word..." I rise on my toes, brushing my lips against the shell of his ear, letting my voice drop, "...is for sex. The rough kind. What you meant to say was a code word, or an escape signal."

His breath catches, and then he laughs, a little sheepish, a little flustered. "Yeah, right. We, uh, probably don't need the first one."

I tilt my head, letting my smile linger. "Was that a question, Rip?"

His expression shifts, his smile falters for a beat, and I can't help but wonder if he saw the video. If he had, he wouldn't even question my need for a safe word. He'd know I'd need one.

"There are just some things," I say, more quietly, "That I'm not into."

He pauses, and then his voice softens. "Not a thing wrong with any of it...if it's between two people who want it. But yeah. I'm not into it either."

Something unspoken passes between us, a mutual understanding in a conversation laced with innuendo.

"Okay," he says, switching gears. "So... a code word that's not casserole, because that apparently is a safe word.'"

I grin. "We need something no one else will question, but we'll know." I glance sideways at him. "Goldilocks? Or Big Bear?"

He stills. Just for a second. Like he's weighing something heavier than a nickname. I know his teammates call him Big Bear. It's part teasing, part respect. But maybe he doesn't want to invite that version of himself into this quiet corner of his life. I let him off the hook. "What about something simple like window? 'Honey, did we leave the window open?' Like, domestic panic, but low-stakes."

"That works." He brightens again, the shadows retreating.

"And if we can't talk, if things get loud, I'll strum the guitar and play..." I pause for a beat to think about it. "California Girls. That seems appropriate and that'll be your cue."

He smirks. "Bold choice. Surf rock as my warning siren. I like it. And if I want out, I'll... I'll just strum. No real tune. Because, in case you forgot, I have zero musical talent."

"Perfect. We're a disaster team with style. Ready?" I ask.

He gives a firm nod, tugging his ballcap just a little lower on his head, and together we walk the gravel path toward Mrs. Callahan's place. As we round the corner into the yard, I greet a few smiling strangers, and clock the way Rip subtly dips his chin, shadowing his face further. The hat. The laid-back clothes. The avoidance of eye contact. He really doesn't want anyone here knowing he's Rip Hart, hockey royalty.

I get it now. He's not just hiding. He's protecting something. His peace, maybe even his heart. So much for the glamor of fame. It turns out even the big, charming guy who can light up a room needs his version of quiet while he heals. Just like me.

"There you are," Mrs. Callahan beams, bustling toward us like a summer storm in florals.

I shoot Rip a wink and whisper out of the side of my mouth, "Did we leave that window open?"

"Too soon, babe," he replies, grinning.

"I brought a salad," I announce brightly, handing her the bowl.

Her eyes practically sparkle as she takes it. But when she notices the guitar in Rip's hands, something in her expression shifts, softens. There's a flicker of emotion there, a shadow of memory.

"Oh, wonderful," she murmurs, her voice going a little wistful. Her gaze drifts past us, toward the fire pit and the gathering crowd. "It's been a long time since we've had music around the fire…"

The way she trails off tells me everything. Whoever used to play here isn't around anymore. I don't ask. But I feel it—the grief, gently worn, like river stone.

Rip adjusts his grip on the guitar. He's watching her, quiet, thoughtful. And something tells me he's not going to let her miss the music tonight.

"Do you have any special requests?" I ask Mrs. Callahan, hoping I can give something back for the way her eyes just gutted me with that quiet kind of longing—the kind that lingers in empty chairs and unplayed songs.

Her gaze floats back to mine, soft and watery, and then her hand lifts, cradling my cheek in a gesture so maternal, so achingly tender, it knocks the breath out of me. Her skin is warm and weathered, and I feel the sting behind my eyes before I can blink it away.

God, I'm not sure my mother ever looked at me with anything but disappointment.

"Whatever you like, darling," she says gently.

Then her attention swings to Rip. "You're sunburnt," she scolds, like she's about to call his parents.

"Yeah," he says with a sheepish grin, rubbing the back of his neck. "Jumped in the ocean. Guess I washed off all the SPF and my common sense."

She lets out an exaggerated *tsk*, and waves a hand. "I've got an ointment for that." But she's already turning, calling out over her shoulder, "Now come mingle."

I stifle a laugh as I follow. Apparently, she has an ointment, but not the time to offer it right now. Ointment by appointment only.

We trail behind her to a long buffet table piled with foil-covered dishes and summer casseroles. I do a quick scan and count about twenty adults and six kids. It's got all the makings of a neighborhood potluck: the smell of grilled meat, the faint screech of kids playing tag, and a lot of very curious eyes landing directly on us.

Mrs. Callahan claps her hands, full hostess mode. The chatter dies instantly. "Everyone, say hello to Rip and Charly," she announces. "They're staying next door at Paisley and Gunter's place."

She gestures to each person, rattling off names. I nod politely while filing absolutely nothing away. There's no way I'm remembering any of this.

Then she pivots dramatically back to us, clutching her heart with all the flair of a Southern drama queen. "These two," she coos, "Are here planning their wedding."

And there it is.

I blink. Rip goes statue-still beside me.

A woman with sky-blue eyes and enthusiastic energy bounces forward, practically squealing.

"Oh, how exciting! I'm a wedding planner! Been in the biz fifteen years."

Lucky me.

I smile so hard I'm about to pull a muscle. "That's... amazing," I say, dragging the word out like I'm buying time. I flick a glance up at Rip. "Isn't that amazing, babe?"

"Uh, yeah," he mutters, clearly stunned.

An elderly man slaps a hand onto Rip's sunburned back and he winces. "Drink?"

Rip straightens but before he moves, he throws me a quick check-in glance. I give him a subtle nod that says, *go, I've got this.*

He walks off toward the drinks table, and I immediately wish I had followed. Or vanished.

"Aww," the wedding planner sighs, watching him. "You can really see the love between you two."

I choke on my own tongue. "Oh, thanks, uh..."

I trail off, not remembering her name even though I'm pretty sure I nodded at her like thirty seconds ago. She doesn't seem to notice.

I am definitely not drunk enough for this.

She slips her hand onto my arm like I'm her new best friend. "I'm Suzanne," she reminds me. "That was my father, Tom." Her eyes dart around the yard. "And that's my husband Jensen," she adds, nodding toward a guy who gives a quick wave before diving back into some deep conversation with a group of men.

Without missing a beat, she steers me toward the wine table — which I'm seriously grateful for right now. "Let's grab a glass, and then I'll introduce you around. After that? We have to talk wedding. I've yet to meet a bride who doesn't want to gush about her big day."

Wanna bet?

"That sounds amazing. Are you from around here?" I ask, trying to sound casual as she pours two generous glasses of red wine.

"New York," she says, raising her glass. "And you?"

"California, actually." Shoot. Why did I say that? I didn't want her adding two and two, especially with the mess that's my past. Plus, Rip and I had totally skipped over the 'how we met' part. There's no way I'm telling this woman I literally climbed through his window and stole his bed.

But you can never steal his heart, girlfriend. It belongs to another.

That thought sneaks into my head like an uninvited guest.

I shake it off and take a careful sip of wine, sinking back into one of the chairs. Soon, a few more women drift over and settle around us. They introduce themselves, smiles wide and friendly. None of them recognize me. Thank God. I'm not ready for the spotlight, not yet. Maybe not ever again.

"So, Charly, tell us about your plans," Suzanne prompts, her eyes gleaming with genuine interest.

Right. Of course. I guess on the bright side of this they're not asking me what I do for a living, the answer of course would be, I'm between jobs. Not a lie at all.

I launch in full throttle, weaving an elaborate story about Italy and a castle—described in lavish detail, though I have no clue if it even exists. Then I gush about colors, cake, flowers, like a pro bride-to-be on a sugar rush. When I finally stop talking, four pairs of eyes are locked on me, wide and starry.

Oh no. Did I go too far? Did any of that sound believable?

"That is absolutely magical," Suzanne breathes, sighing with the kind of wistfulness that makes my heart ache. "I've worked with so many brides over the years, and I'm not sure I've ever heard anyone sound this excited."

I want to laugh. Did I really sound that enthusiastic? Is this even my dream wedding? I don't know. Honestly, everything I just told them is a little fib. But the camaraderie feels real. I miss this — female friendship that's not a competition or a backstab waiting to happen. The kind I never got on The Spotlight.

"It sounds like a real fairy tale," Jocelyn chimes in, leaning back with a warm smile.

Yeah. Fairy tales. The kind Rip and I don't believe in. But sometimes, just sometimes, pretending feels a little like normalcy, in a world where I have none.

I scan the crowd and catch Rip's gaze locked on me. His eyes are hunting for mine, and suddenly my heart flips like it just did a tiny, unexpected somersault. He raises one brow — that subtle, teasing question, then gestures toward my guitar. I shake my head, flash him a quick, knowing smile. He nods, then melts back into conversation with his new friends like it's no big deal.

"Dinner's ready," a guy named Jack, I believe, announces from the grill. We all stand and make our way to the table. I pile my plate with salad while Rip sidles up beside me. I don't even need to turn to know it's him. His scent, warm, familiar, drifts to me and stirs up a need I never knew was there... until him.

Oh boy.

I finally look up, and the second our eyes meet, and his body brushes mine, a flash of heat explodes through me. I can't believe he offered to let me stay longer. And while part of me wants to jump at the chance, I'm not sure it's the smartest move. More time with him might just be trouble. Trouble I'm not sure I'm ready for, for so many complicated reasons.

But dammit, I'm going to enjoy this while it lasts.

●15

RIP

With our bellies full, the sun melting into the horizon, and the sky blushing wild shades of orange and pink, we gather around the fire pit. A salty breeze toys with our hair, while the kids gleefully offer marshmallows to the flames like tiny, sticky sacrifices to the beach gods.

"Want one?" I ask, leaning into Charly, brushing my shoulder against hers.

She rubs her stomach dramatically. "I am so full. I couldn't put another thing in my mouth if I tried."

I shift slightly, adjusting my pants with a silent curse, but then she bites her bottom lip, and that's when I get it. She's messing with me.

"You are so going to get it," I whisper in her ear.

She grins. "Casserole," she fires back. "Wait. No, that's the safe word, to stop. I meant." She puckers her lips. "I'm looking for the opposite. The word that gets us out of here. Because I'm so going to get it..."

The glow from the fire flickers across her face, her blonde hair catching the light like spun sugar. My throat goes tight.

"Did you have fun?" I ask, softer now. I don't want to pull her away before she's ready.

She nods. "Actually... yeah. I'm really glad we came."

"Me too." I reach for her hand, wrap mine around it, and hold tight. Across the circle, I catch a few knowing smiles aimed our way, but right now, I don't care. I'm imagining her alone. Bare. Beneath me. My name on her lips. I'm about to suggest we "go check if we left the window open" when—

"How about some music?" Mrs. Callahan shouts out, holding up a wine glass like a toast.

"Yes, music," a chorus of voices chimes in.

Charly claps once and beams. She's clearly not in any rush to leave now, so I stand, accept our fate, and grab her guitar.

Little Emma scoots closer, her wide blue eyes shining with marshmallow-fueled enthusiasm. "Charly, will you teach me how to play guitar? I'll give you a marshmallow."

Charly laughs. "A marshmallow for payment? That sounds fair."

I lean in and whisper. "Didn't you just say you couldn't eat one more thing?"

She nudges me with a wink. "But how could I say no to that face?"

Honestly, even I would've agreed to teach her, and I have the musical ability of a potato. But that kid is so damn sweet as she looks up at Charly with pure adoration. I get it kid. Trust me, I get it.

"Oh, thank you." Emma flings her arms around Charly, smushing her sticky fingers into her hair. "I'm so sorry," Emma says quickly, eyes round with horror.

"Don't worry," Charly says, laughing. "It'll wash right out."

I hand over the guitar, and she takes it like it's something sacred. Which, to her, it is.

"How about I sing a few songs," she says to the group, "And then I'll teach you a few chords, Emma. You can borrow my guitar if you promise to be very, very careful with it." She smiles at me and it messes with my heart. "It was a special gift."

Honest to God, Charly is the kindest, most quietly extraordinary woman I've ever known, and it pisses me off more than it should that her parents see her as some kind of rebel. How blind do you have to be to miss this? This woman with marshmallow in her hair, children looking up to her as she strums her guitar for the pleasure of others. She's generous. Nurturing. Soft in a way that makes you want to be better.

She catches my eye with a devilish grin. "Feel like singing? I believe this is your go-to jam."

She strums, and oh God I know exactly what's coming before she even opens her mouth. A beat later, Celine Dion's My Heart Will Go On floats into the firelit night. The whole group erupts with glee and joins in. Even me. I'm off-key and half-laughing, but her grin when I butcher the chorus is totally worth it.

I glance over at Mrs. Callahan, who's swaying with her wine glass and singing like she's on stage at a Vegas lounge. The woman still kind of terrifies me, but seeing her this alive makes me weirdly happy. We brought a little magic to this night, or rather, Charly did.

The kids are clapping, twirling barefoot in the sand. The fire crackles. Something about this moment, this whole scene, hits me in the chest. Hard. I've always pictured the white picket fence life somewhere off in the distance. A future thing. A Lyra thing. But right now, watching Charly here, glowing with laughter and warmth and music, I feel...different.

She plays a few more songs until Emma's rubbing her eyes, blinking sleepily. Charly quiets the strings and gently rests the guitar in her lap.

"Want to go find a quiet spot? I can show you a few chords," she offers.

"Yes, I would love that," Emma whispers.

"Thank you, dear," Mrs. Callahan says, and I step back, watching Charly lead Emma a few feet away, sitting cross-legged across from her with all the patience of a good teacher. I'm probably grinning like a damn fool, because suddenly Jensen's at my side, clapping a hand on my back. I wince, my skin sore from the burn.

"Dude," he says, smirking. "She's something special, huh?"

"Yeah," I breathe. My voice is low. Distant. "She really is."

I'm still watching her when Jensen leans in. "You really marrying her?"

I turn slowly, every part of me tensing. There's a look in his eye I don't like. Not one bit.

"You do know who she is, right?" he laughs.

My stomach drops. My fingers curl into fists. "What the hell are you getting at?"

Jensen snorts. "That's Indie Rhodes, man. She can cut her hair, ditch the makeup, wear a Sunday school dress all she wants. But I'd know that face anywhere. And..." He grins, crude and knowing. "Well. Some other parts too."

I'm this close to swinging, fist clenched, heart hammering, ready to knock that smug look clean off Jensen's face. But I drag in a hard breath through my nose, forcing myself to cool down. Hitting him won't help Charly. It'll only bring her more trouble, more eyes, more questions.

"That's not her," I bite out, jaw tight.

Jensen snorts like he's already won. "Whatever you need to tell yourself, man."

My blood spikes hotter. "Does your wife know what you're watching after she goes to bed, Jensen?"

His eyes blink once. Then again. He shifts back half a step, and just like that...I turned the tables on him. Put him in the spotlight and not in a pleasant way—which is what he deserves.

"Does she know what you're paying for?" I add, voice low and lethal.

He says nothing.

I only ever saw the damn video because I'd dropped down beside Theo at a bar in Florida. He was getting off on it like a creep while the Bucks were in his new town, playing his new team. I didn't say a word at the time. Didn't see the point. I recognized her from The Spotlight, but didn't know her personally. If I had... if I'd known who she was back then, I would've broken Theo's nose without a second thought.

But now? Now I know exactly who she is. I know the weight she carries in that bright smile, the bruises hidden under her strength, the way her whole damn career is balanced on a razor-thin edge because of what her ex did. And I'll be damned if I let anyone—anyone—use that against her.

I lean in just enough to make sure Jensen hears me, and only me. "Now, why don't you fuck off and shut your goddamn mouth."

There's a beat. A long one.

"Yeah, okay," he finally mutters. "Maybe it wasn't her."

"It wasn't," I say, dead serious.

"Right." He nods, backing away like the coward he is. "It wasn't."

Just then, Charly comes up to me, her brows pulled together in concern. "Everything okay?"

I tug her into me, needing her warmth like a fix. "Yeah," I say, pressing a kiss to her temple. "Everything's fine."

Her eyes flick to where Jensen stood moments ago. "You and Jensen looked like you were having a very... intense conversation."

I shrug, trying to keep it light. "Just shooting the shit. You know—sports, life, sunscreen application techniques."

She doesn't entirely buy it, but before she can press, Jensen reappears with a grin that's trying way too hard. His arm's looped around his wife like he's the goddamn picture of domestic bliss.

"We're heading out," he says cheerfully. "Great meeting you both, Charly. Rip. Hope to see you around more."

"Night," we say in perfect unison, waving like the happy couple we are—minus the part where I'd still like to knock his teeth in.

Mrs. Callahan swoops in next, wine glass in hand, cheeks flushed with laughter and too much rosé. "Thank you for the music," she says, dreamy-eyed. Then her smile falters. "Wait —you're not leaving, are you?"

"Window," we blurt out at the same time.

I bite my lip to hold back a laugh. Charly recovers first, always the quicker thinker. "I think we left the window open at the cottage," she says sweetly. "With this ocean breeze I don't want sand blowing in."

I yawn for effect, stretching like a man in desperate need of aloe and silence. "Also," Charly adds, patting my arm, "I need to get some ointment on Rip's sunburn."

"Oh, why didn't you say so?" Mrs. Callahan perks right up and plunges a hand into the deep pocket of her floral dress—one that looks like it came straight from a Mrs. Roper fan convention in Vegas—and produces a tube like a magician with a rabbit.

"Here. Miracle cream. Made it myself. Smells like feet but works like a charm."

I take the tube warily, fully expecting the label to read: *Not Approved by Any Medical Board Ever.*

"Thanks, Mrs. Callahan."

She squints up at me like I'm a disobedient student. "You have to reapply SPF after swimming. This is basic stuff, Ripley. Do you want to look like a baked ham?"

"Yes, I know," I mutter, already feeling twelve years old again.

She gives a dramatic huff like she's personally offended by my sun care negligence. Then she turns to Charly and instantly transforms into pure butter. Her face lights up as she cups Charly's cheeks. "You are a treasure. A musical *angel.* If this one—" she jerks a thumb at me "—gives you any trouble, you just pack a bag and come stay with me. We'll drink sherry, and binge-watch Bridgerton. I've got Netflix."

Charly beams. "Thank you, Mrs. Callahan."

"Oh, please." She flutters a hand in the air. "Call me Betsy."

"Betsy it is."

I nod. "Good night, Betsy."

Her head whips around so fast I hear her neck crack. "Excuse me?"

I clear my throat, straighten up like I've just been yelled at for slouching at my desk. "Good night, Mrs. Callahan."

She smirks, satisfied, and walks off with the kind of swagger only a seventy something year old woman in orthopedic sandals can pull off.

As we walk away, Charly sighs, dreamy. "I really like Betsy."

"She's nicer to you than me."

"Probably because I'm teaching her great-granddaughter guitar."

"You brought a salad. If *I* brought a salad instead of a heavy creamy casserole, she'd throw it at me and accuse me of cultural sabotage."

"Like you'd make a casserole. You had oatmeal and pop tarts in your cupboard."

I lift my chin, indignantly. "Fine, be like that and now I'm not going to make you my famous oatmeal, pop tart casserole. You're really missing out."

She laughs. "I don't think I'm missing out on anything. At least...after tonight I won't be." There's heat in her voice and my thoughts are no longer on pop tarts. "She likes you, Rip," she adds. "She just wants to keep you on your toes and make sure you do right by me. She's old fashioned and I think it's sweet of her."

I slide my hand around her back and pull her close. "What if I want to get off my toes, and still do right by you."

A fine shiver goes through her, then a teasing look brightens her eyes. "Wait, you said casserole. Was that your safe *stop* word?"

I laugh. "I actually think we need a new *go* word."

"Wasn't that window?"

I adjust my pants. "Yeah, I just can't seem to think straight tonight."

"That makes two of us," she says breathless. "Ever since seeing you in those water wings." She playfully waves her hand in front of her face.

We reach the cottage, and I quickly open the door. She steps inside and I glance over my shoulder, gauging how far away Mrs. Callahan's cottage is, and if she can hear us.

"While you're standing there, trying to figure out if Betsy is listening, I'm going to wash this marshmallow out of my hair." She steps into the bathroom and doesn't shut the door behind her. Three seconds later, I find her bent over the tub, adjusting the water. She turns around and gasps when she sees me.

"How... Oh my God, Rip."

She's staring at me like I've sprouted a hockey stick—and, in a way, I have. Between my legs. I glance down at my very naked body, my dick standing at full salute for the girl who makes me forget the world even exists.

"What?" I ask, deadpan, trying to play it cool even though every cell in my body is vibrating with the need to touch her.

"You're naked."

"Am I?" I blink, mock-surprised. "Huh. So I am."

She gestures vaguely at the air between us. "You were dressed *three seconds ago*."

I close the distance, steam curling around us, and gently brush my knuckles over her flushed cheek. "Did I forget to mention I hold the title for fastest undresser east of the Mississippi?"

She chokes on a laugh. "Is that even a thing?"

"Absolutely. There's a plaque and everything. Very prestigious. Right next to my third-grade spelling bee participation ribbon."

"Impressive resumé."

"If you don't believe me, I can show you my credentials."

She laughs, but her eyes go soft. I can see it, that flicker of something deeper, something softer in her eyes now. I don't want to just be the guy who gets naked fast, but the guy she can trust.

"You don't need to show me your credentials, Rip," she murmurs, pressing up against me, her lips ghosting the edge of a smile. "I can already feel them."

My body throbs as heat arcs between us, sharp and undeniable. I drop my voice, all humor gone. "You left the door open," I murmur. "I assumed that was an invitation."

My fingers trail down her arms, and I grip the hem of her dress. I lift it slightly, and her breathy sigh is all the encouragement I need. I pull it higher, my other hand sliding between her legs. She parts them instinctively, like her body's already made the decision her mouth hasn't said yet.

"It was," she whispers.

I lean in and growl into her ear, low and rough. "All night, babe. All fucking night, I've been thinking about you."

Her voice trembles with anticipation. "What were you thinking?"

"This," I say. I drop to my knees and hook my fingers in her panties. She lifts her dress, watching as I slowly drag the fabric down her silky legs.

"You've been thinking about my panties?" she asks, a teasing note in her voice.

"Yeah. And the sweetness underneath."

I lean forward, part her folds with my tongue, and taste her.

"Oh, Rip..." she moans, her hips swaying, her body seeking more. I grip her thighs, steadying her, grounding us both in the moment I've been aching for.

"I've been thinking about you too," she breathes.

"Tell me."

"I've been thinking about your hands. The way they touch me. About your mouth, and the pleasure you bring with your tongue."

I drag my tongue from bottom to top and circle her swollen clit.

"Yes...like that," she gasps, her voice unraveling.

I slide a finger inside her, and she whimpers. "You've been thinking about this?"

"Yes. And those two big boxes of condoms, and all the memories we're going to make."

I glance up, and what I see nearly steals my breath. The heat in her eyes. The flush on her cheeks. My heart pounds a little harder.

Memories.

Is it a reminder to me—maybe to herself—of what this is. Fleeting. Temporary. A moment in time?

But as I look at her, this strong, kind, stunning woman giving herself to me I'm suddenly not so sure I want fleeting.

Maybe I want more.

CHARLY

His hands glide over my skin, slick with soap, moving slowly, carefully, like he's handling something precious. Honestly I don't think any man has ever made me feel so cherished before. The scent of citrus and heat swirls in the steamy air, and bubbles burst between us, tiny pops of joy that match the fizzing in my chest. I feel ridiculous and light and overwhelmingly happy, a feeling I haven't let myself touch in far too long.

His thumb brushes over my nipple, the coarse pad dragging across the sensitive peak in a way that's anything but casual. He lingers there, testing my reaction, and I arch into him with a soft gasp. His cock nudges harder against the curve of my backside as he gently turns me beneath the spray. The water is cool, the way we both wanted it, but his touch burns.

God, I love when this man puts his hands on me.

Like he's learning me. Committing every dip and swell of me to memory. Like he needs to remember the shape of my body in his hands so he can recall it when he's back in Boston… and I'm not.

A tiny ache blooms at the thought, and I shove it aside, burying it deep.

Not now.

Now is for joy. For feeling. For this.

I tip my face to the water and close my eyes, letting the rivulets rinse away the soap. It does nothing for the fire crackling under my skin. A blaze lit by Rip. I want him with a kind of desperation that should scare me, but how can I be scared when I'm with a man who makes me feel so safe.

I turn slowly, facing him, pressing my hands to his slick chest as I rise onto my toes and brush a kiss across his lips, gentle, soft, nothing like the storm gathering in my veins.

"All clean," I whisper, letting my words glide against his mouth. My body thrums, greedy for more. I shift him under the water and glance down. "Does the cold water feel okay on the burn?"

"Yes, but I—"

His breath catches as I soap up my hands and wrap them around his cock. Whatever he was about to say is swallowed whole by the sheer heat between us.

"Babe, this is not a good idea," he rasps, voice fraying at the edges.

I look up at him with a grin, slow and sultry. "Really?" I stroke him, once, twice, and he swells even more in my grip. "Because your body seems to think it's the best idea that's ever existed in the entire history of ideas."

He groans, his hands clamping onto my shoulders like he's bracing himself against an oncoming wave. His hips betray him, already beginning to rock in time with my rhythm.

"Yeah. The little fucker is a traitor," he mutters, half-wild with want.

"Maybe he wants my mouth," I tease, flicking my tongue across my bottom lip just to drive him insane.

His head falls back with a sound that's somewhere between a growl and a prayer. "Fuck yes."

God, that sound. That raw, wrecked need...it's everything. A thrill rushes through me at how quickly I can unravel him, how desperately he wants me. But this isn't just power or lust. It's something deeper. Mutual destruction. Because he can reduce me to ash with just one grin, and we both know it.

I start to lower myself, but suddenly, he steps back like I've scorched him.

"Out. Now."

I blink up at him, startled. "Wait, are you...kicking me out?" My voice is half a laugh, half a challenge.

He looks tortured. Beautiful and naked and strung so tight I think he might break. "Charly..."

"But earlier," I remind him, tilting my head, "You said I was going to get it." I soften my voice into something sweet and utterly dangerous. "This doesn't seem like I'm getting it, at all. I'm pretty sure that qualifies as false advertising."

"Jesus, Charly," he mutters, stepping under the cold spray like it's the only way he can keep from ravaging me right here, right now. I wouldn't mind. But we do have his injury to consider. I'd never forgive myself if we did anything that caused more damage.

"You are going to get it," he grits out, water streaming over his head, jaw tight like he's in a battle. "I just... if I don't do some very aggressive mental math right now and get my goddamn dick under control, the first time I put it in you will be over in five seconds. Maybe less. And I want to remember it."

Something in me melts, not from the heat, but from the honesty. The restraint. The sweet, slightly desperate truth tangled in his words. My heart soars, even as my thighs press together by instinct.

God, I love him like this.

Trying to hold himself back. Trying not to ruin it by taking too much, too fast.

And, well, I can't resist poking Big Bear.

I throw him a slow, sassy look over my shoulder, giving my hips a little wiggle as if I'm not currently vibrating with need. "Well," I say breezily, "Guess I'll just have to start without you."

I inch the curtain open, steam billowing around me. I step out slowly, giving him a show, knowing exactly what I'm doing and loving the low, wounded growl that follows me through the room. I reach for a towel and cinch it tightly around my chest, but only for effect.

Then I pause.

"Do you think I should start here?" I ask innocently, spreading the towel just enough to slide my thumbs over my nipples. They peak instantly, betraying the cool air and the hot pulse thrumming inside me.

Behind me, there's silence—*charged* silence. The kind that hums with all the things he's not saying. When I glance back, I find him standing there, still under the water, absolutely stricken—jaw slack, eyes dark, cock harder than any human should be capable of.

Poor man looks torn between worship and weeping.

"Or here?" I ask sweetly, sliding one hand down, slower than necessary, until my fingers dip between my thighs and I let out a soft, genuine moan.

He swears. Just one word, but it's guttural. Maybe I really should be scared, but I think this man is going to wreck me, in more ways than one.

Then the spray cuts off.

I squeal and bolt, laughing as I run toward the bedroom like a thief in the night. My feet slap against the floor, wet and reckless, and I barely make it to the bed before I hear the unmistakable sound of him. Heavy, determined footsteps. Curses. A low growl of impending doom.

Then—

He appears in the doorway, towering, dripping, glorious in nothing but a towel tied at his waist. His body looks carved from stone, every muscle tight with tension, every inch of him thrumming with intent. He's beautiful and lethal, and my playful smile dies the second our eyes meet.

"Rip..." It's all I can manage. My throat is dry, my lungs forget how to function.

He crosses the room slowly, deliberately, until he's standing over me. I crane my neck, eyes wide, every nerve ending buzzing.

"Well," he says, dragging a hand down the center of his chest like he's mimicking what he plans to do to my body. My gaze follows the path, over hard pectorals, down the ridges of his abs, to the trail that disappears into the towel still slung dangerously low. "What did you decide?"

I blink, struggling to form words. "What?"

He leans closer, the heat of him wrapping around me like a second skin. Then, with a flick of his fingers, he unknots my towel. It drops soundlessly to the bed.

My breath catches as the cool air ghosts over my now-bare skin. His eyes take their time, and when they finally meet mine again, they're dark, searing, focused like a man on a mission.

"Where did you decide to start?"

I stare up at him, lust-rattled and trembling, as realization dawns like a thunderclap.

And just like that, the game resets.

But this time, he's in control, and I love it.

Giving him what he's asking for, a smile curves my lips. "Oh," I say. "I thought I'd start here."

I shimmy backward to the center of the bed, and settle my shoulders against the headboard. The sheets are cool beneath me, a contrast to the heat pulsing between my thighs. Slowly, deliberately, I bend my knees and let them fall open, baring myself to him. My hand trails down the slope of my stomach, fingers light and teasing as I touch the skin that's been aching for him all night.

"This," I murmur, pressing just above my mound, "This is the spot that's been screaming at me to use our code word." My eyes flick up to his, dark with hunger and heat, and I give a little breathy laugh. "She's not subtle."

He just stares at me, like he's watching something holy, sacred—and a little dangerous. His eyes are locked on where my fingers move, and I swear he forgets to breathe. I've never done this before. Never had the nerve to touch myself in front of anyone. But with Rip, it's different. He makes me feel powerful and wanted and completely unashamed.

So I keep going, circling, stroking, letting him see everything. A soft moan slips from my lips, and that's what breaks him. With a sharp inhale, he moves, circling the bed with the grace of a predator who's done holding himself back. He drops down beside me and the mattress dips under his weight. His presence floods the space, all heat and want and something deeper.

I lean into him, our skin brushing, and his voice drops an octave, all low, masculine gravel.

"You've been hurting." It's not a question.

I nod, voice shaky. "So bad."

His eyes flick to mine. "We can't have that."

When he reaches for me, I let my hand fall away, surrendering. His thick fingers part me, and when he slides them through my slick heat, I groan, because my wetness has nothing to do with the shower and everything to do with him.

No one has ever touched me the way Rip does. No one's ever seen me like this and made me feel so safe doing it.

"I could barely think straight all night," I confess, breath hitching as he strokes again, so gently it borders on torture.

He lifts his gaze, a grin tugging at his mouth. "I haven't thought straight since I found Goldilocks in my bed."

I let out a surprised, throaty laugh and reach down between us, wrapping my fingers around his thick cock. He groans the moment I stroke him, my thumb gliding through the bead of pre-cum at the tip.

"I've been a mess," I whisper, "Ever since I realized the name Big Bear had more than one meaning."

That grin turns downright wicked. But there's heat behind it. He shifts, moving between my thighs. With a hand on my hip, he inches a finger inside me, his voice gone low and rough. "You need this?"

"No," I say softly. "I need *you*."

And something in him changes. The cocky smirk fades, replaced by something infinitely more tender. Vulnerable. Real.

"I need you too, Charly," he says, the words thick with meaning, no teasing in sight.

Then he lowers himself onto the bed, flat out on his stomach beside me. His hand curls around my thigh and he gives a firm tug, pulling me until I'm flat on my back and spread for him. My breath catches, and then—

His mouth is on me.

His tongue finds my clit with ease, with heat and...hunger. I cry out, arching up against his mouth. My hands dive into his wet hair, fingers threading through the strands as I hold him to me like a lifeline.

Because somehow, somewhere along the way, this man became exactly that.

How did this happen so fast?

His head moves in a slow, devastating rhythm, his tongue drawing circles and his fingers slipping inside me like I was made just for him. I can't think. I can barely breathe. All I can do is feel.

"Yes," I cry out, lost in the sensation, in the way his mouth works me like a symphony he's been dying to play. I give myself over completely. To him. To this. To everything I thought I'd lost—the chance to trust someone, to want someone without fear.

Because with Rip, it's there. That invisible tether. Trust. Maybe it's because we're both hiding, and somehow in our hiding from the world, we don't have to hide from each other.

In no time at all, I break. Using his mouth, his fingers, Rip wrings an orgasm from me so powerful it feels like he's tapping into something deeper than nerves and flesh. It's soul deep. Bone-deep. I cry out, unable to hold it in, as every muscle in my body goes taut.

"Rip...yes...God, that—"

The words tumble out, fractured and unfiltered, until I realize I'm not even making sense. I shut my mouth, but not my eyes. I keep them open, locked on his, needing him to see what he's doing to me.

His lips are glistening, his face flushed with hunger and satisfaction, and he looks like he's on the edge of unraveling just from watching me fall apart. Like my pleasure is his own. And somehow, I believe it is.

As the last tremors fade and I slump into the mattress, he shifts beside me. I reach for him instinctively, my palm sliding over the warm plane of his back, needing the contact. Needing him.

He leans forward, opens the nightstand drawer, and pulls out a box of condoms. I watch as he tears it open, focused and determined, and that's when I reach out and gently take the foil packet from his hand.

He pauses. "What are you doing?"

I meet his eyes, heart pounding, not from fear, but from this. From trust, and risk, and the truth of what we're about to share.

"Trust is hard for me, Rip."

His brow softens. His voice follows. "Yeah, babe. I get that. But I'm still going to suit up. You can trust me on that."

God, the way he says it. Soft but strong. Like a promise. My chest aches.

"Trust is hard for you too, isn't it?" I whisper.

He runs his hand through his wet hair, the motion rough, like he's trying to scrub the truth out of himself. "Yeah." And somehow, I feel it. His pain. Just like I think he feels mine. The invisible thread between us tugs tighter.

"I'm on the pill," I say, voice soft but sure.

He blinks. Once. Twice. "Wait. You mean... we could've done this last night?"

That earns a small laugh from me, even as something tender unfurls in my chest. "Do you usually have sex without a condom?"

"Never. You?"

"I was in a long-term relationship."

He nods. And something shifts in his expression. The reminder of someone else touching me clearly doesn't sit well. And I get it. I don't want to picture anyone with him before me, either. Not when this feels like more than just sex. Like something we're building, even if we know it won't last.

"I'm not saying that to make it weird." I reach and lay a hand on his arm. His muscles twitch beneath my touch. "I'm saying it because... I want to feel you. All of you."

His eyes meet mine, the intensity in them nearly knocking the air from my lungs. "I want that too."

"Without a condom."

Rip draws in a ragged breath and drags his hand through his hair again. His chest rises and falls in a rhythm that's all nerves and desire. His eyes darken with heat and something else I can't quite name.

"Are you sure, Char?" he asks, voice rough, shaky. "I'm clean and tested but I need to know that you trust..."

His words fall off as I run my hand along his arm, feeling every inch of him. But I know what he's asking. He cups my cheek with one hand, eyes searching mine for doubt.

"I never thought I'd get on a boat again," I whisper, the words thick with meaning. A confession wrapped in metaphor. And he knows it. His hand tightens on my face, thumb brushing my cheek.

"Charly…" he murmurs. "I really like you."

I smile, my heart blooming. "I really like you too, Rip."

In return, I don't ask if he trusts me. He doesn't need to say it. His body says it for him—he's staying. He's moving between my legs, without the barrier. We're both doing something completely uncharacteristic, and there's not a man on earth I'd rather do it with than Ripley Hart.

It's reckless, yes. But it's also honest. Real.

We both know this can't last, but right now, I want to wring everything out of this… everything but his heart. Because that belongs to another. But for now, I want to lose myself in him.

I want him to lose himself in me.

That can be our gift to each other—our secret indulgence while the real world waits outside, oblivious.

I toss the condom aside.

He blinks, surprised. "This is crazy, right?"

"If you need to hear me say it," I murmur, lips tilting up, "Then yes. But so was me running away and climbing in through your kitchen window."

That makes his grin flash, but it disappears quickly as he shifts forward, the tip of him pressing against my entrance. He grunts, eyes fluttering closed. "Actually, your body seems to think this is the most fabulous of fabulous ideas in the entire universe."

I gasp, clenching around the first inch of him. "My body would be right."

And with that, he sinks into me.

He fills me beautifully and every part of me stretches around him like he was made to fit. Like my body knew him before I did. He holds himself up, giving me all of him without crushing me, and I wrap my arms around his back, drinking in the flex of muscle, the way he moves just for me.

"So good, Rip," I breathe, my voice wrecked.

"So good," he growls back, and when I drag my nails down his back, he shudders, then starts to move faster, harder, like he's chasing something only I can give him. We're tangled, eyes locked, rising and falling in perfect sync. His jaw tightens, his control hanging by a thread.

And then he grinds just right, sending sparks through me like wildfire. My whole body clenches, pleasure tearing through me as I fall apart around him.

"Rip," I scream, not caring who can hear us.

"Yes, babe," he groans, thrusts stuttering. "Take what you need."

He pushes deep, wringing my orgasm out, prolonging it with every thrust and then he throws his head back and groans.

"I feel you," I whisper, and I do. Every pulse of his cock as he pours into me and kisses me deep, hard, like he can't let go of the moment...of me. I kiss him back and when our bodies come back down, he shifts to the side, pulling me close to him, instead of pushing me away.

"I take it back," I giggle, high on everything now.

His brow lifts. "Take what back?"

"That it was false advertising. You gave it to me." I cup his cheek, drunk on affection. "You gave it to me good."

He kisses me, his voice rough against my lips. "There's more where that came from…"

God help me.

More might just ruin me.

RIP

I roll over in bed, and for a moment, my heart soars when I find Charly there, still asleep. Soft morning light filters through the curtains, falling across her bare shoulder, her cheek pressed into the pillow, lips parted just slightly. Peaceful. Like the world finally gave her a moment to rest.

A wide grin curls across my face, and my chest pulls tight in the best kind of way. I reach out, brushing my hand down the slope of her spine, the curve of her waist, memorizing the shape of her in the quiet. Her skin is warm beneath my touch, like she's holding the sun beneath her surface.

The covers are half-kicked off and bunched at the foot of the bed. As I lean forward to tug them up, something catches my eye, a small, delicate tattoo on her hip. A butterfly made of musical notes. I blink, stunned that I haven't noticed it before. Then again, every time I've had her naked, I've been too overwhelmed to see anything other than how badly I wanted her. How she completely undid me.

"Like what you see?" Her voice is scratchy with sleep, low and amused.

I glance up. She's watching me, a lazy smile on her lips, her eyes still heavy-lidded.

"Always," I say, voice low and honest, then lean in to kiss her. Soft. Slow. Like I have all morning, and really I do, but I don't have forever…not with her. When I pull back, my gaze drifts again to the tattoo. "This is beautiful. I didn't notice it before."

She stretches, breath catching just slightly, and gives me a look that's half shy, half resigned. "Mom and Dad hated tattoos. Said they were trashy, rebellious." She snorts. "That's me, rebellious, remember?"

"I do remember you saying that, but I don't get it, Charly. I don't know why your parents thought you were a rebel or disobedient, or a troublemaker. The first thing you wanted to do was give the guitar back when you thought it was lost. Then there's Emma. She adores you and you're giving up your time to teach her a few notes, and look at 'Betsy'. It only took five minutes with you, before you had her wrapped around your finger. You're kind, compassionate, and everyone who meets you loves you."

Loves you.

She arches a brow, and I say, "Anyway, go on. Tell me about this." I lightly trace the butterfly.

"I knew getting it would only validate everything my parents said about me, and maybe it did. But I wanted it, so I got it somewhere they'd never see it. You'd have to be paying attention to notice."

I don't think her parents were paying close enough attention to what their daughter needed from them, and that makes me sad.

"I'm paying attention," I whisper, fingers brushing gently around the edges of the ink. "The music I get. But the butterfly?"

She hesitates, eyes drifting to the ceiling as if looking for the words. "They always wanted me to be what *they* envisioned. The perfect daughter. Polished, obedient. There was no room for color. No room for flight. But music..." Her voice softens. "Music gave me space to feel. And the butterfly... it's freedom. It's growth. It's mine. I wanted to mark the moment I stopped living in a box and started becoming who I really am."

I study her, not just the tattoo anymore, but the story etched beneath it.

"I like it," I whisper, letting my lips brush over the ink. "Where did you get it done?"

"I was at this dive bar in San Diego..." I cock my head and she blinks like she's rethinking the story and how much to tell me. "Anyway, I met this tattoo artist. His work was beautiful."

"I've always thought about getting a tattoo, but I might be a chickenshit," I half joke. "I really don't like needles."

"Don't people who play hockey take a pounding all the time?"

I stare at her, my brain racing. Am I a fool for thinking, or hoping, she doesn't know I play in the NHL? But it's clear from the way she worded her question, that she's keeping my secret if she does know. Just like I'm keeping her secret.

"A pounding is one thing. A needle." I stop to cringe.

"Don't be a baby."

"Hey, I'm not baby bear, Goldilocks."

She laughs. "Right. Well, if you do decide, and you happen to find yourself in San Diego, I personally vouch for Raze at Rogue Ink."

"Rogue Ink," I murmur. "I guess that's why you liked it. You related to the name, huh?" She nods and I run my finger over the tattoo before pressing my lips to her thigh. "Raze did an amazing job and this suits you. Beautiful, strong, a woman who knows what she wants."

Her smile falters and my heart wobbles as I take in the tears threatening to spill. "I thought I knew what I wanted...but now, I'm a little lost." I stare at her, not knowing what to say, how to make this better. Before I can, she continues, "What's on the agenda today, Rip?" she asks, injecting enthusiasm into her voice that I don't think she feels, but it's a sign that she needs to move on from the hurt. I get it. This time together is about forgetting. "Stretches? Sun? Sand? Sailing?"

"There might be one 's' word you're forgetting," I say, lifting a brow as I try to lighten the mood.

She smirks, eyes twinkling. "Sandcastles, of course. How could I ever forget sandcastles?"

I laugh, and something about her smile, the quiet between us, the warmth of her skin beneath my fingers, it makes me wish that fairy tales really were true.

I drag her beneath me. My lips find hers for a deep kiss and the next thing I know, my cock is inside her and she's chanting my name. "Goddammit, I plan to make you come every day until we have to leave here."

As she clenches around my dick, I release inside her, and we both hug each other, like sex in the morning is something we do every day, and well...we will. Until this is over.

"Oh, wait," she teases. "That other 's' word was sex?"

"No, it was smartass."

She laughs—warm, unguarded, and full of that easy joy that always seems to unravel something tight inside my chest. I swear, her laugh might be the best thing I've ever heard.

"How about breakfast before yoga?" I ask, stretching with a sleepy grin.

"Perfect," she says.

"Why don't you jump in the shower and I'll get it started?" I offer, as her fingers trail lazily down my chest.

"You're not joining me?" she asks hopefully.

I smirk. "If I do, we'll never eat." She shifts to roll out of bed, but I stop her with a gentle touch. "Babe?"

"Yeah?"

I slide my hand down the silky length of her thigh and brush my fingers softly over the slick heat between her legs. My throat tightens at the feeling—intimate, still warm from our bodies. "You know, I've never had sex without a condom before."

"I know," she says, her brows lifting with soft curiosity.

"Can I ask a stupid question?" I glance at her, and for a moment, I hesitate—then I don't. Not with her. She makes it safe to ask vulnerable things, things I could never ask my ex, because I feared it would end up in print somewhere.

She cups my cheek with such tenderness it nearly undoes me. "Ask me anything. Always."

I exhale slowly. "Will I... drip out of you? Will you feel it?"

A slow, knowing smile curves her lips, and something in her gaze turns molten. "Some will, yeah. And yes, I'll feel it," she says gently. "Some of it gets absorbed. Why?"

I swallow hard. "Jesus... just knowing a part of me is still inside you, knowing you feel it... It does something to me. It's like—I don't know. It's intimate as hell, and fuck, it turns me on. I'm not sure I'll be able to walk around today without embarrassing myself."

Her eyes gleam with mischief. "Then I'll be sure to let you know the moment I feel it."

I groan, dropping my head to the pillow. "God, woman. You're going to kill me."

She slides out of bed, still completely bare, and my eyes follow her like they don't have a choice. I groan again, louder this time. "Wait... is that the plan? Seduce me to death so you can have the cottage all to yourself?"

She taps my nose playfully, grinning. "Nah. It'd be boring here without you."

I'm opening my mouth to answer when my phone pings on the nightstand. I don't move, but I go tense. Her smile fades as my phone begins to shimmy across the wood.

"Are you going to get that?" she asks quietly, no longer teasing.

I stare at it. "No."

"It's her?" she asks, voice barely above a whisper.

"Uh-huh."

There's a pause, heavy with unspoken things. "Well," she says, her tone carefully neutral, "I'll leave you in private. In case..."

She disappears behind the bathroom door and closes it quietly, but the sudden silence feels heavier than the room itself. I reach for the phone to silence it, and a strange, gnawing feeling settles deep in my gut—like I'm already doing Charly wrong, like I'm betraying her without even moving. Cheating. The word tastes bitter on my tongue, because nothing about this is black and white anymore.

I hate cheaters. Charly hates cheaters. And yet, what the hell am I supposed to call this tangled mess? I might not currently be in a physical relationship with Lyra, but isn't an emotional relationship...still cheating? Am I even in an emotional relationship? Honestly, I don't even know if Lyra and I have anything at all.

Or if I want anything.

I glance at the message again, heart suddenly pounding in my throat.

Fuck no.

Before Charly showed up, I told Lyra I was holed up at a friend's cottage, resting before training starts. She knows where I am. But now she's talking about coming out here. Coming to a place I'm sharing with Charly. No way. I can't let that happen.

A cold chill goes through me. If Lyra found out Charly was here... if she even smelled it... it'd blow up in ways I don't want to imagine. I don't need that kind of chaos. Not now. Not with Charly.

So I tap out a quick white lie telling Lyra I'll be leaving soon. No point in her making the trip out east. Phone down, I rise and head toward the kitchen. The fridge's still bare, so I head back to the bathroom door and knock.

"I'm going to run to the store. Bacon and eggs sound good?"

"Perfect…" Her voice is soft, hesitant, like she wants to say more—and she does. "I can go with you, if you like."

My chest tightens with an unexpected flutter. "Sure. Maybe we can actually eat at the little café in town." After last night, after meeting the neighbors, maybe she finally feels safe here. Unseen. But then there's Jensen, and the anger coils in me. If he says anything about us, I'll make sure he regrets it. But with my threat hanging in the air, I'm betting he'll keep his mouth shut.

"Okay, give me a minute."

I hurry back to the bedroom, tug on clean shorts and a T-shirt, the fabric cool and soft on my skin. As I head back to the kitchen, the bathroom door clicks open and Charly steps out wrapped in a towel, damp hair clinging to her shoulders.

God, she's beautiful.

"I'll hurry," she says, voice low and steady.

Before I can tell her to take her time, and maybe leave the bedroom door open so I can admire her a little longer, the front door bursts open with a bang like the FBI just kicked it down. Both of us whip around.

"Don't mind me," Mrs. Callahan calls out, strolling in like she owns the place. "Just bringing your bowl back, and I baked some blueberry muffins this morning."

Charly stands frozen, hand pressed to her chest, caught somewhere between amused and horrified. I clear my throat and back up a few steps, positioning myself in front of her, a human shield for her near-naked body.

"Oh, sorry, am I interrupting something?" Mrs. Callahan arches a perfectly gray eyebrow in my direction, suspicion practically dripping off her. "You putting those two boxes to good use?"

Oh. My. Fucking. God.

A tortured groan gets stuck in my throat while a soft chuckle bubbles up from Charly behind me.

"We were just getting ready to go to town for breakfast," I say, trying to sound casual, but failing miserably.

That judgmental eyebrow stays pinned high. "Mmm-hmm. Just checking. I've seen less sexual tension in a romance novel."

I cough, laughing despite myself. "How many romance novels are we talking, exactly?"

"Enough to know a thing or two," she replies, setting the container down on the counter with a satisfied smile. Then, her eyes soften as she looks at Charly. "Now, Charly, I also made some special lemon bars for you. And Ripley?"

"Yes, ma'am?"

She steps closer, reaches out, and pats my cheek with a knowing smile. "If you mess this up, I will personally shave your eyebrows off in your sleep."

"Not messing anything up," I assure her.

"Um, Betsy, you have your own key?" Charly asks.

She holds it up like a trophy. "Of course I do. I check on the place when no one's here."

"Well, I guess there's no need to check on it now. Not while we're here," I say, biting my tongue before adding, "...sullying up the place."

"I hope I get an invite to the wedding." Grinning, Mrs. Callahan turns on her heel, her dress catching a breeze as she disappears as quickly as she came, leaving behind the faint scent of lavender and mischief.

Charly shakes her head, still smiling. "Did she really say, 'less sexual tension in a romance novel'?"

I shiver mockingly. "Out loud. But you get it now, right?" I roll my eyes and groan. "Get why I was so mortified when I heard her say 'sexcapades'—"

We both burst out laughing, the sound filling the kitchen, chasing away the chill left by Lyra. And somehow, right there, everything in our world feels perfectly, undeniably... right.

Except...there will be no wedding.

CHARLY

As the golden afternoon sun slants through the kitchen window, pooling warmth across the counter, I press my hand to the sink's edge and shake my head. One week. Somehow it's already been a week since I arrived, and it feels like I've lived a lifetime here, one that's quieter, slower, and maybe... more honest.

I've spoken to my brother a handful of times. My parents only called twice. I didn't answer them. There's no point— they don't believe anything I say. And I don't have it in me to keep fighting.

But out there, I'm sure most of the world has moved on from Indie Rhodes, the darling of the Spotlight. That's the way it is in showbusiness. But the paparazzi don't forget so easily, which is exactly why I told Rip I'd stay a little longer.

Okay, that's not entirely true.

I'm staying because this beach house has turned into a bubble I don't want to pop. Because when Rip Hart touches me, I forget about performances, and I like who I am with him. Because we've spent lazy mornings tangled in bed, and nights that blur into sunrise. They're full of laughter, aching honesty, and, frankly, the best sex of my life. And the man still hasn't told me what he really does for a living. Maybe I don't want him to. Maybe I like the space we've carved out.

But even beyond that, I see the way he's physically improving. How the swelling has gone down, how he walks easier, breathes deeper. The ice, the stretching, the rehab work I've been quietly guiding him through has been making a difference. He'll be ready when camp starts next month. Assuming they do call it camp. I wouldn't know. I've always been more familiar with stages than rinks.

Then there's Emma. Bright-eyed, hungry to learn, absorbing every note I share with childlike enthusiasm. I didn't expect to love teaching, but somehow it's settled into an empty space inside me.

"Something on your mind?"

Rip's voice breaks through my reverie, low and gravel-rich, as he steps behind me and folds his body into mine. His warmth wraps around me and I turn slightly, my hands still resting on the sink, and he leans in. God. That look. That softness in his eyes that never quite matches the gruffness in his voice. My chest tightens, and I wonder—not for the first time—if I'm falling a little too fast, a little too deep.

"I was just thinking about Emma," I say softly. "And how much I enjoy teaching her."

Rip nods, his gaze warm and steady. "You light up when you teach, Charly."

I blink. "I do?"

The words surprise me, but the truth of them lands heavy and hopeful in my chest. I didn't know it showed. I didn't know he saw that in me.

"You do," he agrees, dipping his head to brush his lips over mine in a kiss. "I've been watching you."

My breath catches. "You're kind of a creeper, Big Bear."

"Yup." He grins against my mouth, then kisses me again, slower this time. "Have you made any decisions?"

I know what he's asking—if I've decided to stay longer. I never gave him a real answer. Maybe because until today, I wasn't sure myself.

"Are you sure you don't mind?" I ask, keeping my tone light even as something heavier settles behind my ribs.

"I wouldn't have offered if I minded."

His voice is steady, sure, but it's his eyes that unravel me. There's nothing casual in the way he looks at me, his gaze lingers, reading every flicker of doubt, every unspoken fear I'm trying to swallow. He sees too much, and yet I don't want to look away.

Lyra, you are such a fool.

"I'm going to stay," I finally say. "Just for a little while longer. I hate to quit on Emma when she's making so much progress. I just..." I hesitate, then add quietly, "I hate quitting..."

Rip nods slowly, and I know he hears the other meaning—my unwillingness to walk away from helping him heal.

He looks past me, his eyes finding something out the window, or maybe nothing at all. I can tell his thoughts have drifted somewhere deeper.

"What's on your mind, Rip?" I ask gently.

He hesitates, like he's weighing whether he has the right to speak the next truth. "I don't want to overstep here, but... I was thinking teaching might be your calling."

The words hit me harder than I expect. I press my lips together, biting down on the sharp swell of rising emotion.

"I don't have the credentials," I say, voice quiet. "I could keep doing one-on-one sessions, sure. But to work in schools or real studios... I'd need a different kind of education."

He brushes his knuckles along my cheek, his touch feather soft. "It's not too late."

My laugh is short, breathless. "It's a lot of work."

His eyes don't budge. "You don't strike me as the kind of woman who's afraid of hard work."

"I'm not. Believe me, I'm not." My chest tightens with the truth of it. I played every dive bar and open mic I could find just to get my name in someone's mouth. I busted my butt for years. I shake my head, eyes stinging with the edges of regret. But looking back... I didn't even like that grind. Not the way I like this. Then, with a quiet sigh, I add, "How silly of me. To skip college just to spite my parents."

"Silly?" he echoes. "Charly, come on. You were young. We all do crazy things when we're young."

"Not getting a college degree when it's handed to you with a bow? That's high on the crazy list."

He leans against the counter, smirking. "You know what I did once?"

I lift a brow. "Please tell me you didn't eat a laundry pod."

He laughs, a rich, low sound that vibrates in my chest. "Nope. That ridiculous trend was way after my time." He pauses, then gives me a look so sheepish it makes me suspicious. "I, uh... once hacked into the school computer system."

My jaw drops. "You did *not*."

"Okay, technically *I* didn't. I just watched my buddy do it. He wanted to change his grades."

I gasp, playfully scandalized. "Ripley Stripley, you are an *accessory to a crime*."

He chuckles. "Thank God we didn't get caught. Otherwise..."

I press a finger to his chest, right over his heart. "Otherwise, it could've jeopardized your future." I don't say NHL career.

The humor fades from his face, replaced by something quieter, more thoughtful. He releases a breath. "Right," he says softly.

I blink up at him, my voice barely a whisper. "I don't want anything to jeopardize your future." He nods, and I exhale slowly, before admitting, "I'm not sure what my future holds. But I *do* know I can't go running back to my parents' house. I can't sleep in my childhood bedroom like I've pressed pause on my life and gone backward."

A beat passes.

Then, almost too casually, like he hasn't thought it through, he says, "You... you could always come back to Boston with me."

My heart slams against my ribs. Boston. With him.

I glance up, caught off guard, and I see the way he straightens

—his shoulders squaring, his posture shifting like he's stepped into something real and doesn't know how it's going to land.

"Roman," he says after a breath. "My buddy, the one I told you about?"

"The one who's going to be your best man at our wedding in Italy?" I tease, trying to slow the pounding of my heart with humor.

He grins, relaxing a little. "Yeah, him. Last year... he helped out an old friend. She went back to Boston with him to get her life in order."

I tilt my head. "This old friend... was it the runaway bride?"

His grin spreads wider, pure warmth. "Yep. That's her. Gabby. She designs clothes now. For NHL families."

He grabs his phone, scrolling quickly, then holds it out. "Look."

The screen is filled with tiny jerseys, glittering team logos on baby onesies and booties.

"These are adorable," I say, but the words catch in my throat.

He's not just showing me clothes. He's showing me a piece of the life he thought he'd have with Lyra. Marriage. Family. Stability. And I can see it, etched in the softness of his expression, in the way his thumb lingers on the edge of the screen, that he still wants that.

"I love them," I tell him, gently. "So this is Gabby, the runaway bride you had to find clothes for? She and Roman ended up together?"

"Married," he confirms, slipping his phone back into his pocket. "I married them, actually. As in... officiated." He gives a crooked smile, then quickly adds, his voice rushed and a little flustered, "I'm not offering marriage, obviously. Just... a place to stay. I have a two-bedroom place. It's not much, but it's safe. No pressure. We could come up with new rules. Like... you know... not sleeping together. If that makes things easier."

I let out a laugh that's half breath, half ache. "I don't think *not* sleeping together makes anything easier." But still, I get it.

He's trying to give me something solid without putting weight on it. Trying to offer safety without strings. But we both know the strings are already there. And then I say the thing I shouldn't, the thing that's been haunting the edges of this whole conversation.

"I know when you get back to real life, when we're outside of this bubble, you'll want to see other women." I try to keep my voice light, teasing even, but my stomach knots at the thought.

Of him with someone else. Of me watching from the other side of a shared apartment wall, pretending I don't care.

The silence between us thickens.

"Take your time to think about it," he says quietly.

I nod, but my mind is already spinning. Is he really offering me a place to stay? A safe space to figure out who I want to be? Or is this just the next version of hiding?

And if I say yes...

What happens when the bubble bursts? When he finds out who I really am? When he sees the video? Will he believe it was fake, or will he look at me differently? Will he see me as the girl the internet says I am—just another fame-chasing, sex-tape-selling scandal? Even if none of it's true, that doesn't mean it won't ruin everything.

I swallow the knot forming in my throat as Rip lightly trails his fingers up and down my arm. "I'm just saying, Char," he murmurs, voice soft, "You could use a friend or two. I know you and Gabby would really hit it off."

His kindness is almost too much. I'm not sure what I've done to deserve it. Honestly, people don't do things like this without expecting something in return—or at least, that's what life's taught me.

"Thank you, Rip." My voice trembles more than I'd like. "We don't even really know each other that well, and this... this goes above and beyond."

He shakes his head, sincere and steady. "It's nothing. And I know enough to know I want to offer you a place to stay."

But it's not nothing. It's everything.

"For the record," I say, lifting my chin. "I do have a friend."

"Yes, your brother, I—"

I rise onto my toes and press my lips to his, cutting him off. "No," I whisper when I pull back. "You. You've been the best friend I've ever had."

A flicker of surprise crosses his face, then warmth floods in. "Do you mean *BFWB?*" he asks, eyes twinkling. I wrinkle my nose and he says, "Best friends with benefits."

I laugh. "It's a great romance trope." I narrow my eyes. "Wait, tell me something, Rip—have you been sneaking those romance novels Betsy keeps stashed at her place?"

He looks out the window and lets out a low, innocent whistle.

I burst out laughing, and something inside me settles. Like maybe, in this moment, I can forget everything else. The scandal. The cameras. The career in shambles. Because this man, this house, this feeling is more real than anything I've known in a long time.

Before I can say anything else, he scoops me up and deposits me on the counter. My legs wrap around his waist on instinct, arms sliding around his shoulders, and he kisses me like he's starving. When his hips press forward, I gasp at the hardness straining between us.

"Rip," I murmur, already breathless.

"Babe," he whispers, voice thick with heat.

And God, I want him. I want to disappear into him for the rest of the day. But... "I promised Emma a lesson this afternoon."

He groans and presses his forehead to mine. "Right." Then he winces, lips quirking. "I could be fast."

I laugh, even as heat pools low in my belly. "Oh, I *know* you can."

"Hey," he mock-offends. "I *resemble* that comment."

He lifts me off the counter and sets me gently on my feet. "Fine. Go. Abandon me. I'll just be here... suffering. Alone." He winks to let me know he's kidding and gestures toward the door. "Maybe I'll go catch dinner. A little solo fishing therapy."

"I just need to finish the dishes first," I say, glancing toward the sink. "I know how you are about keeping this place in order."

He swats my butt playfully. "Go. I'll clean up. You can think about how to repay me later."

That look in his eye says he already has a few ideas.

I hurry to the bathroom to brush my teeth and splash some water on my face. When I return, Rip is still at the sink, forearms flexing as he scrubs a plate. I pause in the doorway. There's something so deeply right about this. It's domestic, intimate... and unexpectedly beautiful. Who knew seeing a man do dishes could make my heart flutter like this?

I thought NHL players had chefs and assistants. Schedulers, handlers. But Rip is just... grounded. A man who fixes things, cooks meals, scrubs pans. There's no ego here, no spotlight. Just him. And I love that about him.

Love.

My breath catches. Nope. Nope, we are not going there. He wasn't offering me marriage—he was offering me space. A spare room. A no-strings arrangement. That's all. Still...

There's a sting in the thought that he doesn't see me as marriage material. But I'm not looking for that either.

Right?

19

RIP

The afternoon sun pours through the open kitchen window, casting golden slats across the worn wood floors and catching in the soap bubbles I swirl lazily with a dishcloth. Charly made us chicken salad for lunch, so it's my turn to clean up.

Outside, the world hums. Kids laughing in the distance, a lawn mower droning somewhere, the kind of sleepy summer background noise that makes you want to lie in bed and nap with your limbs tangled around someone you never expected to find sleeping in your bed.

I reach for a mug too quickly. A few weeks ago, that rookie mistake would have set off fireworks of pain. But now, with Charly's militant 'RICE' (Rest, Ice, Compression, Elevation), it's manageable. Hell, under her care I have no doubt I'll be all ready for camp next month.

The sound of her bare feet on the hardwood makes the back of my neck heat. She's sneaky like that, appearing when I least expect it, usually when I've just regained control of my very male urges. She leans in beside me to slide a plate into the sink, her body brushing mine. If she gets one inch closer, I'm going to lose all sense of decency and bend her over this counter in broad daylight —kids playing, sun shining, my soul leaving my body kind of sex.

I groan and turn to her and she has a mischievous little grin on her face. She loves toying with me, and dammit, I love it too.

"You've got a little..." Her finger grazes the corner of my mouth, wiping away—what? Mayo? Lust? Dignity? Doesn't matter. Her touch lingers, teasing, soft. Sweet torture.

I grab her waist, tug her in, and kiss the living hell out of her. A little gasp catches in her throat as I slide my tongue in and tangle my hands in her soft hair. She wraps her arms around me, giving in to my touches...my kisses.

Honest to God, everything about her, about this moment, is perfect. Easy. Right.

Until...

The screen door creaks open.

We both stiffen. Well, that's not entirely true. I was already stiff. Knowing this, Charly positions herself in front of me, but no one is fooling ol' Betsy.

"I brought muffins!" Betsy announces, crashing through the door like a hurricane in orthopedic sneakers. She stops when she sees us. Her gaze moves over our faces, which are no doubt flushed. "Again?" she asks, eyebrows climbing so high they're practically on her crown. "Lord, have mercy."

I open my mouth to say God knows what, but she cuts me off

with a judgemental finger. "I'll be glad when you make my sweet Charly an *honest* woman."

Honest woman. What century are we in?

But I simply nod and play along.

"Soon enough," I tell her, pressing a kiss to Charly's temple, playing her adoring fiancé. I sigh. "I wish we didn't have to wait until next summer. But there's so much planning to do."

Charly slides one hand behind her back and gives my side a sneaky pinch as we both bite back laughter. I kind of like having secrets with her. But we both have other secrets too, that we're not sharing.

"Well, it's a good thing I brought all these muffins," Betsy declares, marching past us like a woman with purpose and baked goods. "You two need your strength. You burned a lot of calories last night."

Oh no she didn't.

I sputter. "We uh...didn't—"

She waves off my weak defense like she's batting away a mosquito. "Oh, come on, Ripley. These cabin walls aren't that thick."

Charly makes a strangled sound, and folds against me like she wants the floor to open up and swallow us whole. "Oh *God*," she groans.

"Yes, I heard that too." Betsy says, before grabbing Charly's hand. "Where's your ring?" she demands, suspiciously. "Did you lose it?"

Charly blinks like a deer in the headlights, but recovers fast. She pastes on a sweet smile. "Oh. I... I never brought it. It's back home. Getting sized." She gazes dreamily into the distance, like she's smack dab in the middle of a fairy tale. "You should see it, though. It's lab grown, naturally. I'm not into mined diamonds," she says with a frown. But then she casts me a quick smile. "It's not big or flashy. I never wanted or needed that. But it's everything."

And damn. She's definitely spinning a fairy tale here, but her words punch me square in the chest. Not because she's convincing Betsy, but because her words are real and tell me so much about her.

"I can't believe I hadn't noticed," Betsy huffs, scandalized. "We can't have people in the community thinking you two are just..." She lowers her voice, her words for our ears only. "Well, we all know what you're doing. But we tolerate it because you're engaged."

She sets the muffins down, her brow furrowed like she's deep in thought. Then she brightens and raises a finger. "I'll be right back."

She spins on her heel like a woman on a mission and charges out the front door. Charly turns to me, and I pull her to me, eyebrows raised. "Should we be worried?"

She mock shivers. "Very. What if she comes back with a... ring?"

I scrub a hand over my face, grim. "Yeah, I'm thinking that's exactly what she's up to."

"Have we let this go too far?" Charly asks quietly.

"Probably," I say, scratching the back of my neck. "But it's only for a little while longer. And if it makes her happy..." I tilt my head toward the door Betsy just stormed out of, "...we might as well go along with it."

Charlie grins and nudges me. "You like her."

I laugh. "Of course I like her. She likes you, and I like anyone who likes you."

Charly squints at me. "What about... other people, though?" she asks. "What if they see it?"

"She already told everyone we were engaged," I remind her. "No one's going to think or care about us when we leave here." At least, I hope not. I did threaten Jensen, so... hopefully he took the hint. "We'll explain things to Paisley and Gunther. Pretend we broke up." I snort out a laugh. "Not pretend. We can't pretend a breakup if we were never engaged, but you know what I mean."

She nods slowly. "Yeah, I do." But there's something behind it. Something careful and guarded. Worried. Is she worried about her asshole ex? Not wanting him to think she's with someone else because maybe down the road....

"But really," I say, trying to lighten the mood, "Who just has a ring lying around? It has to be something else."

"Let's just hope it's not a judge," she mutters. "Or a licensed clergy." She pokes my chest. "Can you imagine if she knew you were ordained? We'd be married by tonight. Probably right here in the kitchen. With muffins as witnesses."

I laugh. "Fortunately, you can't legally marry yourself."

She fans her face dramatically. "Whew. Dodged that shotgun wedding."

"A shotgun wedding is when the bride is pregnant," I say.

She laughs. "Right. That's not going to happen."

But thinking about weddings, and babies, reminds me I'm not at all where I thought I'd be in life, and maybe...maybe that's a good thing. I think about what life will look like when I return home. Will she be going with me? I'd asked impulsively. I'm not even sure I meant to. The words just slipped out. Like my heart hit send before my brain could run it through spell check. But oddly...I don't regret it. She never answered me. But she didn't run away screaming either. If she does come, we'll need new rules. She mentioned me dating again, like that was even remotely on the table.

The truth is, going back to the usual hookups, hockey groupies, meaningless nights make my stomach turn. The bunnies don't appeal to me anymore. I've met someone who cares about me, the work she's been doing to heal my injury is proof of that. She doesn't want anything more from me. Not like...

My phone rings.

Jesus.

Lyra.

Of course.

It's like she sensed I was thinking about her. Which I was, but not in the usual way.

Charly stiffens at the sound. I see the way her shoulders rise just slightly, the muscle in her jaw tightening.

"She seems to be calling more lately," she says lightly, but I hear the undertone. Feel the shift in the air, the cooling. "Does she... want to be 'on' again?" She says it like it's a joke. Like she doesn't care. But her body language betrays her. She doesn't want me going back to Lyra. Probably because of how Lyra treated me.

But could there be other reasons?

Personal ones?

Like…maybe Charly doesn't just hate the idea of me being with my ex. Maybe she just hates the idea of me being with anyone else. I run a hand through my hair and let out a sigh.

"Yeah. She's been calling."

I drop down into the chair and toss my phone onto the table like it just burned me. Charly doesn't say anything. Just watches me. Watches the phone. And we both still for a moment, the silence louder than any ringtone.

"Are you going to respond?" Charly asks softly, sitting across from me with that careful expression that says she's trying not to judge.

Instead of answering, I reach for her, guiding her onto my lap. She settles, straddles me, everything about her being here with me is right, as her hands slide into my hair, brushing it back, like she's trying to soothe the chaos inside me.

"I can leave," she offers. "Give you privacy."

Like hell.

I glance at my phone, still lighting up with Lyra's name—a neon sign for trouble.

"She was asking if she could come here," I admit, and just like that, I feel her entire body stiffen. I rush to explain. "I told her I was headed back to the city, so now she's just asking when."

Charly nods. "She wants to see you."

"Yeah," I say, my voice flat. "She must need something." That's how it's always been with Lyra. She comes around when she needs something—attention...a story.

Charly slowly climbs off my lap, and the air cools instantly, like she took all the warmth with her. A shiver rips through me that has nothing to do with temperature.

"Maybe it's not a good idea for me to go back to Boston with you," she says.

The words punch me so hard I forget how to breathe. My heart clenches, all fight-or-flight kicking in. "No," I say quickly, too quickly.

She hears it wrong.

"Right," she nods, backing up, putting space between us. "No, I won't go back. I won't come between—"

"Charly, no." I'm up on my feet, pulling her toward me, tangling my hand in her hair. "No, as in I don't like what you're saying. I want you to come back. I want..."

God.

I want everything. I want her in my apartment, her voice in my mornings, her laugh in my bed. I want her songs floating through my kitchen.

But can I say that?

Can I ask for that kind of everything from a woman who just got burned by fame, trust, and love all at once? And what about me? I haven't even really broken things off with Lyra. She still texts. I still check her socials.

So I settle for words that won't terrify either of us. "I want you to," I say simply.

She studies me for a moment. "Tell me something," she says. "What is Lyra looking for from you? You said she must need something." Before I can even breathe out an answer, she asks, "Do you always give her what she needs?"

I groan, the sound rough and heavy. "Pretty much."

Because that's who I've been, a guy unable to turn his back on a woman in need, a woman I once gave my heart to—even if it's not in my best interest. But not this time. Charly—Indie Rhodes—is the only story here in Connecticut, and there's no fucking way I'm letting Lyra near that.

Before I can say more, we hear, "Knock, knock." Mrs. Callahan breezes back into the cottage. She stops when she sees us, Charly flushed, me flustered, and her eyes narrow with curiosity.

"You two at it again?" she asks. But when neither of us speak or move, her gaze softens, like she just realized she walked into the middle of something important and is trying not to stomp all over it with her orthopedic shoes. "I can come back," she offers in a rare moment of grace.

"No, it's okay," Charly says, forcing a smile. "We were just talking about the wedding."

Mrs. Callahan beams. "You are going to be a gorgeous bride, Charly." Then she turns to me and her entire face hardens into a scowl so fierce I wonder if she was a drill sergeant in another life. "We'll have to see how well you clean up," she mutters.

But I see it, the glint in her eye, the almost-smile she's hiding under her mock judgment. She might give me hell, but she's rooting for us.

Dammit, I think I'm rooting for us too.

With that, Mrs. Callahan makes a beeline for Charly, and captures her hand. "This is a promise ring," she announces. "Just temporary." She gives a wink, and my heart stutters because I'm suddenly wondering if she knows what's really going on here, sees through the ruse...sees what I feel. "Until you get yours back."

She opens her palm, and there it is, a delicate little gold ring sitting inside a tiny black box.

Charly blinks, then steps back like the thing might bite. "What? No. I can't wear that."

"Whose ring is that?" I ask.

Betsy's whole face softens, her eyes going a little misty.

"It was given to me by a very good friend," she says, voice gentle now. "After I lost William all those years ago, I never thought I'd find happiness again. Never thought I'd hear music." Charly goes still beside me, the way you do when you sense someone's about to hand you a story they don't share often.

"But Carl," Betsy goes on, her eyes getting distant, "He brought the song back. He made me laugh again. We never got the chance to get married. Life had other plans. But the ring..." She trails off, staring at the little circle in her hand. "This ring reminded me I could still feel joy."

And then she looks right at Charly.

"You brought music back to me too, Charly," she says, her voice cracking. "Now you're teaching Emma the joy of song. Soon she'll be playing around the fire, singing like you do. You gave us that."

Charly's eyes are wide. She opens her mouth. Closes it. "Yes, but I can't—" she tries.

"This would make him so happy," Betsy says. "It would make me happy."

She blinks hard, trying to chase away the tears, but they shimmer anyway.

Then she holds the ring out... to me.

Oh, boy.

Charly turns to me, her eyes damp, wide, unsure. I stare at the ring. It's just a tiny loop of gold, but somehow it weighs a thousand pounds. The thought of disappointing Betsy—and Carl, God rest his soul—sits in my gut like a brick. So I take it. I reach for Charly's hand, my fingers brushing hers. They're trembling. Or maybe mine are.

"It's just temporary," I say, and try to read her face, to understand if she's hearing what I'm saying, or what I'm not saying...or asking.

"Right," she says softly, and her lashes fall like curtains over a storm of emotion. I slide the ring onto her finger. And my heart punches so hard against my ribs, I swear something cracks.

What the hell is happening?

Why does this feel so...right?

It's a borrowed ring. A borrowed story. A borrowed identity.

A fairy tale that neither of us believed in.

But in this moment, it feels like the beginning of everything real.

20

CHARLY

As we follow the winding path into town, the faint sounds of music and laughter drift toward us from the festival ahead. It smells like kettle corn and everything fried. Emma slips her small hand into mine, her palm warm and trusting. I glance down at her, and there she is, beaming up at me with that wide, unguarded smile that could melt stone.

My chest tightens. Honestly, I thought life would look a lot different by now. I imagined a career I was proud of, a little house with a garden out front, maybe even a dog. A family. Laughter in the kitchen. Light in the windows. Instead, I'm somewhere in between what I had and what I lost, trying to pretend it doesn't ache.

I take a moment, and look where I am now, look at who I'm with and that ache subsides. Maybe the universe had other plans. And maybe, just maybe, I'm not mad about it.

Beside me, Rip brushes his knuckles against mine. That

subtle touch trickles through my body and eases the last of the aches.

"You okay?" he asks, voice low and unreadable.

I nod. "I'm good." While I am good—better than good—I can't deny that I'm terrified. Being with him feels too easy. Too right. And it makes me wonder if I could really go back to Boston with him, slip into his world like I belong there. What happens if I fall deeper?

Girl, you've already fallen.

But then there's his ex. The way he still tries to fix things for her. To earn back her love with sacrifices and false starts. He gives her everything she asks for. In return, he gets the scraps of affection he craves. It's a vicious cycle, one I see him stuck in. I wish I could be the one to pull him out. Honestly, it really sucks that love makes fools of us all.

Emma wiggles between us and grabs Rip's hand, her joy effortless and contagious. His eyes flicker down to her, and something in his expression shifts, like he's seeing a future he once wanted, a future that slipped out of his hands.

"Swing me," she squeals, her voice high and delighted.

Rip laughs and checks in with me. I give a nod and he says, "Okay, on the count of three."

We count together, and on three, we lift her into the air. Her laughter wraps around my ribs, tying the broken pieces of myself back together.

"Careful now," Betsy calls from behind. "Don't want to pull your arm out of the socket."

Emma rolls her eyes, but there's affection there. She loves her grandma fiercely. Just like I do.

I glance back at Betsy, walking at a slower pace. I've seen her hustle. She's hanging back on purpose—to give us time alone with her granddaughter. Maybe she sees the loneliness in me. Maybe that's why she pulled me close from the start and offered me something I didn't even know I was desperate for.

A place. A family. A home.

And now, my heart aches with the weight of knowing I'll have to walk away from it all. From her. From this. Because if Betsy ever found out who I really am, what the tabloids say I did, what the internet turned me into, she'd be crushed. And I couldn't bear to be the reason for the disappointment in her eyes. Some goodbyes are hard. Others are cruel.

As if on cue—mind reader that she is—Betsy points to a charming little cottage tucked just off the path. "The Conrads have their place up for sale," she says casually, but there's something there. Something she's not saying...yet.

I stop walking and raise a hand to block the sun, squinting in the direction she's pointing so I can get a better look at the cedar-sided beauty. Quiet. The kind of place where sunsets are sacred and s'mores are aplenty. A dozen brightly painted Adirondack chairs form a loose circle around a firepit, like they're waiting for the next ghost story or singalong.

"Conrads?" I ask.

"They weren't at the bonfire the other night. Their granddaughter just had a baby." Betsy's voice turns all warm and soft, and when I look over, she's smiling at me, like she's in on a secret that I know nothing about.

"They're selling the place and moving closer to their grandkids in Texas," she adds, her eyes practically twinkling. And then—there it is. That look. The one that means she's got an idea I'm going to have to politely decline or die trying.

"It's a perfect spot for newlyweds," she says sweetly, nudging me with her elbow like I'm not already on emotional thin ice. Then she turns to Rip and narrows her eyes. "Or those about to be newlyweds."

Rip throws his arms up. "What did I do now?"

I can't help but laugh. "You haven't made an honest woman out of me yet," I tease, lifting a brow in his direction.

Betsy nods solemnly and huffs out, "Exactly."

"Oh, Charly, Rip, please buy it," Emma gasps, clapping her hands together like she's just solved world peace. "Then we could see you every summer. We'll have bonfires, and sing songs, and go to the festival. And Charly, I'll make you s'mores every single night." She presses her hands to her chest, her eyes full of sincerity. "I promise not to burn them this time."

My gaze shifts to Rip, who's now looking like he might either faint or fake a hamstring injury to escape. I feel you, buddy. We've officially crossed a line, and there's no safe word in place.

"It's lovely," I manage, scrambling for something neutral to say. "Don't you think it's lovely, Rip?"

He drags a hand through his hair and offers a nervous half-smile. "Yeah. Real nice. Super lovely."

"Well, that settles it," Betsy declares. She grabs my hand and starts pulling me off the sandy path, her eyes locked on the Conrads' place like it's already ours.

"Wait, where are we going?" Please tell me we're not going to the Conrads' cottage.

"We're going to the Conrads' cottage," she announces cheerfully.

"Oh God," I whisper, my feet stumbling to keep up. My voice rises a full octave. "Surely, we can't just...Betsy. Don't we need an appointment or... legal permission or... literally anything?"

"Yay!" Emma squeals, sprinting ahead of us.

"Come on, Rip," Betsy calls over her shoulder. "Stop lolly-gagging!"

I glance back and find Rip frozen mid-path, jaw unhinged, looking like he just watched his future flash before his eyes, complete with singalongs, matching sweaters, and...casseroles.

That thought makes me grin. I shrug and give him the most expressive play along or perish look I can manage.

Because in this town, resistance is futile. And if you say no to Betsy, I'm pretty sure the entire zip code shuns you and your descendants for seven generations.

Rip lags behind, his hands in his pockets, kicking at the dirt path as he slowly follows us. Meanwhile Betsy marches me up the stone walkway like a woman on a mission—specifically, a matchmaking, real-estate-closing mission.

Just as we reach the porch of the cedar cottage, the front door creaks open and an elderly woman steps out, squinting into the sun. "Betsy," she calls out, arms wide.

"Marta, it's so good to see you," Betsy gushes, and the two women embrace like long-lost sisters at a family reunion. "How's that grandbaby?"

"Oh, look." Marta's already pulling her phone from her apron. She taps a few times, mutters something about the 'dang cloud,' and then proudly holds up a photo of a squishy little baby in an oversized bow. I glance at the baby, take in the big eyes that say she already knows she's going to become the screensaver.

"She's beautiful," Betsy croons, her voice softening, then promptly grabs me by the elbow to pull me closer. "This is Charly. She's staying at Paisley and Gunther's place."

Before I can even say hi, Marta wraps me in a full-body hug that knocks the big sunhat clean off my head and nearly clips me in the jaw. Then I'm suddenly cheek-to-cheek with a stranger who smells like lemon and unconditional love. Her hug is warm and motherly, the kind of embrace that hits you in the soft places you pretend don't ache anymore.

It makes me miss my family. But not the unconditional love that seemed to flow so freely toward my brother, while I stood just outside the circle, trying not to care.

I reach up to fix my hat, but... what's the point? This heat is slowly melting me into a puddle so I just yank it off and fan myself with it instead. But then I catch Marta giving me a slow once-over, her eyes narrowing just a touch before Betsy throws a hand out.

"This is Rip," she says, voice suddenly tight, like she's trying to swallow so many unsaid words. "He's... the fiancé." I swear there's a tiny growl in there.

Marta's face softens. "Oh, Rip, it's so lovely to meet you."

He steps forward and gives a polite smile. "Nice to meet you, too."

"They're interested in buying your place," Betsy blurts out.

I choke on air and before I can clarify that we are absolutely not house hunting on a random Thursday afternoon, Marta links her arm through mine and starts leading me into the house.

Rip shoots me a wide-eyed *what the hell look* from the walkway. He looks like he's about to run, until Emma grabs his hand. With that, Rip simply shrugs, his eyes telegraphing a message that says: I guess we're doing this.

Okay, this will be fine, no problem. We'll take a look, and kindly respond that it's not our style. Easy peasy.

But then I step inside.

And everything changes.

"Oh my..." I breathe the second I cross the threshold, it's like stepping into someone's memory. The living room is filled with honey-toned wood, soft light, and furniture that says, *'come sit, stay awhile'*. Wooden beams stretch across the ceiling, and the kitchen smells faintly of cinnamon, warmth... home and hearth.

But it's the details that get me. Family photos line the walls, dozens of them on mantels and walls. Smiling faces. Birthday candles. Sandcastles. Laughter frozen in time. Decades of life, love, growth, laughter. Generations layered together in frames.

It hits me like a sucker punch to the ribs.

This is what I want. What I've always wanted. Not the fame. Not the clicks. This.

A life.

As if sensing my emotional free-fall, Rip appears beside me, his hand brushing mine before slipping into it. He gives it a small squeeze. I look up and find him watching me carefully. That's when I see it reflected back in his eyes. That same longing. That same grief for something he's always dreamed of.

Except he'd dreamed it with someone else.

I swallow the lump in my throat and try to speak. "This house," I say softly. "It's beautiful."

"It has three bedrooms," Marta chimes in, all business now. "Plenty of room for a growing family. Just perfect for you two."

My heart clenches. I glance at Rip again and all I can manage is one word. "Yes." Not a commitment. Not a decision. Just... an honest answer to everything this moment is stirring inside me.

Marta sighs softly, and I watch her face shift, as if memories are flickering behind her eyes like old home movies. There's a lightness there, a fondness that both hurts my soul and fills it with longing.

"My kids are grown now," she begins, her voice hitching just slightly in her throat. "I've got grandbabies all over the place now. Gerald and I need a bit more room to fit everyone under one roof. Big summer barbecues. Board games during rainy days."

"That sounds amazing," I squeak out.

She clasps her hands together, and a smile brightens her whole face. "We think we've found the perfect place, but as for our cottage here..." Her eyes flick to Betsy. "...we want the right owners. Someone who will love this house like we did. Not just live in it, but treasure it." She gives Betsy a wink. "If Betsy vouches for you, that's good enough for me."

My stomach knots. Not because I don't want everything she just laid out, but because I do.

It's the kind of place that makes you feel something the second you walk through the door, like it's already waiting to make room in your life. Like it's already whispering, *you belong here.*

Marta gently leads us through the cottage, her hand light on my arm. We pass by the bedrooms. Pristine now, the beds neatly made, the quilts too crisp, too still. But I can feel the echoes. The laughter. The tiny feet pounding down the hall. The squeak of a closet door opened during hide and seek. These rooms were once full of life, chaos and happiness.

And now... they're just waiting for someone to mess them up again.

I glance at Rip beside me. He hasn't let go of my hand since we stepped inside. Emma is skipping ahead, singing a song she appears to be making up on the spot. It involves frogs, popsicles, and something about a dog with a purple bowtie.

She opens cupboards like a realtor-in-training, presenting each empty shelf with flair.

"That one always used to have Pop-Tarts in it," Marta declares with a laugh.

I smile despite myself. Sometimes even grown men keep Pop-Tarts in their cupboards. Especially the ones with strawberry frosting—which I think is an atrocity—and secretly eat them cold.

Everything about this place feels right.

Which is exactly why it's terrifying.

Then Marta slows, narrowing her eyes at me like she's trying to adjust a blurry memory. "You look so familiar," she says.

My pulse jumps. Before I can respond, Betsy swoops in with the speed and precision of a woman who doesn't wear kaftans and orthopedics. "She's been here with Paisley before," she says quickly, her tone breezy but a little too eager.

My heart thuds.

Does she know? No, she can't. If she did, she wouldn't treat me like one of her own. This woman has old fashioned values, and would turn her back on me if she knew. Right? I quietly slip my hat back on, tugging the brim low.

Marta tilts her head. "Yes, maybe that's it," she says slowly, though her eyes are still searching my face. "Or maybe it's because you remind me of that singer who won The Spotlight. What was her name..." She snaps her fingers. "Indie Rhodes."

My stomach somersaults.

"She has long dark hair, though," Marta continues. "And she wears too much makeup." Marta wags a playful finger. "Still, she's a pretty little thing. You're a pretty little thing too."

I force a small laugh. "Thank you. That's sweet of you."

Beside me, Rip makes a sound, a low, gruff throat-clear that almost sounds like a warning or a question or maybe both. I glance at him, trying to read the tension in his shoulders, the stillness in his jaw.

How much does he know?

"Where would we find the listing for the cottage?" he asks casually, but his hand tightens around mine.

Marta's eyes light up. "Give me two seconds." Her voice lifts with excitement as she shifts her focus from me to him.

"Yes, of course. This place is perfect," Rip says, giving my hand a gentle squeeze that somehow reverberates straight through my ribs. "Don't you agree?"

I glance at him, searching his face, but I can't read him this time. My brain races. What does he want me to say? That I love it? That I want this life with him? That I'm ready to dive headfirst into a future neither of us has dared to talk about, to...define?

"It is," I say slowly, "But we're a long way off from thinking about a cottage, Rip. We've got... a wedding to plan. And a lot on our plates." My voice sounds more rational than I feel.

Go me.

Rip doesn't miss a beat. "Right. And I still need to upgrade from my small two-bedroom apartment."

He says it smoothly, effortlessly, like it's always been part of the plan. For a moment, I wonder if it really was. His ability to think on his feet is impressive—and slightly terrifying. It reminds me just how practiced he is at this whole pretending game.

But then I catch something in his eyes. Something quiet. Steady. Real. He's not faking this. At least... not all of it. Had he been planning to upgrade all along? Why? Sure, he asked me to go back with him, until I figured life out, but my temporary presence doesn't require a move. That's when I remember what he said about his ex...she liked Tiffany.

Is he upgrading for her...are they about to be 'on again'?

"Yeah," he adds, more softly now his eyes going to some distant spot, like he's recalling sweet memories—before he met me. "We'll have to start house hunting soon."

"House shopping," I echo with a stiff nod, trying not to let my inner panic show.

"Oh, I can send you all the listing information," Marta says cheerfully, bustling off to the kitchen for a pen and paper. "Just give me your email!"

Of course. Because this fake engagement apparently comes with real estate paperwork now.

Betsy turns to me, beaming like she's won a prize at the county fair. "I knew you'd love it," she says, grabbing both of my hands and squeezing them tight. "I think you two will be a wonderful addition to our little community."

Then, without missing a beat, she spins to glare daggers at Rip. "After the wedding."

Rip's brows rise, clearly caught off guard. "Yes, ma'am," he says, standing straighter like he just got called out by a strict elementary school teacher. "Wouldn't dream of it."

I bite back a smile. I've never seen a man so large look so thoroughly put in his place.

"Grandma," Emma pipes up from her perch near the front door, "Can I have ice cream now?"

"Of course, you can, sweetheart," Betsy says, patting her on the head.

"Just put your information here," Marta says, handing Rip a pen and a flowery notepad. "Or, if you're on your way to town again, the listing's right in the real estate window. Front and center."

Things really are different in this sleepy little community. No apps. No glossy brochures. Just a handwritten note and a spot in the town square window. And somehow… that simplicity makes my chest feel light.

Rip writes down his email, neatly, I notice, and we all step back out into the sunshine.

"Charly," Emma chirps, tugging on my hand. "What's The Spotlight?"

My stomach tightens, but I keep my tone even. "It's a singing show," I say. "People compete for prize money and exposure. It's a big deal if you win. It can change your life."

It did change mine. Just not the way I thought it would.

"You should go on it," Emma says brightly. "I bet you'd win."

Rip makes a low, strangled noise next to me, like he just swallowed a marble. I glance at him, and he immediately looks away, hand suddenly very interested in the back of his neck.

My stomach coils tight.

Okay. So… he might know who I am. But that doesn't mean he's seen the tape. Rip doesn't strike me as the headline-scrolling, scandal-chasing type. He doesn't even post on social media. Most of the time, he's too busy rehabbing his groin, and well, taking me to his bed. The only time I ever see him on his phone is when *she* messages.

I tug my sunhat lower over my eyes, shielding myself from more than just the sun. Rip does the same with the bill of his cap.

As we walk to town, the scent of fried dough, carried on the summer breeze, drifts toward us. Laughter echoes from the town square.

"Oh, look," Emma squeals. "A Ferris wheel." She tugs on my hand. "Charly, please go on it with me!"

"I... uh... I'm not really a fan of heights," I say quickly, my voice a little too high-pitched.

Rip leans in, his breath warm on my cheek as he murmurs, "Really? That surprises me. You know, being a rebel—with a tattoo and all."

I laugh despite myself. "That was a very small act of rebellion."

He grins. "It's only kiddie-size," he adds. "I'll go on it with you guys, if that helps."

He says it so simply, like it's the most natural thing in the world. To volunteer for something just to make it easier for me. And somehow... that fills me with more courage than I expected.

"Pretty sure there's a weight limit for each seat," I tease.

"Yeah, Rip," Emma pipes in helpfully. "You're too big. We don't want to break it."

Rip clutches his chest like he's been mortally wounded. "The only thing you two are breaking..." he says dramatically, "...is my damn heart."

We laugh and just like that, with my hand in Emma's, I start skipping with her toward the Ferris wheel—light as air, like something's finally been lifted off me. Like joy isn't something I have to borrow anymore. It's just... here.

And then I realize I left Rip with Betsy.

Oh, crap.

I glance over my shoulder, half-expecting to see him sweating bullets while Betsy grills him on wedding timelines and repro-ductive plans. But instead, they're deep in conversation —*really* talking.

She's nodding, arms crossed. He's animated, hands moving like he's trying to explain something important.

And that surprises me.

What the heck are they talking about so passionately?

21

RIP

"Come on, Rip! I want the kitty cat," Emma says, bouncing on her toes as I grip the toy gun like it's game seven of the playoffs. I aim at the bullseye target, trying to get the red dot to climb, but the damn thing jerks like a wild bronco. I can land a puck tape-to-tape at full speed, no problem. But this? This carnival contraption is a different beast.

My time runs out with a sad little splutter from the water stream, and the bell stays silent. The guy beside me fist-pumps and hands a plushie to his grinning daughter.

"These things are totally rigged," I mutter, stepping back in defeat.

Charly arches an eyebrow and gives me a teasing shrug. "Mind if I show you how it's done, superstar?"

I wave her forward with exaggerated chivalry. "Be my guest."

Mrs. Callahan, who's standing beside me, shoots me a dry look like I just embarrassed the entire male species. "I could've nailed that thing blindfolded back in my day," she says, bobbing her head proudly.

I chuckle, but my stomach twists. Not because of her sass. But because of the conversation we had earlier. One that's still gnawing at the edges of my mind. I rub a hand over my jaw and shake it off. Not now. Today is for sunshine and ice cream and pretending life is uncomplicated.

The buzzer goes off, and Charly snaps into action. She grips the plastic gun with that same fierce determination I've seen when she belts out high notes that make stadiums hold their breath.

"You're doing it, Charly! You're doing it!" Emma squeals beside me, grabbing my shirt in excitement and tugging. "That's the kitty I want, Rip. Right there."

Charly leans in, tongue caught between her teeth in concentration. Could she be any more adorable? The bell dings. Victory.

Emma explodes in excitement. "She did it. She really did it."

Charly flashes the kind of triumphant smile that makes my chest tighten, and not in the competitive way. She motions Emma over and bends down, conspiratorially whispering in her ear. Emma giggles and nods like a little accomplice.

A moment later, the booth guy pulls down a ridiculous stuffed animal—a sloth wearing a superhero cape—and hands it over.

Charly turns to me with wide, innocent eyes. "For you," she says, biting back a smirk. "Because you were a little... slow on the draw."

I laugh, even as I groan and hold the sloth by one floppy arm. "Really? I had my heart set on that pink unicorn."

"Okay, let me try again," she says, cracking her knuckles.

"I was kidding," I chuckle. "Besides, I think I just got the best prize."

Charly arches a brow, playful and mysterious, her cheeks pink from the sun—or maybe something else. "Oh, the sloth?"

I take a slow step toward her, eyes locked on hers. "No," I murmur, voice dipping low. "The girl who gave it to me."

"Well, you can sweet talk me later. Right now I have a kitty to win."

My God, could I love this woman any more?

Love.

There it is. Shit. I said it.

Not out loud, but in my head. And it's terrifyingly real. Like a puck straight to the chest—no padding.

I lean in closer, dropping my voice just for her. "No, you go ahead. But later, my little rebel, you're going to have to explain these suspiciously honed carnival skills to me."

She tosses me a coy grin. "We'll see."

Charly steps up again, calm and focused, and, of course, wins again. Like the damn game was designed for her. The carnival guy hands over the plush kitty Emma had her heart set on, and Emma squeals in delight. It warms me from the inside out.

"Grandma, I'm getting hungry," Emma says, rubbing her belly.

"Me too," I add, tossing in a groan for effect.

"Food tent," Mrs. Callahan declares, already halfway through the crowd in her orthopedic sneakers like she's training for a senior sprint relay. "Try to keep up."

I blink. "What the hell does she eat for breakfast?"

Sloth tucked under my arm, Emma's little hand in mine, we hustle to catch up, though the image of Charly at that game, completely focused, is still flickering like a firework in the back of my mind.

"I can carry that for you, you know," Charly offers, eyeing the caped sloth clutched to my side.

"Nope. It's mine. Stop trying to steal it."

She laughs. "You're not embarrassed walking around with that thing?" Then she pauses, eyes widening as her hand smacks her forehead. "Wait, what am I saying? This is the guy who wore water wings."

"Proudly," I say, chuckling.

I catch her hand and give it a tug, pulling her into my side. She stumbles a little and bumps against me, soft, warm, perfect.

"Oops. Sorry," she says quickly, brow furrowing in concern. "I didn't mean to jostle you. Are you... okay?"

Her words are careful, layered with that unspoken understanding. She's asking about *me*. My injury. I meet her gaze, heat flickering low in my stomach. "I mean... technically, I've been on my feet too long."

"Damn," she says, guilt threading through her voice. She glances back. "Want to head home?"

I tilt my head, giving her a look that says exactly what I'm thinking, because, obviously, subtlety is overrated at this point.

"Oh," she breathes, her lips curling as her eyes spark. "I get it."

I lean in, murmuring near her ear, my voice a warm whisper just for her. "You get that I want to be off my feet for a different reason?"

Her lips twitch, but she's trying hard not to smile. "Yes, Rip. You don't have to spell it out for me."

I grin and run my tongue slowly over my bottom lip. "You sure? You once told me I was great with the alphabet. Want me to start with *A*?"

"Oh. My. God." She covers her face, laughing, cheeks flushed.

Emma, oblivious to our increasingly flirty undertones, skips beside us singing a made-up song about cotton candy and sloths.

Me? Well I'm floating. On air. On fire. On her.

She rolls her eyes—but doesn't say no—as we turn toward Mrs. Callahan, who's waving us over to a picnic table. But just as we're about to step forward, someone jumps in front of us and flash...a blinding burst of light goes off.

I flinch, blinking stars from my eyes. "What the hell...?"

Emma bolts toward her grandmother. I nearly panic, but remember we're not in the city.

"Getting pictures for the local paper," the guy says as he darts off, already targeting his next unsuspecting victim.

I turn to Charly, and the shift in her is immediate. Gone is the playful tease. Her entire face has tightened with concern, eyes darting like she's searching for escape routes.

"Rip..."

I instinctively start to follow the guy, ready to rip that camera out of his hands and smash it into next Tuesday, but I catch myself. This isn't the city. This isn't scandal-fueled chaos. This is a sleepy, quiet place. *Our* quiet place.

"It's just a local guy," I say gently, breathing through my protective instinct. "A small-town paper. No one's going to recognize us. Especially not in our hats." I don't mention the change in her hair color. She already knows.

She glances down, fingers tugging at the brim of her sunhat. "I just..."

"I know," I say softly. And somehow, it's enough.

Her shoulders ease. I wrap an arm around her waist and pull her in. She leans into my chest as I whisper, "That boring picture probably won't even make it into the paper."

She snorts. "Boring? There is nothing boring about you, Rip. You stand out like... like a giant bear. I swear, if we slapped some plaid on you, people would think you're a lumberjack mascot come to life."

"Okay, so no vacations in Maine next summer," I say with a grin.

She stills, just for a second, and I feel it. That subtle change in the air. Because I said *next summer*. Future tense. Hopeful tense.

Crap.

Her smile falters. Not gone, just... slowed. I suspect she too is thinking about what comes after this bubble, about what she wants. About whether we're both brave enough to chase something real.

My throat tightens.

Look at me. Who knew I still believed in fairy tales?

But then Charly lifts her chin, that wicked glint returning to her eyes.

"You know," she begins, casual as ever, "There are a lot of origin stories for Paul Bunyan. Some say he was born in Minnesota. Others say Wisconsin. And a few even claim he came from Nova Scotia."

"Oh yeah?"

"Mmhmm. So just to be safe... let's avoid vacationing in all of those places."

I stop breathing, because I'm sure that...that was her way of saying she's not ready to let this go either. Please God, don't let me be wrong about that. Maybe I am, but I'm not going to even think about that today.

I'm grinning like a fool when we hear Mrs. Callahan's exasperated voice cut through the moment. "Will you two lovebirds hurry it up? I'm about to die of starvation over here."

We turn to see her standing with arms crossed, glaring at us. I laugh, full and loud. Then I reach for Charly's hand and thread our fingers together. She doesn't let go.

And just like that, I feel lighter.

Hell, I might even be skipping a little.

"Hot dogs all around?" I ask as I reach the table, setting down my sloth prize and eyeing Charly. "Don't try to steal it."

Emma bounces in her seat, hands already rubbing her belly. "I want fries too."

"Well, of course, Emma," I say with mock seriousness. "That's a given."

She giggles, scrunching her nose. "Can I help you?"

"Sure thing. You lovely ladies stay here and hold down the fort. Emma and I will brave the food line."

"Don't try to sweet talk me, boy," Mrs. Callahan says with a suspicious squint, but the smirk tugging at her mouth gives her away.

Then she reaches for Charly's hand, gently turning it to get a better look at the ring on her finger, and just like that, my stomach knots. That earlier conversation with her comes roaring back, twisting me up inside. I watch them for one more second than I probably should—Charly's soft expression, Mrs. Callahan's knowing gaze—before Emma tugs on my hand.

"Come on, Rip. I'm about to die from starvation."

I laugh, unable to help it. She sounds so much like her grandmother it's unreal. Not that that's a bad thing. Not at all. We head toward the hot dog stand, weaving through crowds and cotton candy clouds. I order a dozen dogs, because no way am I getting caught underestimating this crew, and Emma immediately gets to work collecting ketchup and mustard packets.

When she's done, I hand her a tray of drinks. "You think you can carry those?"

She looks up at me with the same indignant glare I've seen a hundred times from Betsy Callahan. "Rip. I'm *seven*."

I hold one hand up in surrender. "Right, right. My mistake. Clearly you're a seasoned professional."

With two big paper bags in my hands and Emma carefully balancing the tray of drinks and an armful of condiments, we start the walk back toward the tent. A few steps in, she lets out a dramatic sigh.

I glance over. "You okay?"

But she's not looking at the tray. She's looking at me. Eyes wide. Serious.

"Rip... when do you leave here?"

I blink. The question lands with more weight than I expect, like she's not just asking for logistics, she's asking about everything.

"In about a week," I say softly.

She nods, eyes still locked on mine, as if she's measuring that answer against something bigger. Then she looks away and walks on without saying another word.

And I realize, it's not just Charly I'd have to say goodbye to if she doesn't come back to Boston. It's this whole world.

She sighs, her little shoulders rising and falling. "I love summers here. Spending time with Grandma is the bestest. But I love spending time with you and Charly too."

My heart gives a little squeeze. "That's great, Emma. Where's home for you?" I ask, realizing, somewhat embarrassingly, I don't actually know.

She juts her head toward the winding road ahead. "That way. My mom and dad work a lot, so I come stay with Grandma in the summer."

"But you love it here," I say, already knowing the answer.

"Yeah." She smiles, then turns her attention to the drinks when they start to wobble in her tray. She's got that concentrated, serious look on her face again. Then, out of nowhere, she hits me with it. "Are you going to buy the cottage?"

I blink. For seven years old, this kid doesn't hold back. "I'm not sure," I say carefully, because what am I supposed to do? Tell her this whole engagement is pretend? That we're living in some fairy tale? That outside this sun-soaked bubble, nothing's been figured out?

But Emma isn't done.

"Can you please buy the cottage?" she whines, drawing out the word in a way only a kid could. And just like that, my heart twists again.

Because here's the truth. I want to buy the damn cottage. I want to fill it with laughter and late-night popcorn and morning coffee on the porch. I want all the memories. With...Charly.

"Let me think about it, okay?" I tell her. It's the most honest thing I can say. I am thinking about it. About all of it. We reach the tent and I set down the bags just as my phone pings.

Charly glances down, the flicker in her eyes unmistakable. But I don't look at my phone. I already know who it is.

"About time," Mrs. Callahan huffs, tearing into the food like we kept her waiting an eternity.

As I ignore the message, my phone pings again.

Lyra.

And something hits me square in the chest. Thinking about Lyra doesn't feel the same. In fact, it doesn't feel like anything at all. No heat. No longing. Just...a hollow sort of pity. Not for me. For her. She's always chasing the next story. Always desperate for her big break. Always one step away from something real. I feel bad for her, honestly. Because I don't think she's ever had what I have right now with Charly.

Warmth. Ease. Laughter. A feeling so effortless, it steals my breath and fills me all at once.

I loved Lyra, once.

But I never loved her like this.

22

CHARLY

I'm not entirely sure what's going through Rip's mind as we walk the sandy path back to the cottage. We're both running on fumes after a full day of sunshine, fried food, and carnival chaos. Yet, there's this low, pleasant hum in my chest, equal parts fatigue and the giddy knowledge that I'll be crawling into bed with Big Bear tonight.

Rip bumps my shoulder. "Something on your mind?" he asks, his voice low and warm as we lag behind Emma and her grandmother. Emma looks like she's about to fold in half from exhaustion. Honestly, same. But there's a tiny thrill bubbling under the tiredness, a fizzy little reminder that there's only one bed back at the cottage.

I shrug, playful. "I could ask you the same. Ever since the hot dog stand, you've been giving me weird looks. Is it indigestion?"

He chuckles, deep and rich. "No, just been practicing the alphabet."

I blink. "The alphabet?"

He bites his bottom lip. Oh, *alphabet*. My body reacts like I just got zapped. "Ripley," I hiss, slapping his arm. "Stop it."

He only laughs harder. "Don't act like you're not a fan of oral... literacy, Goldilocks."

I groan, partly because of his terrible pun and partly because I can no longer think of anything but the letter G. "You're a menace to society."

"And yet, you keep walking home with me."

Ahead of us, the sun dips low, golden light bouncing off the water in a way that makes me sleepier...happier. Emma looks over her shoulder, eyes heavy, limbs dragging.

"Are we going to have a fire and sing songs?" she asks, her voice hopeful even as she covers a massive yawn with one small hand.

Rip slows, rests his hand at the small of my back. It's warm. Steady.

I glance at Emma's grandmother, but she beats me to it. "Might be better tomorrow," she says gently. "Tonight, I think we're all about to collapse."

Emma pouts for a second, then shrugs. "Charly, will you read me a bedtime story?"

The question surprises me, and warms something in my chest I didn't even know was cold. "I... sure. If that's okay?" I glance at Betsy for permission, not wanting to overstep.

She smiles. "Might be nice. Get a feel for what it'll be like when you two..." She waggles a finger between us, "...have your own brood."

"Brood?" Rip echoes, brows lifting as he turns to me with mock horror. "You never mentioned a brood."

I laugh, rolling my eyes.

He taps his temple, pretending to calculate. "How many kids does a brood involve? Like... twelve? Sixteen? Are we talking hockey team or full marching band?"

Betsy snorts. "You keep talking like that and she'll give you a whole damn orchestra."

I clutch my stomach, laughing so hard I nearly double over. "Okay, first of all, I'm not agreeing to anything that involves matching uniforms or recorders."

Rip grins, eyes twinkling. "So you're saying there's a chance."

He looks so adorable my heart does a full somersault. Without even thinking, I give his hand a gentle squeeze. The smile I get in return is so warm, it could toast marshmallows.

"Oh, Rip," Emma scolds, hands on her hips. "It's just a saying."

"That girl is too wise for her age," he mutters under his breath.

Emma straightens, glowing with pride. "I heard that."

"Ears like her grandmother," Rip adds, grinning.

Betsy, a few paces ahead, lifts her chin with matching sass. "*I* heard that."

Rip throws his hands up in mock defeat. "You know what? I'm just going to stop talking entirely."

A laugh bubbles out of me, light and full of happiness. "That'd be my suggestion."

We reach our cottage, and I reluctantly let go of his hand. "I won't be long."

He leans in, aiming for a kiss, but our hats bump like two awkward teens on a first date. He growls in frustration, snatches both off, and plants one on me, soft, unexpected, and hot enough to melt every bit of candy I ate today.

"You better not be," he murmurs against my lips.

"Rip, can you read to me too?" Emma asks, eyes round and hopeful, wielding the full force of childhood charm. No man could survive it. Not even Ripley Hart.

He sighs, already lost. "Sure. What's your favorite book?"

Emma frowns. "I don't have a lot of books here. Just baby ones." She rolls her eyes.

"Hey, nothing wrong with the classics," Rip says.

We follow Emma past our cottage into Betsy's, where she immediately grabs both our hands and tugs us toward her bedroom. She flops onto her narrow single bed and pats the space on either side of her.

Rip stares at the tiny mattress, and I can almost hear his brain working as he calculates the space...and how he's going to hurt something trying to squeeze in. "Uh... how exactly are we all supposed to fit on that?"

Emma blinks at him like he's the village idiot. "Don't be silly, Rip."

I hide a smile as he slowly, reluctantly lowers himself beside her, limbs dangling off the sides. I head to the bookshelf, scanning until a familiar title jumps out and makes me grin.

But then—my smile falters.

From the kitchen, I hear Betsy humming. The tune drifts through the house like a breeze. It's a melody I know well. Too well. I played it on The Spotlight. It wasn't just a song—it was *my* song.

I freeze.

Panic flares in my chest. What are the odds? It's on the radio, sure, but still...

Rip eyes me, sensing the shift. My shoulders tense, but I force myself to inhale, then exhale through my nose. Yoga breath. In. Out. Count four.

It's just a coincidence. It has to be.

I don't believe in coincidences, of course. And up until Rip, I didn't believe in fairy tales either. Feeling steadier, I pluck the book off the shelf and turn to them, holding it up. "How about this one?"

Rip glances over, then groans. He's half on the bed, half off, looking adorable and ridiculous all at once. I bite back a laugh. "You good?"

"Oh yeah, super comfortable," he says flatly.

Emma nods with dramatic maturity. "Yes. It will have to do."

There's a spark in her eyes though. She's trying to play it cool, like fairy tales are beneath her now, but she's all in. I walk over and show the cover. Rip's eyes meet mine, and a slow, mischievous smile forms.

"Goldilocks and the Three Bears," he says, voice low and suggestive. "My fav."

Emma turns to him, wide-eyed. "Really? That's your favorite?"

He shrugs. "Of course. It's a classic. Never gets old."

With Emma now blissfully content, I take off my hat and slide into the tiny bed on her other side, careful not to elbow anyone in the face. I start reading, and it doesn't take long before her heavy lids begin to flutter like she's fighting off sleep just to prove she's still part of the conversation. But honestly, I'm right there with her.

There's this strange, wonderful feeling blooming in my chest, a cozy warmth that feels suspiciously like longing. A child nestled between us, two grown-ups sharing a book like it's our normal, nightly routine. Like once the story ends, we'll tiptoe down the hallway, climb into bed, and fall asleep wrapped around each other while the stars do their thing outside.

And the wildest part is, I want it. All of it. The bedtime stories. The whispered goodnights. The togetherness. I finish reading, and Emma lets out a sleepy little sigh.

"Again?" she mumbles hopefully, already halfway to dreamland.

From the doorway, Betsy's low voice cuts through the quiet. "No, not again. It's late, and someone still has to wash up before bed."

Emma rubs at her eyes and yawns. "Okay. Thanks, Charly. Thanks, Rip."

I slide off the bed to make room for her, and as she scoots across the mattress and around the bed, she apparently makes contact with Rip's baby toe.

"Oof," he grunts, toppling sideways like a sack of hockey gear.

Emma giggles as she darts toward the bathroom, not the least bit sorry.

Betsy shakes her head, and takes a sip from her cup as she watches us like we're the entertainment portion of her evening tea. "Tea?" she asks.

"Thanks," I reply, as I stifle a yawn. "But I think we're going to call it a night too. It's been a full day."

She gives us a warm, knowing smile. "Thank you for being so kind to Emma. She absolutely adores you both."

"We adore her too," I say, and glance behind me to see what's taking Rip so long.

That's when I realize he's still sprawled on the floor. For a second I think maybe he's injured, but nope. He hops to his feet like he's just remembered he has urgent business.

And he does. Between my legs. Heat rushes to my face so fast I'm surprised I don't steam up the windows. Betsy doesn't miss it either. Her eyes glint with mischief as she smirks.

"Well," she says, shooing us toward the door. "I won't keep you from bed."

We step outside, and just as I think we've escaped with our dignity intact, she raps twice on the wall with her knuckles. "Yup. Still thin."

"Oh. My. God," I groan, laughing as Rip groans beside me. He wraps a strong arm around my waist and hauls me close.

"She's going to be the death of me," he mutters.

"You?" I say. "I'll never be able to make eye contact with her again."

A few short minutes later, we're back at our own cottage. The moment the door clicks shut and the lock turns, I feel it... him. That charged silence before the storm.

Rip pins me to the door, his body warm and firm against mine, his eyes simmering with enough heat to raise the ocean's temperature a few degrees.

"Rip," I whisper, but that's all I manage before his mouth is on mine, hungry, hot, and achingly sure. This isn't the usual heat between us. There's something deeper here. Something raw and restless. As he worships me with his hands, his kisses are slower but no less intense.

"I want you," he breathes into my mouth, his voice low and rough. "Today was... incredible. I wouldn't trade a single second. But thinking about being alone with you all day..." He trails off, pressing his forehead to mine. "It's been killing me." He groans, like even talking about it physically pains him. "Fuck, girl," he murmurs.

And just like that, my heart does another flip. Because for all his fire, there's tenderness beneath it. Longing. A man who doesn't just want to take—but to *keep*.

And I might just let him.

Rip grips the hem of my sundress and slowly lifts it, knuckles grazing my skin like he's unwrapping something precious. I raise my arms, breath caught somewhere between a gasp and a moan, eager for the dress to vanish entirely.

The moment it hits the floor, his mouth finds that sweet, secret spot at the crook of my neck, the heat of his breath making me arch into him. His cock presses hard against the aching place between my thighs, and I let out a throaty groan, my hips instinctively seeking more friction.

His lips move lower, tracing a slow, wet path over the swell of my breasts. With practiced, devastating ease, he slides his hand behind me, unhooks my bra, and lets it fall. But this time... his hands aren't rushed. There's no frenzied, frantic tugging. Every movement feels intentional—like he wants to memorize each inch of me.

He pulls back just a little, eyes dark with need, his chest rising and falling like he's trying not to explode on the spot.

"Lose the panties," he says, voice low and soft, but commanding. A lazy grin curves his lips. "Slowly."

I bite my lip just to tease him. His nostrils flare. Good. Sliding my fingers into the waistband, I shimmy my hips, making the removal a whole event. He growls, a deep, primal sound that makes my insides tighten, and watches with rapt attention as I lower them, inch by delicious inch, until they hit the floor. I kick them away with a flick, and they vanish somewhere behind me.

I gesture toward him, smirking. "I believe *you* might be a bit overdressed, Mr. Hart."

In that casually sexy way only men like him can pull off, he reaches over his shoulder and yanks off his T-shirt in one fluid motion. His shorts and boxers follow, landing in a crumpled heap. Then he offers me his hand.

My heart pounds. "What about the mess we made?" I ask, eyes drifting toward the trail of clothing behind us.

He growls, tugging me closer. "Leave it."

I raise a brow. "What happened to my little neat freak?"

He shrugs. "Maybe you're rubbing off on me."

"Funny. I was just thinking I'd like to be rubbing off on you."

That earns me another growl—and a wicked smile. "As long as we're rubbing."

He pulls me into his arms, and I swear my whole body short-circuits. My heart pounds as emotions crash over me, wave after wave, I don't want to swim out of. I want to drown in this man. Let him pull me under. Because with Rip, I feel safe.

And more than that, I trust him. Deep down in a way I didn't think was possible anymore. Not after what my ex put me through. But this? This came easy. Natural. Right. My head should be spinning, but for the first time in what feels like forever, it's *not*. It's clear. This is right.

I don't know exactly what the future looks like yet. But I know who I want in it.

"Yes," I murmur as we walk into the bedroom and he casts a hungry glance my way.

He freezes.

His eyes go from me... to the bed... back to me, panic creeping into his expression. "I—I'm sorry. I just assumed..."

I glance at the bed and laugh softly. "As you should. Because the answer to this?" I point at the mattress. "With you? It's *always* a yes, Rip. But what I meant was yes, I will go back to Boston with you."

Then I pause. Because something flickers in his eyes, a quick blink, a hesitation. Did I surprise him? Or... did I catch him off guard in a way that means he's reconsidering his offer?

Before I can ask, he closes the space between us, capturing my mouth in a kiss that shuts down every overthinking cell in my body. His hands roam, his lips devour, and whatever he might have said is completely lost in the storm he's stirring inside me.

I let myself focus on his touch. On the way he worships every inch of me. Honestly, a man can't touch a woman like this unless he feels something more. Right? Maybe I'm just paranoid. Wounded from the past. Waiting for the other shoe to drop, because that's what happens when you've been betrayed.

But Rip?

He's not that kind of man. He doesn't manipulate. He doesn't deceive. He's steady. Solid. Real. He leads me to the bed and I fall onto the mattress. I spread my legs, but I'm not just offering my body...I'm offering my heart.

He falls over me, slides lower, his breath hot on my skin, and I gasp as his tongue finds my center—slow, teasing, devastating. My whole body trembles as he traces torturously playful shapes. Letters, one by one, like he's writing a love letter only I can read.

"Rip, that is so good."

His voice rumbles against me. "Yeah, baby... it's so good."

I can't help but laugh softly, breathlessly. It always surprises me how much *he* loves this. How much pleasure he gets from giving it. But that's Rip. Passionate. Focused. All in.

And right now, *I need him*.

As soon as those three words leave my lips he's moving, climbing up my body, his mouth claiming mine in a hungry kiss, his big, beautiful body settling between my thighs. And then—

He's inside me.

With one perfect stroke, he fills me completely. I tighten around him, and we both groan. I wrap myself around him, and he does the same, holding me like letting go isn't an option. And in that moment, I feel it...this is different. Not just the sex. The connection.

We move together slowly, unhurried, exploring and savoring, like there's nowhere else in the world we need to be. In no time at all, he makes me come with practiced ease, my body pulsing around him, and I bury my face in his neck, clinging to him like a lifeline. His own release follows, a deep, shuddering surrender.

"I love feeling you inside me like this," I whisper, breath still shaky against his lips.

For a long time, we stay tangled, unmoving, letting the silence settle around us like a second skin. Eventually, he gently slips out of me and rolls to his back, pulling me with him. I drape myself across his chest, lulled by the steady beat of his heart under my cheek.

The next thing I know, I'm opening my eyes to morning sunlight spilling across the room. I stretch, smiling, and reach for Rip. But the bed is empty. My heart skips.

I sit up, expecting to hear the clatter of dishes or the smell of coffee drifting from the kitchen, but the cottage is still. Too still. Then I hear it—his voice. Outside. I step into the kitchen and move to the window. There he is, sitting in a chair, bent forward, body stiff. My heart clenches. What's going on?

My mind spins, racing back to last night. What we said. What I said. *I'll go back to Boston with you.* Did I scare him? Did he change his mind? And then I see the phone in his hand...his words not meant for me but for her.

Lyra.

Was last night's soft lovemaking not about a future, and more about a goodbye?

23

RIP

I grip the phone so tightly my knuckles burn, the plastic casing creaking under the pressure of my frustration as I pace in front of the fire. Jesus Christ. The last thing I want is for Lyra to show up on my doorstep and find Indie Rhodes in my bed.

Not because I want Lyra back. Hell no. I've come to realize that ship didn't just sail, it sank.

But Lyra's not coming here for some heart-to-heart. She's coming because she's lonely, or needs something. Like a new story. I am done with her turning my life into her next goddamn headline. But it's not me I'm worried about. It's Charly. If Lyra finds her here, she'll twist it into something ugly. Use her. Exploit her. Hurt her.

And I'll be damned if I let that happen to my girlfriend.

Girlfriend.

Is Charly my girlfriend?

Goddamn right she is.

When she looked me in the eyes last night and said she was coming home with me, something cracked wide open inside. I was floored. Speechless. Not because I didn't want it, but because I'd been so afraid it was too big a leap for her. Too much, too soon. After everything she's been through, after all the hurt she's had to swallow, I worried she'd flinch at anything that looked remotely like commitment.

But she didn't. She chose me. Us.

Sure we need to talk, voicing the words about who we really are, but that will come. Christ, I'm in so deep, and I'm not even afraid. Leaving our bed this morning was like tearing off a piece of myself, but the phone wouldn't stop ringing. Of course, I knew it was Lyra. I can see it so clearly now, see how relentless and manipulative she is. Being with Charly has helped me take the blinders off.

So I answered, planning to end things once and for all. No more back and forth. No more games. No more being the guy who waited around like a damn stray dog, hoping she'd finally choose me. That guy is dead.

Charly buried him, with nothing but a touch, a look, and the quiet way she reaches for me in the middle of the night. She showed me what love actually looks like. Not headline drama, but steady hands and soft laughter. The way she instinctively tends to my injury, even when I'm sleeping. That's real. Not manipulation. Not someone showing up when they're lost and vanishing when they've found a better offer.

God, how could I have been so damn stupid?

But it ends now.

"Listen, I have to go," I say, cutting Lyra off mid-whine.

"It'll just be a short visit," she presses, voice dipping into that sultry lilt she always used when she wanted something. "I'm in between assignments right now, and I really need you, Big Bear."

"Don't call me that." The words burst out sharper than I intend, but I don't take them back.

There's a pause on the other end, followed by a soft gasp. Like I've just wounded her. Old me might have winced. Might have softened. But not anymore. I drop into the nearest chair, scrubbing a hand over my face. "It's just not a good time, Lyra. Okay?"

"Is there someone else?" she asks, her voice cracking with a practiced sniffle. Like she's crying. And maybe she is. But for what? Losing me, or losing control?

"No. There's no one else." I say it loud, probably too loud, the words echoing off the thin cottage walls. I wince. Dammit. But I have to get that point across to protect Charly. From my peripheral, I swear I see movement in the kitchen window. I turn, but Charly isn't there. My gut tightens.

Shit.

Did I wake Charly?

Did she hear me?

And if she did...how much?

My heart pounds because for the first time in my life, I care more about what the woman inside this house thinks than the one on the phone. And I'll be damned if I screw this up.

"Then why can't I come visit?" Lyra asks, her voice laced with suspicion, as if she already knows the answer and is daring me to lie.

"I'm getting ready to leave," I say, keeping my tone flat, noncommittal.

"You said that last week. And the week before. You're still there."

I press my fingers to my forehead and exhale. "Something came up."

"As in a girl?"

Of course she'd go there. "Lyra, we're over. Okay? I need to go."

Her silence only lasts a second before it breaks into soft, strategic sobbing. Those tears used to unhinge me, and she knows it. I close my eyes, jaw locked tight. I want to hang up. I should hang up. But some part of me, the part that always felt responsible for her feelings, holds me hostage for one more moment.

I push to my feet, and walk down the path toward the edge of the road, needing distance from the house, from the thought of Charly possibly hearing this. The morning sun sparkles off the water, but I'm not really seeing any of it.

"You and I both know this relationship wasn't healthy," I say. "I don't think we can even be friends anymore. I think...it's best if we stop communicating altogether."

"How can you do this to me?" she cries, the words drenched in betrayal.

Do this to her?

I almost laugh. After everything she's done to me? After all the ways she's used me, ghosted me, only to come crawling back only when it served her?

But I can't even blame her anymore. Not really. I'm the one who kept opening the door. Who kept hoping she'd be different. Who let history, habit, and a craving for what I thought we once had speak louder than self-respect.

"Why don't you go visit your parents?" I offer, softening only slightly, because she sounds like she needs someone. But I know it can't be me.

There's a beat of silence before her voice turns sharp, acidic. "You know we don't get along."

Ah. There she is. When Lyra doesn't get her way, the mask slips. The sweetness evaporates. I've never truly seen this side of her before, because with me, she never had to show it. I always gave in. But not anymore.

"I have to go," I say firmly, then press end before she can twist her way in again.

I tuck the phone into my pocket, exhale, and turn back toward the cottage. My chest feels lighter, but still tight with nerves. As I step inside, I half expect to find Charly in the kitchen, arms folded, eyes narrowed. But it's quiet.

I walk softly through the living room and peek into the bedroom. She's still there, curled up under the covers, her hair a mess across the pillow. The tension in my shoulders ease. I let out a breath, my heart filling with all the things I feel for this woman.

I pour myself a cup of coffee, and step back outside. I take a long sip and this time I take pleasure in the beauty before me. The early morning buzzes with kids laughing, joggers pounding sand-packed trails, a dog barking at the waves. Somewhere in the distance, a guitar plays a slow, soulful tune.

For a second, I think it's Emma. But no, Emma's not that good. Not yet.

Under Charly's care, though...

That thought sparks something in me, and I take another gulp of coffee and head back to the cottage. I scribble a note for Charly on the kitchen counter:

Ran into town to pick up a few groceries. Want to do some stretches with you when I get back.

But the groceries aren't the real reason I'm going. And I don't want her knowing what is. Not yet.

I lock up behind myself, careful not to let the screen door slam. Inside, Charly sleeps soundly, her breath soft, her body curled beneath the covers, still tired from yesterday's long, sun-soaked adventures... and the sweet, unhurried lovemaking that followed.

Lovemaking.

Jesus. If Roman ever heard me say that out loud, he'd yank my man card and frame it on his wall like a trophy. Then again, I've seen Roman and Gabby together. I married them in fact, and those two are a walking Hallmark movie, complete with the cozy gazes and sappy grins. They're so sweet it makes my teeth ache... and yet, I wouldn't change a thing about them. They're good together and I couldn't be happier for him.

Thinking about it makes my chest feel full in a way I'm not used to. Because for the first time, I can actually picture what it looks like to hang out with my friends as a couple, not the third wheel. I envision double dates, weekend trips, nights out that don't end in one of us alone at the bar. I can see Roman and Gabby laughing with Charly across a table, clinking glasses, swapping stories. It's the kind of life I wasn't sure I'd ever have.

I stroll past Marta's cottage and stop, letting my eyes linger. There's something about this place that pulls at me. Something solid. Right. The idea of vacationing here again next summer with Gunther and Paisley, hell, maybe even renting kayaks or letting Emma bury me in the sand, it all feels... possible.

Look at me. Making lifelong plans without even consulting Charly. But the truth is, I want Charly in those plans. I just don't know if she's ready for the kind of step I'm about to take. If I told her, she'd probably say it was too much. Too fast. She'd tell me to slow down, to think it through. She's not with me for the fame or glory or even to get the next juicy story. She sees me. The guy beneath the fame, the one who could be taken out with an injury. She's honest. Real. And right now, I won't risk overwhelming her with something that might scare her off. But I also can't ignore this pull.

Just then, the cottage door swings open and Marta steps onto the porch, giving me a wave. Shit. I've been standing here like a total creeper, staring at her house like I'm casing the joint. I lift my hand in return, nod politely, and force myself to keep walking into town.

Heads turn as I pass a few shops. Odd, since no one has paid much attention to me before. I tug the brim of my ball cap lower, hoping to keep a low profile, then step into the real estate office. The cool air inside greets me, along with the jingling laughter of a middle-aged woman wearing a smile almost as big as her hoop earrings. Her bracelets jangle as she gestures for me to take a seat.

"What brings you in today?" she asks, head tilting ever so slightly as she ends the call she was on. Recognition dawns in her eyes, despite my best efforts at laying low.

"I'm here about Marta Conrad's cottage," I say, getting right to the point. "Just down the road."

Her eyes widen, clearly intrigued. "Beautiful property. We actually had an offer on it last week, but Marta turned it down."

"She turned it down?" I blink. "Why?"

"They didn't have the right vibe," she says with a knowing smile, as if she's done this dance with Marta before. "She wants to sell it to someone who'll love it. Really live in it. Not just toss it on Airbnb and call it a day."

"She showed me around yesterday," I say. "We talked for a while."

"Well, that's a good sign," she says, clearly encouraged.

"Betsy Callahan vouched for us."

"Us?" she echoes, eyebrows lifting.

"My..." I hesitate just a beat too long, and then force the word out, steady and sure. "My fiancée."

The word lodges somewhere in my throat. It's not a lie. Not really. Maybe not officially, but in my heart, it feels true.

She's the one.

Now I just have to make her believe it too.

She claps her hands, bangles jingling like wind chimes. "How lovely." She opens a file and begins pulling out documents related to the cottage. The next half hour slips by in a blur of signatures, figures, and official nods.

Once we're done, I stand and hesitate. "Can you please keep this between us?"

"The Conrads have to know," she teases.

I laugh. "Of course. It's kind of a surprise for my fiancée. I'd rather her not know."

She nods. "I can let Marta know that. I can't guarantee that she won't tell Betsy. Those two are pretty tight."

For some reason I'm not worried about Betsy spilling any secrets. One thing I've learned since being here is that she's good at keeping them. When I finally step back into the sunlight, it feels like something irreversible has shifted. I've put in an offer. On a cottage. With Charly in mind.

Damn, it feels good.

I head back, eager to wake Charly with a kiss, or more. As I move through the sleepy town, I catch more eyes on me than usual, recognition flickering in their expressions. I tug the brim of my hat lower. My phone buzzes. My heart jumps, hoping it's Charly.

I swipe across the screen. "Hey."

"Well, nice to hear from you too," Roman chuckles.

"Sorry. I thought..." I pause. "I thought you were someone else."

"Oh yeah?" he teases. "You got yourself a hot little number down at the beach?"

I laugh. "Actually... yeah. But don't call her that." Before he can say anything, I continue with, "I can't wait for you to meet her," knowing that'll get his attention.

I hear a squeaking sound, and can picture him sitting up a bit straighter. "Dude?"

"You're really going to like her."

"Tell me everything. Don't leave anything out."

A deep laugh rumbles from my chest. "You're worse than Elias's grandmother."

"Gabby," he yells. "Come here, you need to hear this—"

"It'll have to wait. I'll tell you when I get home next week."

"Dude, no. You're killing me."

As I pass a man walking his dog, he throws a lingering glance my way. I duck my head. "I have to go. I'll catch up with you later." As he groans, I end the call. When I reach the cottage, I half-expect to find Charly on the porch, coffee in hand, guitar on her lap, humming something soft and sweet. But the porch is empty. I check the time and a strange tug pulls in my gut, a niggling that I think is trying to warn me.

But of what?

I unlock the door and slip inside quietly, just in case she's still asleep. The house is silent, save for the rush of water behind the bathroom door. I head toward it and try the handle. Locked. My stomach drops. She never locks the door.

I knock. "Charly? I'm back." The water shuts off abruptly. I wait. Then knock again. "You okay in there?"

Silence. What the hell is going on?

I'm just about to knock harder, maybe even push the door open, when I hear soft footsteps on the tile. A second later, the door opens, and there she is, towel wrapped around her. She smiles, but it doesn't reach her eyes.

"Hey," I say softly, brushing my fingers over her warm arm. "Everything okay? You locked the door."

"I..." A pause. A beat too long. "...was alone."

"Didn't you see my note?" I ask.

She blinks, then slowly shakes her head. "No. I must've missed it."

I cross to the coffee table and hold it up. She reads it. "I didn't want to wake you. Thought about putting it on your pillow, but I saw how peaceful you looked." I glance past her to the bathroom vanity and spot the coffee mug. "Maybe I should've left it by the coffee maker."

She laughs, but there's a hollowness to it. "I guess I just get nervous being alone," she says.

That... doesn't feel quite right. Is that really it? Or is there something she's not saying? She couldn't have overheard my call with Lyra. She was asleep. And even if she did, it wouldn't have upset her. She doesn't want me with my ex.

"You're not in California anymore, Char," I remind her gently.

"You're right," she replies, though her voice is quiet. Too quiet.

My phone pings and I glance at it. "It's Roman. I was talking to him earlier. I guess he must have forgotten to tell me something."

I step into the kitchen, and look back at her. "More coffee?"

I find her scanning the counter. "No groceries?"

Groceries. Right. Shit. I meant to grab some. I did, after all, leave a note telling her that's where I'd gone. But then the cottage, people recognizing me, and Roman...

Her eyes narrow just a little, her shoulders pulling in. "Rip?"

"Right. I got sidetracked."

"Roman?"

"Ah, yeah."

Her shoulders tighten, and I realize exactly how that sounded.

Like a lie.

...and in a way, it is.

(24)

CHARLY

There's no one else...

Those four words have been looping in my head for the last three days, a quiet echo I can't silence no matter how hard I try. I didn't hear who he was talking to, but I felt it deep in my chest, like a fist closing around my heart. He had to be talking to Lyra. No one else calls him that much. And if he told her I wasn't in the picture, it can only mean one thing. He wants her back.

What other explanation is there? I've turned that question over until I'm raw. And it makes me wonder... was Roman's call the real reason Rip forgot the groceries? Or was that just the moment I stopped being real in his life?

The moment when he chose her?

God, I feel so stupid. Thinking he offered me a place in Boston because he wanted me. That it meant something. That I meant something. I've tried to play it cool, clinging to the hope that I'm wrong. I didn't hear the full conversation, after all. And in the past, whenever Lyra called, I always gave him privacy. But this feels different. He didn't mention the call. Didn't explain the sudden disappearance. Came back empty-handed, because he had other things on his mind. Now, he keeps going on unexplained walks, keeps checking his phone.

Are those red flags or am I letting my past seep into what could be my future?

Truthfully, I want to believe there's still a future for us. But how can we move forward if we're still tangled in lies? He doesn't even know who I really am. Doesn't know the truth about my identity, the video. What will be the fallout when he does find out?

I step outside, letting the warm, salty breeze wash over me. The ocean murmurs in the distance, a rhythm I usually find comforting. Not today. Not when every nerve in my body is pulled tight, like I'm bracing for a storm.

Honestly, I didn't expect to fall for the man who'd been keeping that bed warm before I ever slipped beneath the sheets. But I did. God help me, I fell for him harder than I ever meant to. And if I could go back, I'd do it all over again. Only this time, I'd tell him the truth. From the very beginning. I'd tell him I knew who he was. And I'd let him know just how deeply I was already falling. But there's no rewinding this. Only moving forward. And I pray we're doing that together. Because if he's choosing her... if he's already chosen her... I can't go back to Boston with him. And I sure as hell can't stay here, drowning in what-ifs and broken dreams.

I glance down the sandy path leading into town. Rip left hours ago. Said something about checking on a boat rental and picking something up. What, I don't know. He seemed excited. Hopeful, even. But the longer he's gone, the more it feels like he's slipping through my fingers.

Restless, I wander past the fire pit and pause when I hear a familiar strumming from next door. Emma's playing again. The simple sound threads into my chest, unraveling some of the tension. I follow the path toward Betsy's, and when Emma looks up and sees me, her face lights up with a grin so bright it momentarily makes me forget every ache in my chest.

"Charly, come over," Emma calls, her voice bright with excitement.

"You're sounding great," I tell her, injecting as much cheer into my voice as I can muster.

She pats the empty chair beside her. "Listen."

I settle next to her, and she strums through a tricky chord change—the one that used to frustrate her. But this time, she nails it.

"You've really been practicing," I say, smiling for real now. "I'm so proud of you."

She exhales, her whole face lighting up. That smile tugs at something deep inside me, something warm and achy all at once. Teaching her has been one of the purest joys I've had in my career. It's made me wonder if maybe there's something more I'm meant to do. Something that looks a lot like this—sharing music, shaping young minds, finding fulfillment in the small, meaningful moments. Maybe I could be a teacher. Maybe I could even go back to school.

But the dream stalls in my chest.

Because I'm leaving soon. Even if every part of me wants to stay. It breaks my heart to think about not sitting beside Emma anymore, not watching her grow with every chord she masters. I know there are other teachers out there, but she chose me. She trusts me. And that connection... It's rare. It's real.

Just like what I thought I had with Rip.

I swallow hard and try to push the thought away, but my gut won't unclench. The tension's been living there for days now, heavy and unwelcome.

"Charly," Betsy calls from the doorway, her voice sweet and steady. "I just made tea."

I blink and lift my hand to the brim of my sunhat. "I'd love some," I tell her, grateful for the interruption.

The truth is, I could barely stomach coffee this morning, and breakfast might as well have been air. I forced a few bites, not wanting Rip to notice how quiet I was, how far from okay I felt. I didn't want to make a thing out of it—his sudden absences, that phone call I overheard, the way his eyes haven't quite met mine lately. Maybe it's nothing.

My ex did a number on me, and the damage runs deeper than I care to admit. Still, I keep repeating the same words in my head like a prayer: *Rip is not him.* Rip has never once made me feel unsafe. Unwanted. Unloved.

Not until lately.

A few minutes later, Betsy steps outside carrying a tray with two steaming mugs and a plate of croissants. They smell buttery and warm, and my stomach grumbles. She places the tray on the table and takes her seat. I wrap my hands around the mug and take a sip. The warmth settles in my belly, calming the storm just a little.

When I glance up, Betsy is watching me with that quiet intensity of hers—the kind of gaze that sees far more than you want it to.

I smile, trying to play it off.

She sets her mug down gently. "Have you been getting enough sleep, dear?"

Her question hits me like a soft blow to the ribs. So simple. So kind. But it unlocks something in me I've been holding back too long. Emotion swells, thick and fast, and my eyes sting.

I take another sip to buy myself a moment, hiding behind the cup. Because if anyone can read through my carefully constructed mask, it's Betsy. And right now, I need to hold it together.

I finally lower the mug, pretending to inspect the tray, and take a small bite of croissant. Flaky. Perfect. But the lump in my throat makes it hard to swallow.

"I think I'm just going to miss you guys when we leave," I manage, voice soft and fraying at the edges.

Without hesitation, Emma sets her guitar down and throws her arms around me. Her hug is tight, and I'm not ready for how much I need it.

"Oh, Charly, I'm going to miss you too," Emma says. "But if you buy Mrs. Conrad's place, you can come back every summer, and we can have so much fun."

I smile, but it falters the second those words land. *Buy the cottage. Come back every summer.* My heart lurches. Because in that instant, I envision the cottage, but it's not Rip and me I see inside, it's Rip and Lyra. Just like that, the bite of croissant I'd just swallowed turns to lead in my stomach.

"Darling," Betsy says gently. "You've paled."

"I think I'm just too hot," I lie, forcing a weak smile.

"Go on inside, stand in front of the fan for a moment. There are clean washcloths in the bathroom if you want to wash your face."

I nod, grateful for the excuse to escape before the tears push past my lids. I hurry inside, make a beeline for the bathroom, and close the door with a soft click. The silence wraps around me and I take a few fueling breaths before I run cool water over a washcloth and press it to my face. The sting of the cold distracts me for a second, until I catch sight of myself in the mirror.

Puffy eyes. Pale skin. Haunted expression.

Betsy was right. I haven't been sleeping. Not really. But it's more than that. I'm worn thin, stretched tight by all the pretending. Pretending I'm fine. Pretending nothing's wrong. Pretending I didn't hear the man I love say something that shattered me in four words flat.

I stare at myself harder, searching for the version of me that used to fight for what mattered. When did I become so afraid? Of being hurt. Of being wrong. Of being too much, or not enough. I hate how deeply my ex's betrayal still lives inside me, shaping how I react, how I trust, how I love.

But Rip is not my ex.

And if he and I have any chance at a future, then I need to

stop hiding. I need to talk to him—really talk to him—about what I heard, what I feel, and what I fear.

I suck in a breath. Pull on my proverbial big girl panties and step out of the bathroom. As I move toward the front door, something catches my eye on the small entry table. A newspaper.

My gaze freezes.

It's a photo of...us. Rip and me. Centered. Big. A full-page splash for all to see.

I move closer, heart slamming against my ribs. I reach for it, the edges of the paper fluttering beneath my fingertips. Before I can lift it, Betsy slips inside. Her eyes flick to mine, then to the newspaper. She moves fast. She places her tea directly over the photo, then lets the cup tip just enough to spill. "Oh, look at the mess I've made," she says, far too casually.

I watch her mop up the spill with a cloth, fold the newspaper, and carry it to the trash.

"That was a picture of Rip and me," I say, voice low.

She waves a hand, brushing it off. "There are plenty of photos from the festival, dear. Everyone's in there somewhere."

Maybe. But not everyone was splashed across the front cover, locked in a moment that looked an awful lot like intimacy.

I open my mouth, a thousand questions storming my mind. Did they use our names? Is that why people have been eyeing Rip? But more than anything, one question swells in my chest.

Which name did they use for me?

And just like that, my legs wobble, and I feel the blood drain from my face.

Because if that truth is out there now…maybe that's why Rip is distancing himself.

"Dear, I think you should go home and lie down. You don't look very well today."

There's concern in Betsy's voice, gentle but firm, and I know better than to argue.

"Good idea. I'm getting a headache now." I say quickly.

"Oh dear, I don't have any acetaminophen. Do you have some back at your cottage?"

"No, but I'm sure it will pass once I lay down." She nods and I slip past her. I toss a wave toward Emma, who's already back to strumming her guitar, blissfully unaware of the emotional storm I'm walking through.

But once I'm out of Betsy's line of sight, I don't head toward the cottage. I veer left. The sand shifts beneath my feet as I take the hidden path toward town, my yellow sunhat tugged low to shield my face from the bright midday sun—and maybe from being recognized, too. My steps are quick, urgent, my breath shallow with nerves and something that feels too much like desperation.

I pass a few locals and tourists along the way, offering vague hellos I barely mean. My mind is elsewhere. Racing. When Marta's old place comes into view, my heart gives an odd little stutter. The SOLD sign gleams in the sunlight like a slap. I slow down, staring at it, letting the finality of it settle in my chest.

Behind the curtain, I catch the faintest movement. Probably the Conrads, packing up their lives, making space for someone new. Someone lucky. I force myself to keep walking.

Because it was foolish, wasn't it? All of it. The late-night talks, the stolen kisses, the lazy mornings tangled in sheets and sunlight. The idea that Rip and I could build a future here. That we could buy that cottage and fill it with laughter and memories and love.

A fairy tale.

Something I quit believing in...until Rip.

Which is why, right now, I'm clinging to hope. A quiet, defiant part that whispers—he wouldn't go back to Lyra. Not after everything we've been through. Not after everything she did to him.

There's no one else...

Those words echo again, as I reach town and lift the brim of my hat, scanning the clusters of tourists moving along the boardwalk or walking in and out of shops. My pulse quickens. I move past the shops, peer into the windows of the café, the bookstore, the bakery.

No sign of Rip.

Still, I keep looking. Telling myself I'm just curious, not suspicious. But I know the truth. I'm spying. And it gnaws at me.

What am I even doing?

This isn't who I am. This isn't us. This is what Colby reduced me to—second-guessing, watching for lies. But Rip isn't Colby. He's never made me feel small or paranoid. He's never twisted my trust.

Not until lately.

The realization cuts deep, and shame prickles across my skin. How can I hope to build something real with him when I'm sneaking around like this? When I'm so afraid of what I might find, I can't even ask the questions out loud? I sigh, rub my temple, and turn to head back.

But then—

I spot him through the crowd, weaving his way toward a café with outdoor seating, his beautiful body moving with a new kind of grace, now that he's healing. My breath catches. Relief and excitement bloom in my chest. I lift my arm, mouth parting to call out to him.

But the words never make it out.

Because just then, a woman with long, dark hair leaps from one of the café tables and throws her arms around him.

I freeze.

Rip stumbles slightly at the impact, his return hug stiff and awkward as he glances around, almost self-conscious, before lowering himself into the seat across from her. I don't need to move any closer. I don't need introductions or explanations.

I *know*.

It's her.

Lyra.

From where I'm standing, I can see that they're not just catching up. They're starting something again.

Don't jump to conclusions, Charly. Don't do this to yourself.

My chest tightens, my pulse loud in my ears, but I force myself to breathe. I just told myself we needed to talk. So I need to stop spiraling. I need proof before I let my heart break into a million pieces. With trembling fingers, I pull out my phone and type her name into the search bar, not expecting much. But when her photo pops up, all glossy waves and perfectly curated beauty, the world tips sideways.

It's her.

The woman sitting across from Rip.

But it's not just that.

The bio hits me like a punch: Lyra Truman, reporter for FameWire—celebrity news, gossip, exclusive exposés.

My blood runs cold.

"Oh my God," I whisper, barely able to hear myself over the rush in my ears. My hand tightens around my phone. A reporter. *A reporter.* Which means she likely followed The Spotlight. Which means she might already know exactly who I am.

Is that why she's here? Did she see me in the local paper and follow the trail here, to Rip, to me? No. No, that doesn't make sense. The local paper isn't national. It's not like she'd just stumble across it.

Unless... She didn't see the paper.

Unless Rip told her.

Told her everything because.... it's his way of getting back with her.

I stagger back a step, the ache in my chest blooming fast. My fingers fumble around the edge of my phone, my vision swimming.

When he said he had to pick something up in town, I guess it was Lyra. And the other night's sweet lovemaking, I guess that really was about goodbye. Well, I'll be damned if I'm going to wait around and hear him voice the words.

25

RIP

I tug my hat low as I make my way back to the cottage, my heart still hammering in my chest—for more than one reason. Honestly, I was totally blindsided by Lyra today. If I'd paid more attention to my social media, maybe I would've seen it coming. Someone recognized me in the local paper last week and tagged me. That's how Lyra found the post, saw me standing next to Charly, and decided to "drop by" with a surprise visit.

She had no idea which cottage I was staying in. I only got her text when I was halfway to the realtor's office to pick up the final paperwork. Goddammit. Even now, I'm still a little rattled.

But this time, Lyra didn't want my body for a few nights. She wanted the story. So I gave it to her. Every last piece. And now that she's got what she came for, she's headed back to California. All I can think is: two birds, one stone.

With the contract tucked in my back pocket, I quicken my pace, eager to surprise Charly with the cottage. I hope she's as excited about this as I am. She's been a little off the past few days—quiet, distracted. Going to bed before me. Waking before dawn. I figured she was feeling the same thing I was, the bittersweet tug of leaving a place that's wrapped itself around our hearts.

But leaving doesn't have to mean goodbye.

Warm wind at my back, I step into the yard, my eyes sweeping across the familiar space. She's not out front, so I glance toward the beach, thinking she's probably out for a stretch without me. I took longer than expected. But there's no sign of her by the water's edge.

Maybe she's inside. Or with Emma and Mrs. Callahan. I try the door and find it unlocked.

"Charly?" I call as I step inside. No answer. The quiet wraps around me, and something uneasy scratches at the back of my neck. I do a quick loop through the cottage, check the back patio. Empty. A laugh rumbles in my chest as a thought strikes me. Maybe she's sunbathing nude. She threatened to do that the first day we got here.

Music floats in from next door and my heart lifts. That's probably where she is. I've watched her come alive teaching Emma, like something inside her clicked into place. I think she's starting to realize what I already know. Teaching is what she's meant to do.

I don't even bother locking up as I step back outside and head to Mrs. Callahan's. Funny, she still won't let me call her Betsy. Maybe that'll change after I make an honest woman out of Charly.

That thought stops me cold.

We planned a fake wedding. Picked the location, the bouquet, even the music. None of it was real. But now, well, now I want every last part of it to be real. And I can only pray she wants that too.

"Hey," I say as I round the corner and spot Mrs. Callahan fluffing the cushions on her porch swing. Emma's sitting quietly at the fire pit—no fire going—guitar in her lap as she plucks out soft chords. I scan the yard. No sign of Charly.

"Is Charly here?" I ask. Mrs. Callahan frowns and straightens slowly, and something in me tightens. "What's wrong?"

"She saw the paper," she says gently. "Saw the big spread on you both."

The local paper.

I hadn't even known about it until Lyra mentioned it earlier. I picked up a copy after our meeting and flipped through it. There was no mention of Charly. Not her real name or her alias. Just mine. Still, it was enough to turn heads in town.

"She was upset?" I ask, my voice tighter than I mean it to be.

Mrs. Callahan gives a small nod, her expression full of concern. "She's worried, Rip. But no one else knows... right?"

Do I tell her Lyra knows?

I hesitate. Back during the festival, I was stunned when Mrs. Callahan pulled me aside and revealed that she knew exactly who Charly really was. Said she watches The Spotlight, recognized her even with the changes to her hair, her clothes, her entire vibe. She hadn't seen the so-called sex tape—but she hadn't needed to. Said she'd been around long enough, saw enough, to know that there was no way a girl like Indie Rhodes would do something like that.

This conversation, of course, was long after I told her Charly and I were engaged. Apparently once she saw us together, she went into full matchmaking mode. Charly doesn't know any of this. I never told her. I should have, but I didn't. She would've been mortified to think the kind, nosy neighbor knew who she really was. But honestly, she'd probably be relieved to know Mrs. Callahan didn't believe a single vile word her ex said.

Still, we had this silent agreement not to share our real identities, not even with each other, and I kept my word. Even when I wanted to tell her she had someone in her corner—someone else who saw the truth in her the way I do.

But that's enough of that.

Right now, I need to find her. Because I've got more than just a cottage in my pocket, I've got a future in mind. And none of it means a damn thing without her in it.

We're supposed to be leaving together next week, which means it's well past time we open up about everything. No more half-truths or careful omissions. I plan to do that... just as soon as I find her.

"It's going to be okay," I tell Mrs. Callahan, offering a smile I don't quite feel. She doesn't need to know about Lyra or the story I gave her for her headline. No need to complicate things further. I just have to believe it'll all work out, that when the dust settles, everyone will land where they're meant to.

Two birds, one stone. That's what I keep telling myself.

She nods, but the look in her eyes says she doesn't buy it. "Okay." Her hand lands on my arm, giving it a gentle, grandmotherly squeeze, and damn if I don't feel my throat tighten.

She's everything Charly needs in her life, kind, nurturing, motherly. I hope to hell we get to spend every summer here with her.

"Do you know where she is?" I ask again, fighting to keep the rising panic out of my voice.

Her brow furrows, and she tips her chin toward our cottage. "She said she wasn't feeling well. Went back to lie down."

A chill creeps in.

"I just came from there," I say, glancing toward the beach again. Maybe I missed her. It's a wide stretch of sand, and it's not hard to lose someone in the crowd. But I was looking. I would've seen her... wouldn't I?

Mrs. Callahan twists her hands, anxiety clouding her soft features. "She looked pale. Not like herself these last few days."

I rub at the stubble on my jaw. I noticed that too, noticed how quiet she's been, how her smile doesn't quite reach her eyes. But I chalked it up to the sadness of leaving this little oasis we've built together. Could it be something else? Could she be worried about the photo, her ex or the press finding her?

Well, the press already found her, and they got their damn story. And when I say they, I mean Lyra.

"Maybe she's at the beach?" I say, my voice uncertain now. She doesn't usually go far from the cottage... only heads into town when she absolutely has to.

Mrs. Callahan's expression turns more serious. "She mentioned having a headache. Said I was out of acetaminophen... maybe she went to town to get some."

Town.

My gut twists.

If she went to town, did she see me with Lyra?

No. No way. If she had, she would've said something. She wouldn't have just... vanished.

Unless...

Unless she thought something else was going on. That I was getting back together with my ex. But she knows better than that. Doesn't she? I mean, I do have a pattern, but after everything we've shared, all the things we didn't say but still meant...

God, maybe I should've said them out loud.

She's a songwriter. She pours her heart into her lyrics, finds a way to say the unsayable. And me? Well, I kept it all inside. Let her feel it instead of hear it. Maybe that was my mistake.

"Okay, well, I just came from town and didn't see her," I tell Mrs. Callahan, trying to keep my voice steady. "But I'll check again. I'll hit the beach first."

I head toward the sand, fighting to push down the rising dread. My gut is screaming at me that something's not right. I walk the familiar stretch until I reach the water's edge, the same spot where we do yoga every morning. The breeze is warm, but it hits my skin like ice as I scan the beach, eyes darting from face to face.

Nothing.

I keep walking, past the dunes and all the way to the rocks where we went fishing that first morning. Still nothing.

Maybe she *did* go to town. But then why wouldn't she text me? Ask me to grab her something for the headache?

Because maybe you've been acting secretive. Distant. And maybe she went to town to find out what you've really been up to.

And what would she find, dude?

Just me. With Lyra.

Christ.

I make the trek back to town, checking every overcrowded shop, slipping in and out of boutiques, cafes, and corner stores, scanning every face. Nothing. No sign of her. The unease twists tighter inside me.

I rush back to the cottage, half hoping—praying—that I somehow missed her, that she's back in bed, resting like Mrs. Callahan said. I burst through the door, take the hallway in three long strides, and throw open the bedroom door.

And then I see it.

The ring.

Sitting on the nightstand like a slap to the chest.

Holy fuck. No.

My legs nearly buckle, but I force myself forward, snatching it up with a shaky hand. It's warm from the sun streaming through the window, but it feels cold in my palm.

Did she forget it?

Or did she leave it on purpose?

What the ever-loving fuck is happening?

My heart pounds painfully as I spin and bolt out the door, straight to Mrs. Callahan's. I find her still on the porch swing, staring out at the ocean like she's been waiting.

She jumps up when she sees me. "Did you find her?"

"No," I say, and hold out the ring. "But I found this."

Her expression shifts instantly—shock, confusion, then fear. "Rip?" she breathes, her voice thin and trembling.

A sound catches in my throat. Her gaze meets mine, full of questions she doesn't ask.

"Yeah," I manage. "I know."

Charly's gone.

Where, I have no idea.

But she's gone.

I fumble for my phone and fire off a text: *Where are you?* I wait, watching the screen like my life depends on it. No reply.

I call.

Straight to voicemail.

My stomach clenches so violently I nearly double over. The silence on the other end is worse than anything I imagined.

Then—

"There you are!"

We both turn at the sound of Marta's voice.

"Marta," Mrs. Callahan says quickly. "Let me put on the tea."

Marta waves her off. "No need. I just wanted to stop by and

tell you and Charly how thrilled I am that you bought the place."

"You bought the place?" Emma jumps up and throws her arms around my waist, hugging me tight. "That's amazing! I'm so happy! Where's Charly? I want to hug her too."

"She's not here?" Marta asks, glancing between us. "I thought she'd be back by now."

The words hit like a puck to the faces.

"What do you mean?" I ask, the panic I've been holding back crashing straight into my voice. "Back from where?"

"I spotted her walking to town earlier," Marta says. "Thought I saw her headed back home too. It's hard to miss her in that big yellow sunhat." She laughs softly, unaware that the sound shatters something inside me.

Jesus.

She *had* to have seen me. Had to jump to the worst possible conclusion. And can I really blame her? I told her myself that Lyra and I had been on-again, off-again for years. What the hell was she supposed to think?

"I have to go," I blurt, already turning.

"Make this right," Mrs. Callahan calls after me.

I race back to the cottage, pulse pounding. My thoughts spiral. What do I do now? Stay and wait? Go looking? Looking *where*? If she went anywhere, it would be to her brother's place. Only problem? I don't even know the guy's goddamn name.

I pace the small living room, heart pounding, hands shaking, until I finally force myself to start tidying up, anything to give my hands something to do. When that doesn't help, and still no message comes in, I grab my phone, lock up the cottage, and call a ride to the airport.

I book a one-way ticket home.

Not that I expect her to be in Boston. I never even told her where I live. And if she really believes Lyra and I are back together? She won't come anywhere near me.

Fuck.

She ran because of what she saw. Because I didn't get the chance to explain. And now she probably thinks I sold her out or did something equally unforgivable.

It kills me—kills me—that she'd believe that of me. I know her ex did a number on her, but after everything we shared, after every touch, every word we didn't say but still understood, she'd believe better of me. No, I never told her who I really was. Just like she never told me who she was. But I always had the feeling she knew. Just like I knew. And I thought that mattered. I thought *we* mattered.

But now all I can do is hope that when she sees the article, when she reads the truth I gave Lyra, she'll understand. That she'll come back. Or at least... answer the damn phone.

Over the next few hours, I check my screen a hundred times. When I finally get back to my apartment, my body healed—thanks to Charly—there's still the matter of my wrecked heart.

I toss my bag down, head straight to my room, and send off another message. No reply. But I'm not giving up. I won't. I lie awake most of the night, chasing the memory of her laugh, her voice, her smile. When sleep finally takes me, it's restless and broken.

The headache greets me first thing the next morning. The second thing I do is grab my phone.

I open FameWire. And when I see the article, I jackknife upright in bed. I scroll. Fast. And then slower. And with every word, the hope I clung to curdles into rage.

What the fuck did Lyra do?

She made it worse, dude. Way worse.

This isn't what I told her. Not even close. But I get it. The angle she saw on social media, that's the juicy stuff. That's what sells. But she didn't just sell a story. She sold us out.

Are you really surprised?

I shouldn't be, but goddammit. I am.

I tried to do right by Charly. I gave Lyra the story. The truth. I thought I was protecting and making things right for the woman I'd fallen for. Instead, I torched the whole damn thing. I grab my phone and hit call.

Roman answers on the first ring. "You finally ready to tell me about your girl, or what?"

"I need your help," I say, my voice rough. "I've got a runaway bride of my own... and I need help catching her."

# CHARLY

For the third night in a row, I lie motionless in my childhood bedroom, staring blankly at the cracks in the ceiling like they might offer some kind of answer. Downstairs, the clatter of dishes echoes through the floorboards, sharp, angry sounds that say more than words ever could. My parents cooked extra again. I didn't touch a bite. I couldn't. And now they're upset. Not just about the wasted food, but about what's become of me.

What *has* become of me?

I left Connecticut like a ghost, not even sure where I was going. Jason offered me a place to stay, of course. He always does. But I couldn't bring myself to pull him into the wreckage of my life. Even though he's the only one—the only one—who believed me when I said it wasn't me in the tape.

Would Rip have believed me?

That question burns more than I want it to. I don't know the answer. But I do know what it felt like to see the look in my parents' eyes when I showed up on their doorstep. Not relief.

Not love. Disappointment, like I'd failed them again in some unspeakable way.

I wish it didn't hurt. I wish I didn't care. But I do.

Worse, I care too much. Because now, after seeing Betsy with her granddaughter, with me, and even Rip—teasing, tender, full of that quiet, unconditional love—it hit me like a freight train. That's what I want. Not the spotlight. Not the noise. Just... someone to love me, respect my choices, believe in me.

I know I haven't always lived the life my parents wanted for me, but I've always followed my heart.

And look where that got you.

A bitter groan slips out as I roll onto my side, but no tears come. I've cried myself dry since the moment I saw Rip with Lyra. I keep asking myself: *How could it have meant nothing to him?*

The sweet, sleepy mornings. The laughter in the middle of nowhere. The yoga. The fishing. The silence that wasn't empty, but full of ease. Every soft brush of his fingers. Every look that lingered too long. It couldn't have meant nothing.

Could it?

Maybe not, Charly.

That voice, small and traitorous, curls into my mind before I can shut it out.

Maybe... maybe he was ending things with her.

My breath stumbles in my throat. The thought, so simple, so easy, spreads inside me. After I saw them together in town, I did what I always do. I ran. Fast. Far. Before the pain could catch me. But what if...what if I misunderstood? What if he wasn't choosing her?

What if he was letting her go?

My heart beats faster. Panic or hope, I can't tell. My fingers fumble for my phone. I don't even know who I'm calling. There's no one. No one to lean on. No voice that will talk me down. So, I do the stupidest thing I can think of. I open social media. Not aimlessly. Not really.

I type in her name. Lyra.

God, if she posted a picture of them together, if she's already out there parading around in some smug victory lap, I don't know what I'll do. But that's not what I find. No. It's worse. A headline. An article. Her name beneath the byline, bold and bright like a slap.

I click.

I read.

And my stomach turns over so violently I almost throw up. My breath becomes sharp, shallow gasps, until the edges of the world begin to blur. I collapse back onto the bed as the screen slips from my fingers. The tears come back. Hard. Ugly. Unstoppable.

Because whatever I thought I knew... just changed.

This...

This is why Rip met with her. To tell her I was Indie Rhodes and that we've been cozying up together and pretending to be a couple. Why? Why would he do that?

Oh, girlfriend, you know the answer.

He gave her what she wanted…to get back together with her. Here I was beginning to think I'd made a mistake by running, but now I'm thinking I haven't run far enough. Downstairs the door opens and closes, and I push from my bed, thinking I have the house to myself, only to hear Mom come up the stairs.

"A package for you," she says, barely able to look me in the eye as she hands it over.

Who would be sending me a package? The only one who knows where my parents live is…Colby. Please God, don't let it be another sex tape. But the package is too small for that.

"Thanks," I manage, and she continues to stand there, arms crossed. I walk into my room and quietly close the door. I stare at the package for a long time before I get the nerve to open it. When I do, and find a key I don't recognize, I hold it in my palm, completely confused.

Who would send me a key, and why?

As I try to puzzle that out, I hear Mom go to the door again, but this time, when I hear a male voice, a very familiar male voice, I jump from my bed. I hurry to the bedroom door and open it, sure I'm hearing things, or hallu-cinating.

But no…

Rip is here.

At my parents' house.

Why?

Oh, maybe to say his final goodbye, to get his closure.

"Charly," Mom calls. "There's someone here to see you."

I take a deep breath, and then another, my legs frozen in place.

"Charly, either you come down or I'm coming up there," Rip announces, a seriousness to his voice.

Forcing myself to move, I grip the handrail and carefully walk down the stairs. I square my shoulders, try to compose myself. But the second I see him, the dark circles under his eyes that match mine, the hair a dishevelled mess, clothes that have no doubt been on his back for three days, I nearly collapse. He's not here to say goodbye to my face. For closure.

He's here for something else.

"Rip," I push past a thick tongue.

"I'm Rip Hart," he begins. "I play hockey for the Boston Bucks. I was in Connecticut healing from an injury that could have killed my career." He hands me a manila envelope. "I need you to read this."

"What is this?"

His eyes—bloodshot and raw—search mine with quiet desperation. "Please," he says, voice low and frayed. "Just read it."

With trembling fingers, I take the envelope, the flap already loosened. Inside is a single sheet of paper. One. I unfold it and scan the words once. Then again, slower this time.

My heart starts to pound—not just in my chest, but in my throat, my ears, my fingertips—as the truth unfolds line by line, each word a light cracking through the darkness I've been lost in for days. I look up. Rip hasn't moved. He's just watching me, like the paper in my hands holds his fate too.

"Rip," I breathe, barely a whisper.

"That's the story I gave Lyra," he says quietly. "I didn't even know she was in town until she showed up. After that photo of us surfaced... She tracked me down. But I wasn't going to see her. I swear."

My brows draw together, confusion battling with hope. "I don't understand."

"She sold me out. *Sold us* out," he says, anger pulsing beneath his words. "I told her everything—told her to check with your tattoo artist if she didn't believe me. Because that girl in the video?" He shakes his head. "She didn't have a butterfly-shaped music note on her thigh."

I blink. "Rip..."

He steps closer. "This article...it goes live tomorrow. My buddy Jaxon hooked me up with someone legit. Not a tabloid rat. A real journalist. Someone who cares about the truth."

I clutch the paper tighter.

"I...I heard you on the phone. I heard you say there was no one..."

He blinks, and then understanding dawns. "I told her that because I didn't want her coming to the cottage...finding you. Not because I wanted her back. But because I wanted to protect you from her."

My heart races. "You were...protecting me."

"Yes, and I told Lyra we were over," he continues. "I'd already ended things with her before she came to town, but when she showed up, I didn't leave room for doubt. I gave her the truth to clear your name. I thought I could kill two birds with one stone—getting your truth out there, and ending things with her for good..."

There's a long silence, and then, "You knew," I say at last, voice small, eyes stinging. "You always knew it was me... that I was Indie Rhodes."

He nods. "Just like you always knew it was me too. Right?"

I let out a breathless, bitter laugh. "Yeah." I stretch out a hand like it's the first time we've met. "Hi, I'm Charly. Also known as Indie Rhodes. I won The Spotlight. My ex hated that I was rising and he wasn't, so to steal the attention—and ruin me—he made a sex tape, with someone who wasn't me."

Rip doesn't flinch. "I never once thought it was you."

"Really?" I swallow. "You always knew it wasn't me in that video?"

He nods, jaw tight. "I did."

"I guess that means you watched it."

"Not by choice," he says grimly. "Some douchebag player I know was watching it. I saw enough to know. Anyone with half a brain could see it wasn't you."

A sharp intake of breath draws my attention.

I turn and find my mother standing at the bottom of the stairs, face pale, lips parted. My father slips an arm around her waist.

Rip turns to them. "Oh," he says flatly, not even attempting to hide the edge in his voice. "Right. No offense. Well, maybe just a little."

I bite the inside of my cheek, but a grin teases its way forward. Rip is here. He came for me.

"How did you find me?" I ask softly.

He exhales a laugh. "You didn't exactly leave a trail. But I had one lead. Your tattoo artist." He jerks a thumb toward the door. "Roman's in the car, by the way. While I kept the artist busy getting inked, he went through the files and found your address."

My eyes widen. "You... got a tattoo?"

Rip lifts a brow, something glinting in his eyes—mischief, affection, maybe even love.

"I'd do a hell of a lot more than that," he says, "if it meant finding you."

My breath catches when I see it—my name—inked into his bicep in delicate, graceful script. Not a flashy design. Not a show. Just *me*, etched into him like a vow.

The sob escapes before I can hold it in. "Rip..."

He moves closer, his big hands warm and steady on my shoulders. "Roman once had a runaway bride," he says softly, eyes shining. "And I helped him catch her. This time... he returned the favor."

My laugh is broken, wet. "Runaway bride?"

His smile—God, that smile—spreads slowly across his face, full of boyish charm. I swear my heart might burst right out of my chest.

"Well," he says, "We *are* engaged, aren't we?"

I blink at him, confused. "Well, no. That was—"

But before I can say another word, he drops to one knee. My world stops.

"This might not be the time or the place," he says, voice rough, but warm. "But I can't wait another second.

Charly, will you marry me and make me the happiest man alive?"

Behind me, Mom gasps. "How well do you even know this man?" she blurts out.

But I don't look at her. I can't. My entire world is standing— or rather kneeling—in front of me.

I smile through my tears, hand outstretched. "Since the plans are already in place," I whisper, "Yes. I'll marry you." My heart soars as Rip slides the ring onto my finger. It's small, not at all flashy. A perfect lab grown diamond. It's everything I've ever wanted and he remembered.

Then he shakes his head. "No."

I blink. "No?"

He gives me a crooked grin. "I don't want to get married in Italy. If that's okay with you."

I open my mouth, confused.

"I mean, I want to honeymoon there, absolutely," he says. "But I want us to get married somewhere that matters. Somewhere that feels like home."

His fingers gently uncurl my right hand, the one still fisted around the mysterious key.

"Our cottage," he murmurs. "You're holding the key."

My breath hitches. "Rip..."

"I was on my way to town that day to pick up the deed and the key," he explains, eyes searching mine. "That's what I'd been sneaking around about. The phone calls. The late nights. I wanted to surprise you. I just... I didn't know if it was something you even wanted."

My voice cracks as I choke back a sob. "It's everything I've ever wanted." And then I throw myself into his arms. He catches me instantly, holding me like he never intends to let go.

"You're everything I've ever wanted," he whispers into my hair before kissing me with everything he has, every promise, every heartbreak, every ounce of love he's been holding back.

A throat clears behind us. Dad.

Rip straightens and turns to face them, still keeping an arm wrapped around my waist.

"I'm in love with your daughter," he says, strong and steady. "She is smart, and beautiful, and talented. She's fearless when it counts, and kind when it matters most. You should be proud of her." He glances at me. "She's a handful," he adds with a smirk, "But she's *my* handful now. And I'm taking her home to Boston." Eyes still on me, he continues, "I can promise you both this, I will always love her, and believe in her and never hurt her." He pauses, then looks at my parents again, more softly this time. "She makes great decisions. Well..." he chuckles, "Except when it comes to windows."

"Hey," I say, laughing through my tears as I swat at him.

Rip grins but turns serious again. "No matter what she chooses in life, I'll be behind her. I hope you will be too."

My parents don't speak right away, but after a beat, they both nod—small, uncertain gestures, but enough. Enough to begin something new.

Rip turns back to me. "I'd like them to come to the wedding. You would too, right?"

It's a truce. A small one. Fragile and imperfect, but a beginning.

"Yes," I say gently. "I'd like that very much."

Mom and Dad share a look, then return a faint smile.

Rip claps his hands together. "Great. Because we've got a plane to catch." He pulls two tickets from his pocket.

"You bought tickets?" I ask, startled.

"Of course," he says. "I wasn't leaving here without you. And if I had to, I'd have thrown you over my shoulder and carried you out."

I arch a brow. "Confidence. I like it."

He pulls me close again, gaze locked on mine, lips curving with heat and affection. "Right. And I'm also confident that when we get back home, you'll once again find my bed just right, *Goldilocks*."

I smile. "I'm pretty certain you're right... Big Bear."

My parents look at us like we're speaking another language. But it doesn't matter. Because as I stare up at the man I love, wrapped in his arms and surrounded by the pieces of a broken life we're finally stitching back together, I feel it down to my bones.

Fairy tales aren't fiction.

And happily ever after...it's real. It's right here.

And it's mine.

Rip

As the warm ocean breeze curls in off the waves, I pace slowly on the sand, my shoes long abandoned, my heart thudding in a rhythm that matches the tide. Somewhere nearby, gulls call, and waves kiss the shoreline, but all I can hear is the pulse of anticipation building in my chest.

I glance at Roman. He's grinning like a fool.

He warned me this would happen—told me that one day I'd find myself standing at an altar, lovesick and shaky, waiting for *her*. I hadn't believed him.

Not then.

But now?

Now I know he was right.

Off to my left, sweet Emma sits on a driftwood stool, barefoot and radiant, strumming the soft notes of the song Charly chose. When we asked her to do the music for our beachside wedding, she lit up like it was the greatest honor she'd ever been given. I think maybe, for her, it was.

I scan the crowd and see only joy—our friends smiling, eyes already glassy with emotion. My chest tightens with so much happiness I think it might just split wide open.

Who would've thought that Big Bear would fall head over heels for his Goldilocks?

And yet, here I am. Changed. Humbled. Made whole.

My gaze finds my brother, standing proud and emotional. Then my parents, hands clasped as if holding each other up. I follow that line across the aisle to Charly's family—her mother, standing a little stiffer than the rest, but *here*. Her brother and his fiancée, beaming. A fragile bridge has formed between Charly and her parents—tentative, but real. And I know how much it means to her.

I want that for her. A future where she's not just tolerated but *celebrated*. Where her family believes in her, trusts her choices, loves her as fiercely as she deserves.

And let's be honest—she's got pretty impeccable taste. After all, she chose *me*.

I smirk at the thought, and Roman lifts a brow like he knows I'm thinking something cocky. I just shrug, all innocence. My eyes move again, landing on a familiar figure in the second row. Mrs. Callahan. She's glowing.

Of *course* she wanted to officiate. The second she saw Charly and me together after she followed me home from my condom-buying adventure, she probably ran home and signed up for an online ordination course, convinced she'd be the one to make us official. And truthfully, we'd considered it. But in the end, I wanted her to sit back, enjoy the view, and take it all in without the pressure. She deserved that much.

Then, a shift in music.

Emma strums a new progression, soft and steady. The signal.

The crowd turns. So do I.

And there she is.

My breath catches.

Charly.

Beautiful. Luminous. My *bride*.

I take in the gorgeous ball gown made by Gabby as Charly's bare feet sink gently into the sand as she walks toward me, sunlight dancing in her hair, her father steady at her side. That sight alone—*that her father is here*—makes my throat tighten. Not because of old wounds, but because of hope. Because of healing.

And somehow, even as the tears press hard behind my eyes, I'm smiling. Because against all odds, we made it. After everything—the scandal, the whispers, the heartbreak, the past that tried to swallow her whole—she rose. Stronger. Softer. Braver.

Jaxon's journalist friend published the truth, and just like that, the world remembered who she really was: not the girl in the video, but the woman with fire in her voice and gold in her heart.

America's sweetheart, once again.

The offers came flooding in. A tour. New endorsements. A chance to reclaim the spotlight and take the world by storm.

But...

She had other plans.

Plans that involved Boston. Going back to school. Me.

I would never—*ever*—keep her from her dreams. That was one of the first promises I made to her. But something happened over the course of last summer. Slowly, quietly, like the tide rolling in, her dreams shifted. She stepped out of the spotlight and realized she didn't miss it. The noise, the pressure, the weight of being *watched*. It turns out, the limelight wasn't made for Charly—it was something she carried like armor, not something she basked in.

She's happiest when things are quiet. When she's with her small, tight-knit circle of friends. When she's barefoot on the beach, or sitting cross-legged on the floor, teaching little ones how to find their voice through music. That's where she lights up. That's where she shines.

We bought a big house—not to show off, but to grow into. A home with laughter in the walls already. One near our friends, with space to breathe. We turned one of the sun-filled rooms into a studio for her, where she can give private lessons when she's ready. But her heart right now is set on school, on getting her degree, on becoming a music teacher. In an actual classroom. To some, that might seem like a step down. To Charly, it's a step toward something real.

Her parents were thrilled, obviously. But this time, she didn't do it to please anyone else. She's doing it for *her*. For her peace. For her joy.

And I wouldn't want it any other way.

As for me, our NHL season ended. We didn't hoist the Cup, but we left everything we had on the ice. And thanks to Charly—her hands, her care, her constant belief in me—my groin healed fully. She never let me push too far, but never let me give up either. She knows me better than I know myself sometimes.

Charly.

My wife.

I used to watch the other guys scan the stands during a game, eyes searching for someone. I didn't get it then. What that meant. What it felt like. But now, when I skate off the ice and catch her smile, when I see her clapping, yelling, eyes bright with pride, I know.

It's the best kind of adrenaline rush. Like scoring a game-winner. Like flying. Like home.

She's beside me now, standing in the sand in a dress that made me forget how to breathe. Her dad just kissed her cheek and whispered something that made her tear up, and now she's at my side, where she's always belonged. She passes her bouquet to Gabby with a wink. I knew those two would hit it off the second they met. Charly fits in like she was always meant to be one of us. The WAGs adore her. And honestly, when she opens her studio, she's going to be booked solid just from our team's kids alone.

Speaking of kids...

We're not in a rush. We want time. Time to finish school, time to settle, time to soak each other in. But yeah, we want a family. Maybe not a full-blown brood, but at least a couple. A little team of our own. After seeing her with Emma, the way she gently braids her hair and sings silly songs that somehow make everything better, I know she's going to be an incredible mom.

As for me, I'll admit it. I'm nervous. I've never really been around kids much. I don't know how to swaddle a baby or change a diaper or make up bedtime stories. But I do know how to love. And with Charly at my side, and a locker room full of guys ready to offer unsolicited parenting advice, I'll figure it out. We'll figure it out. Together.

The officiant clears her throat, and we turn toward her, hearts pounding. We read our vows, voices shaking, laughter slipping through the tears. We make quiet references to Goldilocks and Big Bear, our little inside joke wrapped in forever promises. She cries halfway through hers. I nearly do too, but manage to keep it together...until she whispers, *"you're just right"* and I break.

When it's time to kiss the bride, I don't hesitate. I pull her into my arms like I've been doing it for a lifetime and press my lips to hers, slow, deep, full of every promise I've ever made her. Every future I see with her.

"Love you, Char," I murmur against her mouth.

"Love you too, Rip," she whispers back, her voice soft, her smile dreamy and sure.

The crowd erupts into cheers, we turn to face them, and I swear I've never felt so full—of love, of gratitude, of sheer, blinding happiness. Charly also wanted to get married right here, exactly where we met, and I can't imagine a better place. It's not just a location, it's a memory etched into the sand, the beginning of everything. Sure, we'll head to Italy for our honeymoon—wine, history, sunsets over the Amalfi— but this place? This is sacred. This is ours.

Tonight, we'll celebrate on a sunset cruise. Something Charly used to be terrified of. But she's worked through that fear, let the water carry her instead of drowning her, and I'm so damn proud of her. Of us. Of how far we've come. And just because she's brave now doesn't mean I won't slip on my ridiculous water wings, because nothing—nothing—makes her laugh harder. And her laugh is everything.

We weave our way through a tunnel of friends and family, hugging, laughing, holding on to every second. When we reach Mrs. Callahan, she's standing there, lips pursed, eyes glinting like she's about to give me a lecture.

"What?" I ask, already grinning.

"About time," she says, then gives me a playful smack on the cheek.

"That I finally made an honest woman of Charly?" I say, tugging Charly closer into my side.

"Yes, Rip." She pauses, then softens. "And I suppose... you can call me Betsy now."

I laugh, pick her up like she's light as air, and spin her in a full circle. Her surprised squeal is pure joy, and I hold her for a second longer, just to soak it in. "Thank you, Betsy. For every-thing. You've been more than a neighbor. You've been a friend. A protector. A nosy, pot-clanging guardian angel."

She grins, but then points a warning finger. "Don't thank me just yet. Remember, those walls are thin. I still have my pots. And my ears."

"Ohmigod," Charly groans, hiding her face.

"But we're not your neighbors anymore," I say, nodding toward the little beachside cottage we were lucky enough to buy last summer. The one I promised I'd fill with memories, real ones. The kind that echo through a home long after the doors have closed for the night.

"Well, that's true," she concedes.

"So technically," I say, inching closer to Charly, "We can make all the noise we want."

Betsy plugs her ears. "I've lived a long life, Rip. I've heard it all. But there are some things I don't need to hear again."

Charly's face is bright red now, and I swear she might combust.

I lean down, my lips brushing her ear. "What do you say, Mrs. Hart? We head back to our place, and I show you some of my best moves, while you practice those new high notes you've been working on?"

She bites her bottom lip, her voice a whisper. "Do we have time?"

"I can be fast," I murmur.

"Oh, I know," she teases, arching a brow.

I laugh—loud and unapologetic—sweep her into my arms, and head down the beach with my bride, the love of my life, cradled against my chest.

Marta wanted this little cottage to be filled with life again. With laughter. With morning coffee and midnight popcorn and baby socks on the floor. And we're going to give her that.

Eventually.

But first...

A quickie.

. . .

***

Thank you so much for reading, **STICK BREAK in my Boston Bucks series.** I hope you loved this story as much as I loved writing it. Stayed tuned for Penn and Jaylynn's story in Peppermint Stick Break.

Interested in leaving a review? Please do! Reviews help readers connect with books that work for them. I appreciate all reviews, whether positive or negative.

Happy Reading,

Cathryn

ALSO BY CATHRYN FOX

Boston Bucks

Stick Move

Sticking Around

Sticking Out

Hook 'em Hard (Written in the Boston Bucks World)

Stick Play

Stick Magic

Stick Work

Stick Fight

Stick Break

Scotia Storms

Away Game (Rebels)

Warm Up (Rebels)

Crash Course (Rebels)

Home Advantage (Rebels)

Shut Out (Rebels)

Moving Target (Rivals)

Face Off (Rivals)

Scoring Fast (Rivals)

Opposing Teams (Rivals)

Fake Out (Rivals)

Deal Breaker (Rebels)

Hard Burn (Rivals)

End Zone

Fair Play

Enemy Down

Keeping Score

Trading Up

All In

Blue Bay Crew

Demolished

Leveled

Hammered

Single Dad

Single Dad Next Door

Single Dad on Tap

Single Dad Burning Up

Players on Ice

The Playmaker

The Stick Handler

The Body Checker

The Hard Hitter

The Risk Taker

The Wing Man

The Puck Charmer

The Troublemaker

The Rule Breaker

The Rookie

The Sweet Talker

The Heart Breaker

In the Line of Duty

His Obsession Next Door

His Strings to Pull

His Trouble in Talulah

His Taste of Temptation

His Moment to Steal

His Best Friend's Girl

His Reason to Stay

Confessions

Confessions of a Bad Boy Professor

Confessions of a Bad Boy Officer

Confessions of a Bad Boy Fighter

Confessions of a Bad Boy Doctor

Confessions of a Bad Boy Gamer

Confessions of a Bad Boy Millionaire

Confessions of a Bad Boy Santa

Confessions of a Bad Boy CEO

Hands On

Hands On

Body Contact

Full Exposure

Dossier

Private Reserve

House Rules

Under Pressure

Big Catch

Brazilian Fantasy

Improper Proposal

Boys of Beachville
Good at Being Bad
Igniting the Bad Boy
Bad Girl Therapy

Stone Cliff Series:

Crashing Down

Wasted Summer

Love Lessons

Wrapped Up

Eternal Pleasure Series

Instinctive

Impulsive

Indulgent

Sun Stroked Series

Seaside Seduction

Deep Desire

Private Pleasure

Captured and Claimed Series:

Yours to Take

Yours to Teach

Yours to Keep

Firefighter Heat Series

Fever

Siren

Flash Fire

Playing For Keeps Series

Slow Ride

Wild Ride

Sweet Ride

Breaking the Rules:

Hold Me Down Hard

Pin Me Up Proper

Tie Me Down Tight

Stand Alone Title:

Hands on with the CEO

Torn Between Two Brothers

Holiday Spirit

Unleashed

Knocking on Demon's Door

Web of Desire

ABOUT CATHRYN

New York Times and *USA today* Bestselling author, Cathryn is a wife, mom, sister, daughter, and friend. She loves dogs, sunny weather, anything chocolate (she never says no to a brownie) pizza and red wine. She has two teenagers who keep her busy with their never ending activities, and a husband who is convinced he can turn her into a mixed martial arts fan. Cathryn can never find balance in her life, is always trying to find time to go to the gym, can never keep up with emails, Facebook or Twitter and tries to write page-turning books that her readers will love.

Connect with Cathryn:
Newsletter https://app.mailerlite.com/webforms/landing/c1f8n1
Twitter: https://twitter.com/writercatfox
Facebook: https://www.facebook.com/AuthorCathrynFox?ref=hl
Blog: http://cathrynfox.com/blog/
Goodreads: https://www.goodreads.com/author/show/91799.Cathryn_Fox

Pinterest http://www.pinterest.com/catkalen/